KNIGHT OF SWORDS

IAN BRECKON

First published 2009 by Old Street Publishing

This edition published 2010 by Old Street Publishing Ltd
40 Bowling Green Lane, London EC1R 0NE
www.oldstreetpublishing.co.uk

ISBN 978-1-906964-12-2

Copyright © Ian Breckon 2009

10 9 8 7 6 5 4 3 2 1

A CIP catalogue record for this title is available from the British Library.

Printed and bound in Great Britain

KNIGHT OF SWORDS

1

HE WAS DREAMING about chess when the attack began. Chess, and his old school, and he could not see his opponent. Doors slammed in the cold corridor, somebody was shouting in a foreign language, and he stared at the chequered board, the hands of his enemy moving the pieces, and could remember nothing of the rules of the game. A slow bleed of defeat. Birds rose black and panicked from the icy quad, battering at the windows.

Alzatevi! Alzatevi tutti, veloce!

He woke suddenly, disorientated in darkness. Blindly he reached out, expecting to find Carla still lying beside him. The hut was filthy with the stink of sour bedding and paraffin, and he heard the flat cracking of the rifles before the door banged shut again. Swinging himself upright, he threw the blanket aside. A turmoil of shadowy figures stumbled against each other, cursing. The last shreds of the dream slipped from him as his palm closed over the barrel of the Sten beside the bed.

Outside, the mountains were roaring in the cold leak of dawn. The valley was iron grey under the clouds and his breath plumed before him as he ran across the yard. Against the low wall on the far side, three men were crouching. The rifle fire was continuous, and he tried to gauge the distance. Close – almost at the village. From directly below came the sudden metallic rip and crash of an MG42.

He was in one of the outlying picquets, a clutch of farm buildings dug into the mountainside, high above the village where the main force of the partisans was encamped. He crouched low, shoulder to the wall. The man beside him had a Beretta machine-carbine resting on the parapet, sighted down into the grey of the dawn forest; the man's teeth were chattering, a staccato porcelain tapping, and his knuckles were white as he gripped the gun. He knew the temptation, felt it himself – to fire at something, shoot blind. He had cocked the Sten as he left the hut, but now he eased it off, the spring relaxing in its steel tube.

'Don't fire,' he said quietly. 'Nobody fire.'

He knew they were scared, shocked from sleep, already exhausted by months of struggle. There was no fear in him, only a pin-sharp lucidity. The air smelt keenly of wood resin, damp soil and rain, and in the hard-edged silences between the gunshots sounds came to him clear and distinct: a clatter of birds from the valley below, the whispers of the men beside him, the sound of blood and his own breathing. The man with the Beretta lowered it from the wall. Figures were moving below them, streaming up the steep path from the village in full retreat. There was the distant cough of a mortar, then a moment later the dull concussive thud of the explosion. The noise rolled back off the mountains.

'Let's go,' he said.

At a break in the trees the track levelled out. The column of retreating partisans, nearly two hundred men of the Garibaldi Division *Fratelli Varalli*, bunched and slowed as the men turned to look back into the valley. Cigarettes were passed around, a flask of grappa. He took a cigarette, cupping dirt-printed palms around a sulphur flame. The rawness of the smoke tasted real, and he held it down, expanding his lungs. Staring along the column of figures climbing towards him from the valley, he tried to pick Carla out amongst them, but their faces were indistinguishable, pale smudges in the dawn shadow.

There was a breath of snow in the air. The first sun angled below the lid of clouds and the mountains blazed apricot and rose. Soon, as they climbed further, they would reach the sunlight themselves: a perfect target for shellfire. He knew where they were going: their only route out of the sharp-sided valley led over the shoulder of the mountain. The track was marked on the maps, the *Passagio Mazzaferro*. The enemy had the same maps.

He tensed, nerves awakened. Close-pressed, the column was an easy target – two machineguns could scythe them down. The partisans passing steadily up the pathway seemed indifferent, too tired, too glad to have escaped the death below, and he had the quick dizzying sensation that he alone was awake, he alone aware of the danger. He felt the rage mounting inside him, barely held, his own fierce self-control powerless now to effect what surely must happen. The enemy gunfire was so certain he could almost hear it.

Compulsively his fingers went to his throat, and he felt for the British Army identity discs hanging against his chest. If the enemy were German regulars, even SS, he might stand a chance of surrendering, but the fascist militia rarely took prisoners and in a gun battle his hopes would be slim. He began moving again, pushing his way upwards past the climbing men, wanting to find the commander of the detachment, wanting to find Carla, wanting to find anyone who might listen to him and follow where he led. The air was icy, but sweat poured down his back.

As the track doubled and rose higher through the trees he glanced back at the men behind him. Kicked from sleep, weary and unwashed, dressed in scraps of military uniform, berets and battledress jackets, winter coats and alpine caps, fur hats and rolled blankets, they resembled refugees more than soldiers. Six weeks ago the troops of Mussolini's fascist republic and their German allies had crushed the Liberated Zone of Ossola; since then the partisans had been harried through these mountains, camping in the bare woods and the winter-abandoned villages, alert to the insect drone of the reconnaissance planes. Exhaustion had blunted their bravery.

As they met his gaze, he saw the mistrust in their eyes. He looked like them – lean-faced and unshaven, hair a little too long, dressed in the same collage of mud-coloured clothes. He spoke their language fluently but he was not a partisan, not an Italian; he was a foreigner, an *allied co-belligerent* in the accepted formula. He had been with them for eight months, he was a professional and his skills made him valuable, but this was not his war. When he looked at them he saw not soldiers but the men they had once been: farmers and railway-men, students and factory workers. He saw their fervour and their fear and the depths of their grief, and knew he could share none of it. But they were civilians, and he was not. War was his country, and they were the strangers now.

As he climbed he stopped every third or fourth man he passed, asking if they had seen the commander, and every man was shaking his head, sucking his cheeks, shrugging, non-committal. And always he looked for Carla. The evening before he had argued with her – argued until he felt sick and rotten inside – then packed his bedroll and hiked up the hill to the farmhouse. Now, in the chaos of the retreat, he had no idea where she might be, no idea if she had even left the village alive.

He was nearing the head of the column when he found her. In the shadow of the trees she was another drab figure in oversized military fatigues and a woollen cap pulled down over her ears. She glanced back down the path, her slim face boyish beneath the cap brim.

'Carla!' he shouted, quick with relief. 'Wait there!'

Somebody shoved him from behind. A hand clasped his wrist, fingers clawed at his shoulder, then there were men pushing all around him. No chance to struggle before they had him pinned between them – the Sten was slipped from his back and they hauled his left arm up hard. Bright pain at the back of his head as a pistol butt clipped him, then a hand at the nape of his neck forced him down and forward. Twisting, squinting against the pain blooming in his skull, he saw Carla with her hands cupping her face, eyes wide and bright, slowly shaking her head.

His voice was rasping in his throat, trying to form words.

'What are you doing?' he said. 'What the *bloody hell* are you doing?'

Between four trees, in a brief clearing out of sight of the path, they dragged him upright. When he blinked the sting from his eyes he saw Commissar Bruno standing before him with a pistol in his hand. Bruno's uniform was neatly pressed, his moustache clipped, the red enamel star glinting on his cap, but he was nervous beneath the glaze of authority. Whatever they were about to do would be done quickly. Reason had evaporated.

'We know you're a traitor,' Bruno said, his words chopped and unconvincing.

'This is a mistake,' he forced himself to say. 'It's a mistake, believe me,' trying to argue though he knew there was little point.

'Two days ago you left your position without authorisation. Where did you go?' The pistol in Bruno's hand rose and fell. He seemed afraid of it.

'I went to San Gaudenzio, I told you that.'

'You didn't go to San Gaudenzio! Where did you go?'

At the far side of the little clearing Carla was staring at him. A man in a leather jacket, the man who had held his head down, was urging her back towards the path.

'I don't have to tell you anything,' he said. 'I'm not under your orders.'

'You're under the orders of Brigade Command, who know all about you.'

'I'm not under your orders. I'm not in your army. I'm a British soldier.'

'You're a traitor!' A catch in Bruno's voice, a moment of genuine spite.

'Fuck off,' he said.

His mind was clear and sharp now, every colour of the forest loud and distinct. He had faced death before, but this death was so sudden, and lacked all meaning. There were so many other things he could have died for.

Bruno's eyes flicked left and right, unable to meet his, with almost a look of apology. He had admired Bruno in the past – a calm man and a steady leader, a university lecturer in Novara before joining the partisans. But the Commissar was neither calm nor steady now.

'I have my orders,' he said carefully, speaking in English so the others would not understand. 'You've already been judged. This isn't my decision.' Then, as if he feared he had betrayed himself, Bruno gestured angrily with the pistol.

The guards to either side of him stepped away, gripping his wrists and dragging his arms out straight. For a moment he thought they meant to tie him to the trees, crucify him, but they were just standing clear of the blood spray. A boot kicked at his legs, trying to buckle them and make him kneel, but he hardened his muscles and stood stiffly upright. Seconds died. And now, he thought. And now this is my death.

He turned his head and saw Carla looking back at him over the shoulder of the leather-jacketed man.

'*Traditore!*' she cried out, harsh and bitter.

Bruno's pistol swung up level with his face, the muzzle black and empty. It was a German gun, he realised, a Walther P38. Bruno's face looked sick.

I am about to be shot with a German pistol, he thought. Everything was suddenly hilarious. He choked back dry laughter, grinning into the muzzle of the Walther. Bruno's hand shook, the pistol weaving.

The first gunshot was a quick snipping sound. One of the trees burst fleshy pale, showering splinters; then volley fire from the slope above crashed through the forest. The man behind Bruno dropped with blood lacing from his head. Bruno turned, the pistol in his hand arcing, firing into the trees.

The guard to his left had slackened his grip and he hauled against him suddenly, kicking his boot up hard into his armpit. Cartilage cracked and the man released him. The second guard stumbled, thrown off balance, and they fell together onto the mat of slimy leaves. He drove his knee up into the man's jawbone and dragged himself free. A snatched breath, then he was leaping for the trees. Bullets whipped close around him. He plunged through the undergrowth, colliding with trunks and hurling himself onwards, zig-zagging, throwing the forest from his palms.

Ferns grew densely between the trees and beneath them the ground was uneven, treacherous with dead wood. Chest high, the ferns were a waving sea of brilliant green in the slanting sunlight, and he was swimming through them, kicking out at the submerged ground. His arms scooped and swirled, his boots crushed and stamped, and his blood was loud in his ears. The momentum of escape had carried him down the mountainside, the path and the partisan column left far above him. Braced against a tree, its trunk ringed with black and silver stripes like range markings on a gun-sight, he crouched low and listened for the sounds of pursuit. The shouts, the noise of the fighting, were fainter now, and he was hidden.

Then he made out another figure away to his left, stumbling through the undergrowth, almost invisible in the submarine light. A figure running alone, panicked and disorientated – a moment more and he recognised her, the brief flashes of her white tennis shoes clear in the shadows as she ran. He should stay put, he should let her go. There was nothing he could do to help her. For a moment he hesitated, hugging the wet bark of the tree. Then he began moving towards her, surging through the ferns.

She turned as he called her name, and he saw the garnet of blood below her right ear – she had been hit, or fallen against something. As he approached, she lurched towards him suddenly and he raised his arms to catch her. The first blow struck his cheek, but he snatched at her wrists and pulled them down to her sides.

'*Bastardo! Bastardo traditore!*' she shouted, her voice ragged with shock and tears. '*You* did this. You led them here!'

'Carla, Carla be quiet,' he was hissing, strangling the words. She fought him, kicking and grappling as he tried to control her, then he gave up and hurled her away from him.

'Don't touch me,' she screamed. 'This is your fault!'

There was another sound now, the steady crack and swish of men moving through the bracken. A line of soldiers climbing up steadily between the trees. They were fascist militia of the *Guardia Nazionale Repubblicana*, young conscripts in leaf-patterned smocks, their Beretta carbines levelled and ready. One carried a machinegun, the belts of ammunition a gleaming brass cuirass.

Carla's eyes were wild and delirious, her body heaving with panic. She had her back to the approaching enemy, oblivious to them, but the distance was closing fast.

He turned to run and she followed, striking at his shoulder. He ran three long strides into the ferns and she came after him. The voices of the enemy soldiers were hard and taut with nerves, calling to each other as they advanced.

'Who are you?' she sobbed. '*Who are you?*'

He calculated a moment, then lunged at her, bearing her down with his whole weight through the ferns and into the soaked blackness beneath. One of her legs was pinned under him but still she struggled, kicking at him and trying to knee him, her free hand boxing twice at his face. He tasted blood on his lips.

'I trusted you,' she spat into his face, 'You betrayed us. You did this.'

'Be still, be quiet.' His palm found her face as he leant onto her, trapping her. Wood crackled around them, and the ferns waved slowly above. Out of sight he could hear the enemy moving around them, their steady tread, and the noise was pouring water, or fire blazing, a gathering rush. She was still fighting, but his hand was clamped tight over her mouth and his body pinned her. Sucking back blood he raised his head a little, but saw only the rusty tracery of dead ferns, the green freshness of the tall stalks. Carla's body writhed and twisted beneath him, her hand clawing at his shoulder.

'Be still, be still,' he was whispering to her, dropping his head to breathe into her ear, 'we're safe here, but you must be still.'

A clatter of gunfire, a volley of shouts off to the left somewhere. He lay with the girl trapped beneath him, his body rigid, teeth clenched tight.

'Don't worry,' he breathed to her, 'we'll be alright. Lie still, don't move.'

The ferns sighed and bent as a breeze passed, the green waves shifting and covering them, and the soldiers moved on.

Voices called through the forest, punctuated by rifle shots. A bird screeched, loud and repeatedly. Holding his breath, he listened for the last shot's echo. Silence. He eased his grip; Carla didn't struggle. He rolled from her and knelt, head raised to scan the forest. Empty. He looked back at the girl.

Carla lay still, legs crooked, arms bent, one eye open and glassy. He knelt above her for a moment, not moving. He laid a palm on her cheek, then held it above her open lips. He felt no breath. He felt no pulse in her slender wrist.

Violence was pouring through him, a sudden sick heat. He pressed down on her chest, trying to force the life back into her body. He gulped air and put his mouth to hers, pushing it down into her lungs again and again. Fresh blood pooled in the hollow of her ear.

'Carla,' he said. Shaking, he took the body in his arms, held it clasped against him, lying in the black muck. Her one open eye stared up through the waving ferns. Her face was smooth and soft, skin eggshell-textured. He laid his palm on her cheek, trying to feel a little of the warmth still remaining. Her skin was cool beneath his hand. He pushed back her woollen cap and smoothed away the black curls sweated to her forehead. He kissed her brow and kissed her dead lips. Then he fell beside her, crawling into the twisted S of her body, clinging to her as the sickness punched at him from inside.

Downhill, he was walking blindly, reaching out to steady himself. He had tried to bury Carla, he supposed: the dirt was dug in under his nails. He remembered nothing of it. He moved without thinking, without feeling. Light rain flecked down through the weave of bare branches.

Something split the air beside him and smacked into a tree, bursting yellow shards. He tensed, legs locked, telling himself not to move though his body was feverish to run, or turn, or fling itself down. Any movement now would make him a clear target.

A shout, then a sudden lash of pain at the top of his thigh, his leg buckling beneath him. He heard the sound of the first shot as the second bullet split the tree beside him, ricocheting, and as he turned his head from the stinging splinters it struck him full in the back, punching him forward and down.

He fell noiselessly, dropping into the slough of rotting leaves, and dirt filled his mouth.

2

He awoke gasping, and everything was blue. Voices boomed and receded, lights flashed bright then snuffed out into plunging darkness, leaving him sick and reeling. Sometimes the lights and the voices converged and there were faces around him, hands that mauled and probed, slicing at him with tiny, bitter blades. The pain was like noise, like twisting steel; like the scream of the railway girders at Gattinara, tearing as they fell. In a moment of clear focus he felt the morphine in his blood, recognised the sickening glassy slide of it. He tried to speak, but his words were animal grunts and whines.

Commissar Bruno sat beside his bed, then a short, round-faced man in pin-stripes who shook his head sadly and caressed his thin moustache. A woman was crying in the lamplight. 'I don't want him to die,' she said. 'I don't want him to die.'

He was in his father's study, Florentine sun splashing the tiled floor.

'Now,' his father was saying, 'have you learned the lesson for today, eh? Conditionals. Tell me what you *should* do. The verb is *to believe*. Go on!'

'*Crederei, crederesti, credebbe,*' he said. '*Crederemmo, crederesti, crederebbero.*'

As he spoke, the sun flared brighter, burning away the room and the image of his father. He closed his eyes against the glare, and when he looked again Carla was bending over him.

'Don't try to talk,' she said, her face in shadow, her breath warm.

'It was a mistake,' he whispered. 'It wasn't me. I never betrayed you.'

Shh, she said. *Shh now.*

'But I killed you . . . I killed you.'

'Don't be silly,' she said. 'I'm alive, aren't I?' And she leant across him and lightly kissed his forehead.

'Sleep now.'

The smell of burnt charcoal and ashes as he woke again. He was in a circular chamber twelve feet across, with walls of pitted plaster. A room in a tower, perhaps. A castle tower, and he thought of the castle in the Walt Disney pictures, a fairytale place of pointy turrets, witches, evil dwarves and captive princesses. A fire smouldered in a little grate, and the wind was driving the smoke back down the chimney.

His mind was clearer now. On the far side of the morphine there was the memory of pain – snatches of sensation, vivid as nightmares. Days and nights he had walked, a crooked shape on the howling mountain, the rush of the fever driving him on. He remembered the lead slug caught in his back, grating against bone, huge and vicious as a cannon shell. He saw himself lying in a pool under a white cascade, drinking freezing water until his throat seized and he could drink no more. He saw clouds massed huge in the sky overhead, slow rolling, as stripes of pale sun moved across the bare slopes of the mountains above him and the colours of the trees were russet into grey into deep evergreen.

He ran his fingers over the edge of the sheets. They were clean, rough with starch, and smelt slightly of camphor. His right leg was bound up and huge as a log. A jolt of fear, and his hand went to his throat and found it bare, the identity discs gone. A moment more and he remembered dragging the leather strap over his head and holding the discs clutched in his fist; he had hurled them away from him somewhere out there on the mountain. Nameless now, lost and alone. He wished to remember no more of the past – he wanted to erase it all from his mind. There was a breeze around his head, and he crawled an arm from under the bedcovers to touch his skull, feeling bare bone under a light rasping stubble. His head had been shaved.

Rising panic sped his blood. He turned his head to stare at the narrow door, expecting it to open and his torturers to return, then forced himself to breathe slowly. But he could feel the weakness in his body – the slightest movement pained him, and he had barely the strength to raise himself from the bed. He could do nothing, and there was no possibility of escape.

Eyes closed, he let the slow wash of morphine carry him, bringing random disconnected images. He was back in school, the emptied daytime dormitory in wet rainy light, sharp white sheets up to his chin and the bedsprings hooking into his back. Outside the bleary windows a landscape of heavy suet and damp wool, cows placid under drizzle. Then he was sitting beside a fire in a mountain valley far away, and Bruno was explaining why he had to kill him. He nodded his head, took one of Bruno's cigarettes, understood everything.

Some time between day and night, he rolled, wincing, and craned his neck to look around the room. The fire had gone out. Beside the bed was a low table and a chair with a coat draped over the back. On the table an unlit oil lamp stood beside a bowl half filled with some sort of grey porridge and a big earthenware jug. Feeling stronger now, and very thirsty, he twisted himself up from the bed and stretched across to take the jug. It was heavy; his arms trembled as he tipped it to his mouth, lips on the thick glazed rim, gulping back water.

As he lowered the jug he noticed for the first time what he was wearing. Pyjamas in striped blue and grey, with a worn monogram on the breast pocket. Of his own clothes there was no sign, but when he replaced the jug he saw his wristwatch lying curled on the table. Beside the door were his boots, filthy and blackened. They looked like meat.

Carefully, he lifted the piled sheets, quilts and blankets aside. He was weak, painfully thin. One of his legs was encased in bandages above the knee, another bandage circled his chest and left shoulder. His hands were raw and blistered from the cold, and his feet stuck up grey and knotted at the end of the bed. As quietly as he could, he shifted himself from the mattress, tentative as his legs took his weight, and slowly stood up. There was no sound from the door, no cough or shuffle of a guard outside. The bound leg flamed with trapped irritation as his blood began to circulate. He reached out to the chair to steady himself, took four paces across the room, then began lacing his boots over bare feet. Beneath the bed he saw the curve of a bedpan and felt a quick pinch of shame.

The coat was heavy serge in some dull shade, a man's overcoat with wide lapels and nothing in the pockets but fluff and crumbs. As he shrugged himself into it he noticed the pair of crutches leaning in the corner beside the door. A bakelite switch on the wall too, but when he snapped it down nothing happened. The darkness was gathering, and he could barely make out the shape of the bed against the white of the wall. He tried the door, was surprised when it opened. No sentry stood waiting on the far side. Instead he saw the angle of a dirty wall, dusty cobwebs hanging over a spiral stairway. Even with the dead fire the room had been bed-warm, body-warm. On the stairs the cold was unchallenged, harsh as old iron.

Swinging himself awkwardly on the crutches, he dropped down the stairs to a corridor, stone paved and shadowed. A door to his right, large and studded with metal, opened to the outside. Misty drizzle fell luminous in the last of the daylight. Breathing in ice, breathing out fog, he descended a flight of stone steps into a wide courtyard.

Opposite rose the bulk of a tower, a cube of massive old masonry beneath a low peaked roof; directly in front of him was a ruined structure that might have been a small chapel. Gravel grated under his boots as he crossed the courtyard, and the keen air tightened his shaven scalp. Other buildings were ranged around the far end, fronted by a two-storied structure of squat stone arches, a portico with a loggia above it. Broken walls enclosed the courtyard on all sides. From the loggia, distinct in the massive gloom, a sliver of firelight showed through a part-opened door. A pale shape stood in the angle of the yard: an arched wellhead capped with the statue of an angel, weathered now and almost faceless. It made him shudder to see it, the form almost obscured by misty darkness. He should return to his room – if discovered, he would be too weak to run or to fight – but still he moved forward.

Crutches cracking at the stone, he scaled the wide steps to the loggia. Through the arching shadows he reached the door, iron-studded oak with the light behind. At the threshold he paused, listening, thinking there should be voices or sounds of life. Nothing but the same uncanny stillness. He raised his hand and pushed gently at the door, tensed for the whine of a hinge. He hesitated – the warmth on his face drawing him, the ice at his back pressing him forward – then crossed the threshold.

The room was heavy with the heat of the fire. Dark wood panelling, a long table set with candles, cups, plates. He stood in the open doorway swaying on the crutches, seeing shadows and smoke. He felt he was looking through a thick pane of clouded glass. At the far end of the room an inner door was opening and he shifted, meaning to escape back outside. A figure stepped into the room: a young woman carrying a loaded tray who glanced across the room and saw him there. She cried out, once and suddenly, and the tray fell from her hands.

'Carla!' he said, then fell against the wall as the heavy door swung shut behind him.

'You gave yourself quite a shock there. Quite a shock indeed! And I'm not surprised either. Very stupid of you to go wandering about in your condition, no?'

The man – a doctor, apparently – stood over the bed with his hands in the pockets of his double-breasted pinstripe suit. He was a small man with a broad fleshy face and a neat moustache. The suit looked too big for him, a pre-war cut; perhaps he'd lost weight in recent years. 'What did you think you were doing, eh? Creeping into the house to rob us? Thought you'd murder us all in our beds maybe?'

He was speaking in Italian, with a pronounced Turinese accent. Now he carefully removed the covers from the lower part of the bed. 'Ought to get those bandages off, no?' The shutters were closed, the fire burning and the lamp lit, and the air in the room was close and stale.

Lying still in the bed, he watched the doctor attending to the bandages. The man talked as he worked, a staccato stream of Italian he gave no impression of understanding.

'So . . . so,' the doctor said, rolling back the bandage with scrupulous care. 'Not as bad as I'd feared. You're a lucky man, eh! Lucky we found you out there when we did – another day or two and you'd be dead. Filthy wound, that was, but it looks like you can keep the leg after all, heh heh!' He spoke softly, as if to himself. The sort of man who laughs at private jokes.

'Now,' the doctor went on, 'I should take a look at your back. Move onto your side please.'

A long pause, eyebrows raised.

'*Non capito.*' He spoke with a distinct British accent. 'No understand . . . *non parlo Italiano.*'

'Hmm? Don't understand me? Well well, a foreigner!'

The doctor looked away smiling – his private joke – then made a gesture for him to loosen his shirt. His fingers were numb with cold and fumbled at the buttons, and the doctor, tensely fastidious, leaned down and snapped them open one by one. Then, prodding with his fingertips, he rolled him over onto his side and pushed up the back of the pyjama shirt.

'The wound here was badly lacerated,' the doctor went on, speaking as if to himself, not caring if his patient understood him or not. 'The bullet entered obliquely, clearly deflected, judging by the deformed tip, but it missed your vertebral column by only a few centimetres.' The dressings tightened suddenly and then eased, and the doctor's hands were crawling over his back, cold on his skin. The sudden physical intimacy felt invasive and he tried not to flinch.

'There was some suppuration. I had to cut away the flesh around the wound to reach the abscess and drain it, but the bullet itself was lodged quite neatly so I didn't attempt removal. If it shifts, you may experience extreme pain, even paralysis, but there's not much I can do about that.'

He paused, pressed down slightly. Pain lanced from the wound. 'I'd feared septicaemic fever, possibly also pneumonia. I treated for both, although I'm happy to see you're recovering well. I've used most of my supplies, hydrogen peroxide and carbolic and so on. And I can spare no more morphine for you either . . . I had to rely on chloroform for the principal anaesthetic.'

The doctor was swabbing at the wound now, breath warm against his shoulder. A sharp smell of alcohol, then he applied another dressing. He seemed too quick, nervous even, whistling through his teeth when he wasn't talking. 'Your clothes, of course,' he said, glancing up from his work, 'we had to burn. Lice, you know. Therefore the shaved head too. I might ask how you came to be in such a shocking state, eh? Ah, but you don't understand me . . .'

He said nothing as the doctor slipped a fresh bandage beneath his ribs and across his back. A light touch on the shoulder, and he pulled the pyjama shirt back around himself.

'The soup, then,' the doctor said abruptly, when his patient was lying flat again. 'You must eat!' He took the bowl from the table, brown fluid to the brim, and a large wooden spoon.

'Eat, eh? *Food?*' he said, stirring the spoon in the bowl then raising it towards him.

He lifted his head obligingly, sucking soup off the spoon. It tasted of burnt meat stock, and the salt stung his lips. 'That's it,' the doctor said, holding the bowl well away from his suit. 'I'm not a nurse, you see. Not too good at this sort of thing. Odetta's been looking after you all this time, but after her shock last night we thought it best she didn't see you. Thought you were a ghost, eh! Died and come back to haunt us! Young women, you know. Their nerves, not good. Something about them at that age, no?'

He continued to drink the soup as the doctor spoke, careful to show no sign of comprehension. The doctor didn't seem to care.

'Good,' he said, placing the bowl down. 'Now you should rest a little more, no? Perhaps tomorrow we might allow you out. My brother, the Barone, is keen to meet his guest. I'm sure, hmm, you'll find him a more . . . *obliging* host than me!'

The doctor brushed lightly at his sleeves, then made for the door. Before leaving he looked back; a safe distance from the bed now, a slow hauteur squared his shoulders inside the boxy suit.

'Don't think,' he said, 'that we trust you.'

Blinking, expressionless, he lay in the bed without moving until he heard the key turn in the lock. *I don't trust you either.*

3

ARRAYED IN CANDLELIGHT, they were waiting for him in the dining room.

Earlier that evening the doctor had led him, dressed in pyjamas and overcoat, down the spiral steps from his room to the stone-flagged corridor, then into a room fogged with welcome steam in the glow of a paraffin lamp. An ancient bathtub, its enamel chipped and cracked to oxidised zinc, stood by one wall, a chair with piled towels and clothes by the other, and between them a washstand and a toilet. He was glad to see that at least: no more of the humiliating bedpan.

The doctor removed his bandages and dressings, then left him standing before the misted mirror. Painfully he mapped the bruises and the scars, turning and craning to look back at the raw wound below his left shoulder, a fierce red comma incised into his flesh, ringed with purple and blue. He looked at his face and saw age cut deep into the features. The rough stubble that covered his head and jaw gave him a savage look. Beside the bath was a cake of good soap, a shaving brush and a set of antique razors in a calfskin wallet. He shaved sitting in the bath, angling the mirror to his hollowed face.

The clothes that had been set out for him were a strange assortment: white dress shirts in dated styles, their detachable collars slightly grubby, trousers from long-separated suits, tweed plus-fours, a jacket in garish checks. Some of them fitted and some did not, but in the end he assembled an outfit – heavy twill workman's trousers, a flannel shirt and a roll-neck sweater of dark grey wool. The rest he left on the chair, reeking of mothballs. In the mirror he had stroked his fresh-shaven jaw, blinked and tried to look agreeable. He brushed his teeth, gargled and spat. Then he pulled the overcoat back around him, picked up the crutches and waited for the doctor to take him to dinner.

Fire-warmth wrapped him as he passed through the arched doorway from the loggia. The doctor conducted him with a light touch to a chair at the end of the table, a throne-like thing of hefty black wood and worn upholstery. Crutches propped to either side, he dragged the coat from his shoulders and lowered himself down to sit. For a minute there was silence – only the snapping of the fire, the gentle rush as cinders collapsed into flame.

'Well, he looks amenable enough to me,' the Barone said at last. 'Not quite the wild beast after all!' He sat at the head of the table, his back to the fireplace, a boy to his left and a girl to his right. With the glow behind him he looked somehow insubstantial, a figure of dark smoke. The doctor circled the table and took his seat. The sixth chair remained vacant. The fire was scattering sparks up the chimney.

'*So*, then,' the Barone said, his crisp English only faintly accented, 'welcome, sir, to my home.'

A leap in his blood, and for a moment he stared. The dread of discovery was deep in him and it was unnerving to be addressed so directly.

'Don't be surprised, please,' the Barone said, smiling and leaning forward into the candlelight. 'I spent many years in England. I studied at Trinity College, Cambridge, in fact. Oh, but I am assuming that you *are* English? I hope so, or I'll look rather foolish . . .'

'I am English, yes,' he said, finding the words difficult, the language thick and heavy in his mouth.

'Splendid! Then we can be civilised *Englishmen* together, no?' The Barone sat up straight again, spreading his hands on the table. To either side, his family gazed at him.

'My name,' he announced, 'is Paolo Cavigliani, Barone di Salussola, Signore di Briasco, and master of Castelmantia, which is the name of this place. My brother Umberto you have already met, of course.' He gestured to the doctor, who inclined his head politely.

'This is my daughter, Odetta, and my son Pietro. And my wife . . . well, she will be joining us shortly.'

The Barone resembled his brother only superficially: while the doctor wore an evasive, ill-fitting discomfort, the Barone exuded calm assurance. He was slim and angular, well dressed in a charcoal-grey suit and a tie of gold silk weave, and aged somewhere in his late forties. His hair, the same shade as his suit, was brushed back smoothly from a narrow, half-smiling face and thick black brows. A handsome man, though slightly unsettling in the frankness of his gaze, he seemed perfectly in keeping with his surroundings. The candles lit his face starkly, giving him the look of a sorcerer armoured with powerful magic.

He recognised the daughter, Odetta: she had been with him often during his illness, and she was the girl he had surprised when he last entered this room. Actually she looked nothing at all like Carla. She was in her mid teens; her features had the rounded softness of adolescence, and her dark curls were cropped short of her shoulders and pinned behind her ears with silver slides. She glanced between him and her father, as if wanting to speak but uncertain how to begin. Opposite her sat the boy, Pietro, clearly the younger child. He looked about eleven or twelve and was thin and withdrawn, barely lifting his eyes from the table.

Only seconds had passed since the Barone last spoke, but already the sound of footsteps came from an adjacent corridor. The door near the fireplace swung open, and the last member of the family walked into the room.

Maybe it was the deliberate effect of her delayed entrance, maybe the sense of expectation that had preceded it, but the Baronessa's appearance was a surprise. A tall woman, taller apparently than her husband, she moved across the room in a long evening dress of midnight-blue silk. A fox-fur stole draped her shoulders, framing a necklace of pearls. She wore her hair elaborately waved, scraped back from her temples and gathered in a gleaming mass at the nape of her neck. As she passed the Barone's chair he took her hand and lightly kissed the back of her wrist, almost in congratulation.

'My wife,' the Barone said. 'The Baronessa Teresa Cavigliani.'

She was not quite beautiful, he saw now as she took the vacant chair between him and the boy – maybe forty years old, with a thin and high-boned face, a long aquiline nose and deep-set eyes. Not a pretty face, but striking in its austerity: the face of a Byzantine icon.

'My family,' the Barone continued, 'will not understand us, but I can translate for them if necessary.'

An expectant hush. The need for caution pricked at his skin, the need to guard himself without appearing guarded. He sensed that the same game was being played by the man at the far end of the table. He cleared his throat, shifted in his throne.

'I should introduce myself then,' he said. 'My name's Brookes. Francis Brookes, and I'm a captain in the British army.'

'*Il nostro ospite è un ufficiale inglese,*' the Barone said to his family. They looked with quiet faces from him to Brookes, as the Barone nodded for him to continue.

'I confess I don't remember much of how I came to be here, but I'd like to thank you all for looking after me so well. Particularly your brother and your daughter here.' He gestured to them, half smiling at each in turn. 'I understand they did a lot for me.' He had to force the politeness, keeping his tone neutral.

'Ah yes, Umberto was very . . . *exercised* over your condition when we brought you in,' the Barone replied. 'He's not actually a surgical doctor by profession, you see. He usually deals with the issues of women, shall we say. Formerly he attended to some of the most noble ladies in Turin. I'm afraid your case rather threw him back on his medical-school training – I only hope he didn't hack away at you too grievously!'

A pause then while the Barone translated what had been said. His brother merely glanced up briefly, then resumed his scrutiny of the tabletop.

'But I am being a terrible host!' the Barone declared suddenly. 'We should have *un aperitivo* before eating.' In Italian he asked his brother if it was safe for their guest to drink alcohol.

'I suppose so,' the doctor said, 'in moderation.'

The Barone signalled to Odetta, and the girl got up and went to an open cabinet where bottles stood ranked in shadow. She returned with a tall red, pouring the wine inexpertly into the glasses. The bottle dripped as she lifted it, and wine splashed the curve of his glass; Brookes watched it as it ran, black in the candlelight.

'And so you are an English officer, Captain,' the Barone said, breaking his reverie. He lifted his glass and swirled it, inhaling the scent. 'But how did you come to be here?'

'I was captured in North Africa, back in '42,' Brookes replied. He sipped the wine and felt it rushing immediately in his blood. Paused to steady his words. 'I was moved between a few POW camps in southern Italy, then brought to another one near Vercelli, shortly before . . . the armistice.'

'Before Italy surrendered, you wanted to say?'

Brookes glanced at the Barone quickly, but he was still smiling, still urbane.

'Some of us escaped,' he went on. 'Actually it wasn't much of an escape, we just walked out of the gates while the guards were playing cards. That was before the Germans showed up and took control of everything. We headed for the mountains, aiming for Switzerland. The paths were harder than we'd expected. I twisted my ankle and was laid up for a month, and by the time I'd recovered, the passes were snowed under. Some of the others tried to make the crossing. I don't know if they got through . . .'

Difficult to keep his voice calm, his tone natural, stop the tension stealing in – his mouth was dry and he took another large gulp of wine.

'Sorry, it's been a while since I've spoken to anybody,' he said. Already he had betrayed himself to a degree: the penalty for sheltering escaped prisoners of war was death. About the Barone and his family he knew nothing, but how much did they know about him? He might have talked while he was delirious with fever and morphine. He wondered what language he had used, and the thought suddenly unbalanced him. As he drank his wine, he considered how much he could allow himself to risk.

'Be assured, Captain,' the Barone said, 'you are safe with us. You are our guest. The *Tedeschi* will not come to look for you here. But what then?' he went on, angling his head, inquisitorial. 'You have lived in the mountains all these months?'

'Yes, I have.' Trying to strike the right note of defiance. 'We moved around a lot, of course. There were quite a few of us by then: a couple of South Africans, a Polish officer from the RAF. In a few places we were given shelter, but we didn't stay anywhere long. Then we voted to have another go at crossing into Switzerland. We were separated. There was a patrol. Somebody fired at us, and I was hit. I . . . fell. After that I'm afraid I don't remember very much.'

A pause then, as the Barone gave his brief commentary. Brookes noticed that the Baronessa seemed to be gazing at something over his shoulder. Despite himself he turned but saw only darkness, and when he looked back her eyes were on him. Suddenly he realised he was sweating. Like an amateur, he thought. Seated furthest from the fire, he felt the great gulf of cold and shadow at his back.

'It's surprising to me,' the Barone said, 'that you and your friends were able to live undetected for so long. Over a year, you say? You must be aware that there are many others in these mountains. There are a great many – how should one call them? – bandit gangs operating in this area. Did you see nothing of them?'

'I suppose you mean the partisans. If you don't mind, I prefer that term.'

'As you wish. Did they not assist you?'

'No. We saw some of them, but our duty was to escape from enemy territory, so we kept ourselves apart from them.'

'I quite understand,' the Barone said. 'We know so little, you see, of what happens outside our walls. We have no wireless here, and very few visitors to bring us news. You might say we live rather cut off from the world and its problems.'

'Then I would say you are very lucky.'

A strange, condescending smile from the Barone; his daughter was asking something now, speaking to her father but gazing at Brookes.

'Odetta would like to know,' the Barone said, 'whether you saw any wild animals during your sojourn in the wilderness?'

'Well, yes,' Brookes replied, addressing himself to the girl. She stared back at him with uncomprehending fascination, eyes dark-rimmed and alert. 'We saw quite a few,' he said. 'Deer, of course, and mountain goats. And sometimes we heard wolves howling at night, although we never actually saw one.'

'Wolves?' the Barone said, and raised an eyebrow. 'How unusual.' Then he turned to his daughter and gave a translation.

All this time the Baronessa had sat silently at Brookes' right hand, upright in her chair. A palpable tension about her – she seemed uneasy, perhaps angry, certainly apprehensive. As if she feared some outrageous act at any moment. Now she stirred herself, tapping her son on the shoulder and pointing towards the fire. The boy left the table without a word.

The fireplace was an enormous edifice, filling half of the rear wall of the room. Below the massive stone chimney-breast and the ledge of the mantelpiece the fire itself looked distant, deep in its sooty cave. Tall irons on either side might once have held a spit for roasting meat, but now supported a blackened grill where several heavy pots stood over the heat. Wrapping his hands in a rag, the boy took one of these pots and carried it with quaking arms back to the table, setting it down on a woven mat at the centre. Greasy steam from the pot, and the smell of vegetable broth.

There was no ceremony, no piety before the meal was served. It was Teresa, the Baronessa, who leant across to the pot and ladled out food into each of the dishes. Something aggressive about the way she moved, the contrast between her elegance and her actions; it seemed deliberate. Only when the dishes were all filled did the family pause, glancing towards the Barone.

'*Buon' appetito*,' he said.

Macaroni floated glistening pale in the broth. Brookes ate slowly, conscious of his hunger, the almost painful easing of the tight knot in his gut, but still wary. The food, thin and oversalted but hot after stewing over the fire, made him sweat again. The glasses had been refilled and he drank. Easy, he thought; don't let yourself relax.

'Maybe it's rude to ask,' he said, 'but I notice you've nobody to help you here. No servants, that is.' He was already sure of the answer – the kitchen set up over the fire, the piles of crockery on the sideboard. The family had moved everything into this one room.

'No, no servants,' the Barone said as he ate. 'We had to send them away. It seemed cruel to keep them from their own homes and families in times like these. They were from Turin, you see, city people.'

'No electricity either?'

'No electricity, no running water. There is a pump in the yard, but it's fed from our own cistern, and often it's quicker to use buckets from the well. I suppose to you our lives must seem very primitive, no?'

'You forget, sir. I've been living in a mountain hut for over a year.'

'Oh, but of course,' the Barone said, with a dry flicker of amusement.

'Then I need not apologise for the lack of luxury! This is, after all, only a mountain hut on a larger scale.'

The rest of the family said nothing while they were eating. Only the daughter, Odetta, whispered sometimes to her father. When she thought he was not looking, she watched Brookes with keen observation, but when she got up to clear the plates she would not meet his eye.

After the macaroni came a rice dish, boiled with roast chestnuts. When he was with the partisans Brookes had eaten chestnuts almost every day, and the smell alone made him queasy. The wine had gone straight to his head, and despite the poor scanty food his stomach already felt full.

As the Barone and his family ate Brookes looked around the room. What had before been a vague space of firelight and shifting shadow now took form and substance: not as large a chamber as it had once seemed, probably not the largest in the castle. A servants' hall or living room at one time, perhaps. The walls were panelled with smoked wood, under a ceiling of heavy black beams. On the side opposite the door to the loggia were two deep window alcoves, piercing the thickness of the outer wall – nearly six feet of masonry sloping towards the sealed and shuttered windows. Dim pictures hung on the walls, prints and old photographs. Brookes saw dogs, horses, portraits of men and women alike in anonymous murk. There was a side table with an antique wind-up gramophone, the curved trumpet matted with dust, and a squat black telephone. Cabinets held bottles, ornamental plates and racks of cutlery. He noticed the heavy spoon he was using – old silver, with a crest on the handle. The fork beside his plate had a different crest. There was something, he thought, mismatched about the whole room: no chair was the same as the next, and even the plates were odd.

Over the fireplace was a thick wooden board with a carved armorial crest – the same as the one on the spoon handle. The sculpted shield was painted black, and bore the silver blazon of an armoured knight on a caparisoned horse with sword raised. Above the knight was a double eagle on a band of dirty yellow.

'You are looking at the crest,' the Barone said, catching the direction of his gaze. He turned in his chair to regard it. 'The arms of the Cavigliani family,' he said. 'You can find the same motif carved on some of the arches around the building. You see we also carry the eagle of the Holy Roman Empire.'

'Your ancestors must have lived here for many years,' Brookes said.

'Since the early fifteenth century, in fact,' the Barone told him. 'We were granted the castle by the Visconti of Milan when they took over this land. Although in fact it was originally built by the Counts of Biandrate, back in the twelfth century, I believe.'

The Baronessa glared at him as he spoke, but said nothing.

'We used only to come here in summer,' he went on, 'for holidays, you know. The place has always been rather shabby, and I intended to have it restored. But with the current conflict, we decided to leave Turin and move back here.' He shot a smile at his wife, who did not return it.

'The current conflict?' Brookes said. 'You make war sound so ordinary.'

'An effect of living here,' the Barone said. He swept his hand lightly before him, indicating the circle of firelight and the dark castle beyond. 'This place has seen so many wars. It was besieged by the Imperial army, the Lombard League and the Dolcinian heretics, occupied by the French, the Spanish and the Savoyards . . . Wars have swirled around us. But here we are still.'

On the sideboard close to the door Brookes noticed a single photograph in a silver frame, quite distinct from the forgotten objects that cluttered the walls. The photograph showed a young man in his early twenties, grinning and handsome in an open-necked shirt.

'Is this a relative too?' Brookes asked. There was a short pause.

'My eldest son, Vittorio,' the Barone said. 'Sadly he was killed.'

'I'm sorry to hear that.'

'Yes, he died in North Africa, in Tunisia. Killed by the English.'

The Baronessa dropped her fork. It clattered into her dish. Across the table, her son looked up abruptly, alert for the first time since the meal began.

'What the hell did you tell him that for?' – she spoke in Italian, using the Piemontese dialect, but Brookes understood. And he knew that she had understood everything all along.

'Don't get upset, my dear,' the Barone replied to her. Then, in English, 'I'm sorry, Captain, my wife cannot bear to hear his name mentioned.'

Teresa was frozen, only a pulse working in her jaw. 'You're hideous,' she said, then picked up her spoon again and resumed eating.

Brookes lifted his empty glass, then set it down again. 'War is never just, I'm afraid,' he said quietly.

'Please,' the Barone replied. 'We won't mention it again.'

Dinner had been cleared, the rest of the family had retired and Brookes and the Barone sat together. Their two chairs were drawn close to the heat of the dying fire. A coffeepot stood on the grill above the glowing coals, and the Barone poured coffee into small porcelain cups. He took a silver case from his inside pocket and opened it on a side table – four Calypso cigarettes and a book of matches.

'Help yourself,' he said. 'They are in short supply here, but they compensate for the bad coffee, I find.'

Brookes lit one of the cigarettes. The taste was rank and made his head reel after so long without smoking, but he was tired and craved the alertness of nicotine. The Barone stared into the fire, his face cut from shadow.

'I must apologise for my wife,' he said at last. 'She is not in the best of tempers. It was never her idea to come here, you see – she would have stayed in Turin and made the best of it. Teresa is a woman who needs . . . the finer things, you could say.'

'I had that impression,' said Brookes.

'Then you are a man of sensibility yourself, Captain. I'm pleased to hear that. You realise that for a long time I've had so little company here. We, all of us, feel very isolated.'

There was something hypnotic in his voice, his words so smooth and slightly accented that Brookes felt he could slide between them. But was there also something mannered and artificial about it? When the Barone had spoken in Italian there was none of the same elegance.

'But the isolation is self imposed,' Brookes said. 'You admitted as much yourself.'

'True indeed. But hard to bear nevertheless.'

For a while they sat in silence. Brookes drank the bitter coffee.

'You may stay with us as long as you choose,' the Barone said. 'As long as it takes you to recover fully from your injuries, certainly.'

'I don't want to burden you,' Brookes said. 'I should leave as soon as I'm able.'

'But,' said the Barone, turning from his scrutiny of the embers, 'soon the weather will become very bad. We will be snowed in! I couldn't possibly turn you out into a mountain winter. Where would you go?'

'I'd find somewhere. Thank you, but I really should leave as soon as your brother pronounces me fit.'

The Barone stared at Brookes a moment, one hand cupping his chin. A gleam of firelight was trapped in his left eye.

'You must understand, Captain,' he said, 'that I put my family before all. Even, I'm afraid, before courtesy. I know there are things that you don't wish to tell me, things that perhaps it's safer I do not know. But still I wish to know a *little* more about you.'

Brookes ground out his cigarette in the ashtray and frowned.

'Forgive me,' the Barone said. 'I too have been a soldier, and I know the prohibitions that imposes. But I've explained about myself and my situation. I just wish, for the sake of my peace of mind, you see . . . I am not your enemy, Captain. I would hope to know a little more than name, rank and number.'

'I was born in London, if that's the sort of thing you want to know,' Brookes said. 'My family moved around a lot when I was young – my father was in the diplomatic service. I joined the army young, and I suppose it became my real home. I was posted to Alexandria when the war broke out: 550 Company, Royal Army Service Corps, attached to the 7th Armoured Division. I was in charge of supply depots – ammunition and fuel convoys, that sort of thing. Not very glamorous work at all, not very . . . heroic, you know. My unit was surrounded near a place called Bir Hacheim, in the Libyan desert. We never fired a shot. After that, things went much as I told you.'

The Barone was smiling again, the light flashing in his eye. 'Very good,' he said, 'very good.' He eased his shoulders back, stretching in his chair, and Brookes had the uncomfortable sensation of being weighed, measured and understood. 'I'm sorry if I seemed to doubt your credentials, Captain, but in these times one can never be too sure.'

'That's certainly true.'

Laughing quietly, the Barone poked at the remains of the fire.

Brookes had the distinct impression that his display of candour was assumed, and that he was supposed to realise as much.

'I must ask a few considerations of you,' the Barone said. 'While you are here, however long that may be, you can move about the castle as you wish. But, please, you must not show yourself at the windows, nor at the gate. It is a precaution only.'

'I understand.'

'I'm glad of that. I said that we hold the world outside our walls, but sometimes it comes nevertheless, sniffing about. Rather like those wolves you mentioned, perhaps.'

'Perhaps.'

A sound from the darkness of the room made them both glance up then. The Baronessa stood beside the table, a coat pulled over her gown and a paraffin lamp in her hand.

'Paolo,' she said to the Barone. 'Come on. It's time.'

The Barone got up with a show of fatigue. He straightened his jacket. 'You must excuse us for a short while,' he said. 'Please help yourself to cigarettes if you wish.' The far door closed behind him, and there was the sound of a bolt being drawn.

Brookes sat still beside the fire, counting slowly. After twenty seconds he got up and went to the door, supporting himself on a single crutch and the edge of the table. A thin blade of lamplight showed beneath it, but there was no give when he leant against the panels. Listening, he heard feet shuffling, the creak of a shutter, no voices. Silently he crept back across the room. He lifted the receiver of the telephone and heard nothing: the line was dead. He returned to the fire, lit another cigarette and waited.

Seventy-six seconds, and the door opened. Umberto, the doctor, walked across the room to the fireplace, then pointed to the outer door.

'Bed now,' he said. 'Understand? *Sleep.*' He mimed a pillow, folded hands against his cheek.

Brookes nodded, tossed the cigarette into the hearth and hauled himself up onto the crutches. When he glanced back, the door at the end of the room was closed once more.

4

D AYS PASSED, UNCOUNTED, before Brookes felt strong enough to walk without the crutches. The doctor brought him a stick, iron-hard grey wood polished by many hands, and he exercised each day in the yard, pacing in the cold mist. He had not eaten with the family since the night of his introduction; instead food was brought to his door, left on the threshold with a polite knock: bowls of thin minestrone, chestnut polenta, sometimes a jug of wine. Once he reached the door quickly enough to catch sight of the daughter, Odetta, retreating back down the steps – she turned at the curve of the stairway and waved up to him, smiling.

If the Cavigliani family seemed to be avoiding him, he had no reason to resent it. Intimacy brought the risk of disclosure, and he did not want to test the boundaries of their hospitality either. They were exiles from the world, and whatever intrigues motivated them were none of his concern. It was almost amusing, Brookes thought, to watch them deploying themselves against him, shutting him out when he had no wish to be let in. But his nerves were stretched by the unusual confinement, the weakness of his body, and his patience was growing short. He tried to clear his head of thoughts; he was safe, and nobody could find him. He would stay at the castle as long as it took him to recover fully, and then he would leave, whatever the Barone might think.

In his room, he cracked open the inner shutters and dragged himself up to the cold embrasure of the window to look outside. Below him lay a steep valley, bare trees scratchy though the bank of mist and rain. Everything was smudged and formless, and he felt the weight of it, damp scented emptiness. Death's landscape. Beneath the window was a fifty-foot plunge down buttressed walls and raw rockface; when he leaned further, pressing his face to the glass of the window, he could see a road rising from the cleft of the valley towards the jutting block of the gatehouse.

The road would lead to a town, and a bigger road, maybe a railway line along a larger valley. He pictured himself walking away down the road, away from the castle until he vanished into the grey mist. Another two weeks, he thought. Maybe three – then I'll be gone.

Beneath the faceless stone angel, Brookes sat on the coping of the well in the centre of the courtyard. He had walked the hundred paces from the ruined chapel to the well six times. A dull day, the year declining steeply into winter; freezing wind soughed off the mountain slopes, and the courtyard was lagooned with puddles. From where he was sitting, Brookes could take in the dimensions of the whole castle. It was neither large nor impressive, but strong and compact, gripping an outcrop of the mountain like a curled stone fist. The road from the valley passed through the toothless arches of a sunken gatehouse, then rose again on a steep mossy incline within the walls before curving up into the courtyard.

His gaze travelled to the square tower: the original keep he supposed, the nucleus of the castle. No glass showed in its narrow windows, and the slates hung from the roof. Around the base of the tower was a mess of dilapidated sheds, filled with rubbish, old doors sagging from hinges fastened with twine. The main buildings were ranked around the other two sides of the yard with a single turret jutting up at the angle. The dereliction of the place was obvious; the moss that chased the cracks in the stone, the decayed mortar, the sagging roofs full of rents and cavities.

Brookes' own room in the round tower lay at the end of a withered arm of buildings extending past the gatehouse. Outside stood the ruined and roofless chapel, and beside it the lower end of the courtyard was bounded by a low stone balustrade with a ragged garden beneath. Beyond the furthest tumbled wall the flanks of the mountains were dark and snow bright through the mist. Brookes knew that he must have come down from that direction, stumbling and feverish. The recollection made him shudder.

Leaning, he gazed down the throat of the well: bright green moss on wet black rock, and the glint of water far below. When he looked up again, the Baronessa Teresa was standing at the head of the steps from the loggia.

At first he didn't recognise her. The immaculate mask had been dropped, and instead of silk gown and pearls she was wearing a thick cable-knit cardigan buttoned to the neck, a pleated skirt and rubber boots. In her hand she carried a tin bucket. Brookes waved a greeting, and she pointed to the bucket and began to descend. As she approached, he noticed her lined face and the rings beneath her eyes. She wore no make-up, and looked more attractive for it. Even in the rubber boots she moved gracefully.

'Hello,' he said, in English.

Clasping the cardigan tight to her throat, the Baronessa placed the bucket on the coping of the well. Fixed beneath the arch of the wellhead, under the weathered angel, was a pulley with a rope and an iron-bound pail. Without a glance at Brookes, she lifted the pail and dropped it down the well – it boomed into the water far below.

'*Vous parlez Français, peut-être, Madame?*' he asked.

'*Bien sûr,*' she replied quietly, after a short pause. She began hauling on the rope, drawing up the loaded pail. When it was clear of the well she swung it across and tried to tip it, splashing the water into the tin bucket.

'Let me help you,' he said in French.

'You don't have to, Captain,' she said. 'You are still an injured man.' Tired dignity in her voice; her French was academy-perfect.

'I can manage. Please.'

He hefted the pail in both hands and tipped it over. Some of the water splashed onto his hands, ice cold. Teresa held the bucket steady until it was full.

'I'll carry it for you,' he said, taking the handle. She stepped back, folding her arms.

'Are you sure that you're strong enough for that?'

'Quite strong enough,' he said.

She walked ahead of him as they crossed the yard, head down, hugging her chest. Brookes leaned heavily on the stick, the bucket swinging in his left hand, and the wound in his back burned and throbbed. As they climbed the steps to the loggia he felt pain shooting up his injured leg.

At the top she turned and took the handle of the bucket.

'I can carry it now, thank you,' she said. He shrugged, keeping hold of the handle and for a moment their hands touched.

'As you wish,' she said, letting go, and stepped through a door.

Brookes followed her into a small chamber, much smaller than the dining room: a scullery or back kitchen, with a pot of water over a fire in the grate and a heavy ceramic sink piled with sheets and clothes. Heaped along one wall were sacks of rice and flour, pyramids of tinned food; in the corner was a large bathtub with a folding canvas screen pulled partway around it.

'Put the bucket there,' the Baronessa said. She checked the pot of water over the fire, but it was not boiling yet. Sighing, she leaned back against the sink, took a cigarette from the packet on the table and lit it.

'I haven't seen the Barone for a long time,' Brookes said. 'Is he busy, perhaps?' He picked up the packet of cigarettes, extracted one and put it between his lips.

'Help yourself,' the Baronessa said coldly. She took the matches from her pocket and tossed them onto the table. 'My husband has been busy, yes,' she said. 'Busy and sleeping. They all sleep a lot. It's the best way to keep warm in this horrid place.'

'And you? You don't sleep?' He lit the cigarette, inhaled sharply.

'I can't sleep,' she said.

For a while they stood smoking, waiting for the pot of water to boil. Brookes scrubbed fingers across his scalp, through the coarse, yellow-brown stubble.

'He likes you anyway,' Teresa said. 'He claims to, at least. It's strange, because he's always detested the English.'

'Really? Why?'

She looked at him with a wide-open, credulous expression. 'Many people in Italy do,' she said. 'They find you cold, deceitful, arrogant and lacking sensibility.'

'I suppose I should laugh at the irony of that.'

The Baronessa shook her head, then extinguished her cigarette.

'Don't forget, your planes are bombing our cities,' she said.

She lifted the bucket of water and hefted it onto the rim of the sink, then poured the water onto the clothes. She had overfilled the bucket, and it was almost too heavy for her – she must have known Brookes would offer to carry it for her. I won't help her now, he thought.

The pot over the fire was boiling, and Teresa lifted it carefully from the grate and added it to the water already in the sink. Steam filled the room. She removed the rings from her fingers, rolled up her sleeves, then scattered soap powder from a cardboard box, stirring the heap of clothes into the water with a stick. A scum of suds formed around the islands of wet fabric.

'Apparently you want to watch me doing the laundry,' she said, raising an eyebrow.

'Perhaps I just want to watch you,' he replied.

Colour flushed her cheeks at once, and for a moment she could not speak. Then she laughed and went back to stabbing at the wet clothes. Rhythmic slop of water, and the crack of the stick against the ceramic. Brookes squatted beside the fire and warmed his hands over the coals. Abruptly she stopped stirring the clothes and stood still, staring down into the sudsy grey basin.

'You should leave here,' she said. 'Leave the castle, as soon as you can.'

'I intend to, as soon as I'm fit enough.'

'You don't understand,' she told him, with careful emphasis. 'My husband doesn't understand either. It's dangerous here, both for you and for the rest of us. You have to leave.'

Brookes stood up, picked up his stick.

'As soon as I can,' he said, 'I'll be gone.'

She turned to him, a hard and level gaze. 'I'm entirely serious, Captain. There is more here than you know. Leave as you would leave a house on fire.'

He nodded once, then turned on his heel and went outside. Down the steps to the courtyard, the icy wind whipped the heat from his face.

That night he could not sleep, as if the Baronessa's insomnia were contagious. He lay awake on his bed in the dark room, still wearing the overcoat under the heavy blankets. The wind whined and shoved at the shutters, and in the grate a famished fire guttered in the blasts of air down the chimney.

Getting out of bed, pulling the blankets around him, Brookes crossed the room and sat on the floor beside the fireplace. He was cold; colder than he had been for a long time, even in the winter bivouacs of the partisans. In the stone houses of the mountain villages, in the packed warmth of bodies under the dripping eaves, there had at least been clarity – the enemy was known, there were maps, there was a sense of time and consequence. Together they had gathered around the hissing wireless set, crouched close to hear the news of war. He remembered their faces – Bruno and the rest, men he would never see again – and wondered if they were still alive. If they had survived the ambush on the mountain they would be searching for him. All the partisans in the area would be hunting him; the fascists and the Germans too.

But the attack, the accusation and the attempted execution had been no accident. It was planned, intentional, and he knew the names of his enemies. They had wanted him dead. Carla had died in his place.

Her memory rose suddenly, keenly. He could almost feel her, a physical presence in the room: her musky scent, unwashed and earthy, campfire smoke tangled in her hair; her breath warm against his cheek as she told him of her perfect socialist future that would never, now, exist. To allow himself to think about her was painful – the shock of it stabbed deep within him. He closed his eyes, turning from the fire, and forced himself to focus, to conjure her more vividly.

That last evening together before the attack they had been arguing about her fiancé, Giorgio, taken away to a labour camp in Germany. Carla was a believer: she believed her man would return to her after the war, after the People's Victory. She was twenty-one and her family were all dead and he didn't want to argue with her, but she made him angry and he hated it. She had not been stupid, just young and surviving on belief. He remembered the gold crucifix necklace she wore, the girlish blouse of thin cream cotton beneath her combat jacket. Light brown freckles across the bridge of her nose, only visible in sunlight.

He remembered the days he spent with her at the abandoned ski resort in the mountains near Mottarone. A four-star hotel, polished wood under heavy eaves jutting from the evergreen slopes; it had been closed for the off season, and they felt they had broken open paradise. Clean white sheets, running water and a big white enamel bath with gilt taps. A bedroom with a polished floor and French doors opening onto a balcony of fretted woodwork and long, smoky views over the summer mountains.

They had bathed together then slept together. After they made love for the first time she cried; she had not been a virgin, she told him, but she had always been faithful to Giorgio. They bought fresh milk from the dairy in the village down the valley; she poured a saucer of it and crouched naked on the bed, bowing her head to lap it up. Her cropped hair curled black at the nape of her neck, and her spine curved long and slender. He embraced her, wrapping himself around the curve of her, and when he kissed her he tasted cream.

She held up a hand to his face, palm flat across one cheek, covering one eye.

'I see you like this,' she said. 'Just a half, and the rest hidden. Like you're half in shadow. You like to appear like that, don't you? What are you hiding?'

Shhh, he had said, and ran his thumb across her mouth, sealing her lips.

Brookes felt closer to Carla now than he had when she was alive. Now there was no need to conceal himself from her. They had been lovers for barely three months; that was all. He had known next to nothing about her, and everything she thought she knew of him was wrong. He scrubbed at his face, trying to drive her memory out.

He should have died in the battle, or the execution, or out on the mountain; all the odds had been against him, but somehow he had survived. It seemed unnatural now. Lying beside the fire, he could almost suspect that he had died, and that the castle was some afterlife, a shadow world of smoke and phantoms. It was a comforting illusion, almost. He could imagine that the man he had been was gone, dead and forgotten out in the night and the forests; he was somebody new, reborn without earthly concerns, without the need to conceal himself. But he could not allow himself to think like that. He had enemies, and the castle could become a prison yet.

He remembered the Baronessa's parting words, and they seemed more of a taunt than a warning. Stupid to speak to her at all, but solitude and long incapacitation had made him reckless. Dread was creeping through him, deep in his bones, and he felt the lack of a weapon keenly. Near the door was the tray with his supper dish, and he crawled across and took the knife that lay there. It was blunt thing of heavy tarnished steel, and he rasped it against the stone of the fireplace to try and give an edge to the blade. Stretching himself out beside the fire, facing the door, he drove the point of the knife into the floorboard beside him. Twice that night he reached out and grasped it, the touch of steel an anchor in the darkness.

In his dreams he saw the railway bridge at Gattinara, the span over the river a geometry of shadows in the moonlight. Again he felt the polished coldness of the rail under his palm as he placed the detonators between the sticks of gelignite – below him the river, a black sliding sheen. Then he ran crouching back along the line to where the rest of the sabotage squad lay concealed. The sudden crack as the charges went off, the engine plunging, shrieking, down from the rails and into the river, jetting smoke, dragging the carriages after it. That noise again – the scream of buckling steel.

The dream was clear as a memory, as reality relived. Nobody had spoken as the group drove up into the mountains again before dawn. Sitting in the back seat of the stolen car, he could still smell the explosive on his hands. The man beside him was weeping quietly, muttering prayers under his breath, He wished that he too could pray. He wished he had a God he could believe in.

Soon after dawn he woke, strangling a shout. He was lying curled on the floor beside the dead fire with his hand locked around the blade of the bloodied knife. Numbed by cold, he only felt the pain as he eased his grip and saw the gashes in his fingers and palm. The blade was stuck to his skin with clotting blood, and he had to peel the metal free. Outside, he dragged the bucket up from the well, then washed the blood from his injured hand and bound it with a damp rag. The cuts were not deep, but throbbed with a regular sharp pain.

The day had a battered look, the same low colourless cloud pressing in around the mountain flanks. Flocks of birds wheeled black around the roofs of the castle, and all the shutters of the main building were closed. Brookes sat on the edge of the well. He peered down the shaft, into the black throat of old stone and damp moss. There was nothing there, not a blink of reflected light. He felt the cold strike up through his body; his leg ached and the wound in his back felt sharp and new. Exhausted, clutching the bound hand to his chest, he returned to his room and slept most of the day with the blankets pulled over his head.

In the afternoon the doctor arrived, bringing a note written in neatly flowing script. Brookes read, keeping his injured hand beneath the covers, then propped the note on the table beside the bed.

Dear Captain Brookes,
My apologies for having neglected you these last days. May I invite you to join us again for dinner this evening?
Sincerely – Paolo Cavigliani

'At seven,' the doctor said. '*Seven*, understand?' and held up seven fingers, grimacing meaningfully.

Brookes nodded, waiting until the man had gone before sinking back beneath the covers. He had several hours before dinner. He slept, dreamless and warm.

5

WASHED, SHAVED AND freshly dressed in a suit of serviceable grey wool only slightly shiny with age, Brookes presented himself in the dining room at the appointed time. The doctor had returned to fetch him half an hour before, and had attended to Brookes' hand without comment – a raised eyebrow as he washed the cuts with disinfectant, a grunt of disapproval as he wrapped them with gauze, but nothing more.

Once more the table was laid and the candles lit; once more the family were gathered and waiting for him. The Baronessa was already at the table this time, dressed again in her silk evening gown. Brookes tried to catch her eye as he took his seat, but she ignored him.

The meal was roast chicken with potatoes in grease, eaten in near silence. The Barone asked Brookes about his bandaged hand,

and seemed satisfied by the answer – a glass broken on the bedside table. He commented on the weather, expecting the snow to move down from the mountains very soon. He asked if Brookes was keeping warm enough: the doctor had reported that he had a slight cold. Brookes stifled a cough and replied that he was as well as he could hope to be. He could feel the knife pressing against his right leg; after the bath, he had cut a strip of bandage and bound it there, just above the top of his boot. It was a reassurance.

The chicken was dry and fibrous, the potatoes boiled almost to pulp, but Brookes was hungry and ate with enthusiasm. It occurred to him that he had not seen any chickens around the castle, no animals of any kind. He was about to ask where the bird had come from, but decided against it.

This time the rest of the family departed quickly, as soon as the meal was done, Odetta taking the last of the dishes with her and retreating through the door leading to the scullery. Brookes and the Barone were left facing each other down the long bare table. The Barone stood up, taking one of the three-branched candelabra.

'This room is very draughty, don't you think?' he said. 'With you feeling the cold so much, I thought we could retire to my study. I have a few bottles of warming tonic.'

Brookes nodded. After sleeping all day he felt awake, alert and in no mood to return to his room in the tower. The Barone crossed to the small door at the back.

'This way,' he said. 'Bring a candle.'

The door led to a wood-panelled corridor. Immediately to the right was a low arch opening onto a spiral stair. At the far end of the corridor stood another door, set deep in an alcove in the wall; it would have to be the external wall of the castle, Brookes thought. They were high above ground level here, and he guessed it must lead to a balcony. The Barone was already moving away along the corridor, the light of his candelabra throwing slanted reflections across the polished wood.

There were framed pictures on the walls. Brookes paused to examine one showing a castle on a high rock above a valley with snowy mountains beyond. It was a photograph, he saw now, an old albumen print or daguerreotype; the castle was square and white, and the date was written in looping script below: 1882.

'All the pictures here show the castle, at various times in its history,' the Barone said. He returned to where Brookes stood looking at the picture.

'This photograph was taken shortly after the building was restored by my grandfather,' he said. 'There was a fire here back in the 1860s and the whole place was gutted. It stood empty for many years. My grandfather repaired the damage and had this picture taken as a commemoration. He used the castle mainly as a hunting lodge. Sadly, since those days it has declined somewhat. I'm sure you must have noticed. And this is the earliest picture we have . . .'

He moved his candelabra to the next frame, which held a yellowed woodcut print. The castle was small and blocky on its spur of rock, surrounded by the sheltering arms of the mountains. Spilling away from the walls was a string of tiny cubic houses; stiff little figures toiled in the fields that covered the hills. The date below the print was 1556.

'I rather like this picture,' the Barone said. '*Suggestivo*, don't you think?'

'Is there a village below the castle then?' Brookes asked.

'Oh yes, it's still there, but it's almost completely deserted now. Only a few houses occupied. When this picture was made it was a populous place; all these valleys were full of life in those days, had been for centuries. Very isolated, of course. The Lords of Castelmantia were always vassals of one power or another – the Empire, the Visconti or the Dukes of Savoy – but they ruled supreme over the villages around here. Rather a tyrannical sort of rule, by repute. My ancestors were robber barons of the worst sort, I'm afraid to say!' His grin looked villainous in the candlelight.

Brookes scanned the other pictures as they passed: there were photographs, etchings and drawings, the castle seen from every elevation and every angle. None showed it as decrepit as it was now. He was looking for details of the surrounding area: roads or railway lines, evidence that a large town or city might be close by, but there was nothing. Then the Barone turned aside to a smaller door flush with the panelling. He passed through and Brookes followed.

'But those people who remain in the village,' Brookes said, 'they sell you food and supplies?' He began to suspect where the evening's chicken might have come from.

'Oh yes,' said the Barone airily. 'Although they *give* rather than sell. I am still, after all, the Lord of Castelmantia!'

The chamber they had entered was far smaller than the dining room, and seemed correspondingly cluttered. A deep window-seat was set into one wall, and a fireplace stacked with kindling occupied another; the walls themselves were obscured by ranked display cabinets with dusty glass faces, a tall clock, shelves of books. A pair of crossed swords with dull and dented blades hung above the fireplace, and the heads of stuffed animals gazed down with glass eyes on a desk and a pair of worn leather armchairs.

The Barone knelt beside the fire and used the candles to kindle the sticks and charcoal in the grate.

'On the side table there is a bottle of very good cognac,' he said. 'Perhaps you might bring it, and two glasses?'

Brookes brought the drink and poured it, holding the bottle carefully with his bandaged hand, then settled himself into one of the chairs while the Barone applied a pair of old and creaking bellows to his little blaze. Something comical about him, Brookes thought, crouched over the grate, creaking away with the bellows, a look of intense concentration on his thin face. The Lord of Castelmantia!

'You're a keen hunter, then,' Brookes said, pointing to the mounted heads. The glass display cases held further trophies of the gun and the snare: a weasel arched over a dry log, several birds with moulting plumage, a hare posed in mid flight. There was a gun rack on the far wall, but where he might have hoped to see shotguns or hunting rifles there were only empty spaces.

'My father's, mainly,' the Barone said. 'Although some date from my grandfather's time. Both were sportsmen, although I never shared their enthusiasm for slaughter. I prefer to restrict myself to the running of the estate. I've been meaning to clear all the relics out of here, actually. There are a lot more throughout the castle. I believe my son finds the trophies rather unnerving.' He eased himself up with a grimace, then settled into the chair opposite Brookes.

'All the same, your setup here seems a bit feudal, if you don't mind me saying so.'

'Feudal?' the Barone said, giving the word an awkward twist. 'Well, you could say that. But perhaps not such a bad thing, in today's world, don't you think? *Feudalismo*, after all, was based on trust and responsibility. Living here, you know, one can feel that the Middle Ages are not so far distant. Only a touch away. I feel a great affection for those times – humanity was more comfortable with the unknown then. They did not demand answers and rational explanations of the world, but trusted in God and their masters. All was illuminated by the clear light of the unseen. I often think that the loss of trust, of . . . *order*, has led us to our current sad condition.'

Brookes sipped at the cognac. It was as good as the Barone had suggested, and spread a sweet fire down his throat. The cuts on his hand ached every time he raised his glass, but the warmth of the alcohol was soothing. Sticks in the grate snapped and spat, and the Barone lit an oil lamp with a tall glass flue and placed it on the table between them.

'And who do you trust, Barone?' Brookes asked. 'Where do your loyalties lie?'

'What is loyalty in a country like Italy?' the Barone said. 'We Italians are the most cynical people on earth, Captain. We seem young, but we are ancient and wise and know the folly of things. You English are mere children compared to us.'

As the Barone spoke, Brookes caught the memory that had evaded him since he entered the room. The master's study at his old school: the same meagre, flickering fire, the same surrounding cold of empty stone rooms, the seeping odour of old books and dusty upholstery. Even the Barone's attitude had something of the crafty don, circling a presumptuous student, waiting to deliver the cutting blow.

'Your wife,' he said carefully, casually, 'told me you detested the English.'

'Did she?' the Barone replied, but Brookes was certain that his expression of surprise was a sham. 'I wouldn't say that, no. She exaggerates a great deal, sometimes.'

'She also gave me a warning,' Brookes went on. He kept his gaze locked on the Barone. 'She told me I was in danger here, and should leave as soon as I could.'

The Barone was nodding, frowning. He reclined into the shadows, then abruptly started forward again and laid a hand on Brooke's knee. 'I must tell you something in confidence, Captain,' he said.

Brookes raised an eyebrow, waited for him to continue. 'My wife,' the Barone said, 'is not in the best of health. I am speaking about her *mental* condition. My brother, you know, is able to treat the worst of the symptoms, but she . . .' He broke off, covering his face with a hand. His distress seemed genuine, but Brookes was still wary.

'Shortly before we came here, my wife suffered a nervous collapse,' the Barone said. 'A mental breakdown, I think you call it. Our son's death, the difficulties of war . . . even now she is very unstable. She has a certain *paranoia* . . . and may become hysterical at times. She does not lie deliberately, but I must beg you not to put great faith in anything she tells you. Treat her with care, and please, never mention anything of what I've said to you . . .'

'I understand,' said Brookes.

'I'm glad. I'm glad you understand. You are safe here, I promise you that. Please have no thoughts of leaving until you feel completely restored to health. Now . . . of what were we speaking? Of England, no?'

'Your dislike of England.'

'Not dislike . . . I am, I could say, very disappointed in England. Disappointed in what England has become, when it had so much potential. It is the materialism of England that I detest, Captain, the scorn for all that is mysterious and unquantifiable, the quality you call *pragmatism*.'

Brookes smiled into his glass. It was a fairly inept form of goading, he thought, and he'd heard much the same and very much stronger from the partisan commissars. He remembered those interminable arguments with Carla: the future shaped and waiting, free of foreign oppression, full of bliss. The Barone was waiting for a response.

'But you are a patriot?' the Barone said. 'It angers you that I speak in this way?'

For a moment Brookes contemplated the question. 'England means very little to me now,' he replied thoughtfully. 'It's been years since I was last there, and I've forgotten most of what I knew of it. A few things I remember – voices on the radio, the smell of Lifebuoy soap, certain unavoidable gestures of reserve in social situations, I suppose . . . not enough to create a sense of belonging or loyalty.'

'Then you have no past. You are a blank, a homunculus.'

'Better to say that I have no time for the past. I believe only in the present, Barone, the *now*, in what I can touch and scent and see. What I did or felt yesterday or last year or when I was five years old has no relevance.'

'But your ancestry . . .' the Barone began.

'I have no ancestry,' Brookes cut in sharply. 'No ancestors that I acknowledge, Barone. Family trees bore me. If I were to jump out of this chair and kill you right now then my act wouldn't be conditioned by the past or the future or anything else. The present is all we have.'

If I were to kill you – where had that sprung from? Brookes felt calm, the alcohol warming him gently, but inside him a sullen resentment was building slowly, edging close to anger. He had become engaged in a contest he had no wish to fight, and no idea how to win. His bandaged hand smarted, but he forced himself to smile, and saw that the Barone was impressed.

'*Al contrario*, Captain,' he said. 'I would argue that the present is precisely what does not exist. What you call *now* is merely a liminal state between the past and the future, a medium of time in which we are suspended. If your view were correct then all would be chaos. You have a past, certainly. You choose to deny its existence, that's all.'

'I have a past, yes, of course, but it doesn't affect me now. It doesn't control me.'

'But it does! You are a soldier, you have your training in the army, your experiences in war. All the soldiers and all the wars of history have combined to create you and form what you are. You have, I think, been injured, Captain. I don't mean just the wound in your leg or the bullet in your back – you have been damaged by this war . . .' He trailed off with a quizzical air, but his eyes held an eager intensity.

Brookes reclined in his chair, looking up at the stuffed animal heads arranged around the walls: deer with curly horns, leering foxes, a bear; dead tusks and dry fur and dust. He knew the Barone expected him to reply, to continue the debate. But he had no desire for that.

'Let me ask you something, Captain,' the Barone said after a pause, gazing at him over steepled fingers. 'Consider our situation here, the two of us sitting talking beside this fire. Do we not inhabit preordained roles? You must recall stories from your past – if you can acknowledge that such a thing exists – certain stories that recur throughout the ages. A soldier, wounded in war, escaping unknown enemies, seeks sanctuary in an isolated castle . . .'

'A reclusive nobleman gives him shelter?'

'Exactly. Already we are playing certain roles dictated to us by the shared mythology of humankind. I am content that you will not, as you suggested earlier, leap up and murder me in my own home. There is nothing in the story to necessitate this.'

'Not yet, anyway. I don't recall how some of those stories end. Perhaps you have a princess hidden in a glass coffin somewhere?'

The Baron laughed silently.

'I want to show you something,' he said as he got up. He went to the mantelpiece and took down a slim case of black wood, which he set on the table. 'These have been in my family for a great many years.'

The lid of the case lifted on tiny hinges and the contents were wrapped in black silk. The Barone unfolded the silk very gently, revealing what looked like a very old pack of playing cards, larger and longer than usual and hand-painted in enamels. He slid the cards from the box, and Brookes thought he recognised the symbols painted on them – he recalled an excruciating drinks party, years before the war.

'What's this?' he said. 'Fortune telling?'

'They can be used for that,' the Barone said. He held the cards carefully as he spread the black silk on the tabletop. 'Although that is usually an amusement at travelling fairs and suchlike.'

Brookes didn't try to hide his disdain. 'And next we'll be trying spirit boards, I suppose?' But the cards were beautiful, and had their own appeal.

'Oh no, not that. Foolish games, I believe. They were rather fashionable for a time while I was at Cambridge. Largely amongst the English students, I might add. The *Tarocchi* are altogether different.'

He was laying the cards out on the black silk, an odd formality in his movements. Like a pianist, Brookes thought. The lamp was turned down low, and the cards were lit mainly by the glow of the fire. Gold leaf shone against blood-ruby, garnet and brown. Brookes had to lean in close to see them clearly. The cards showed cups and coins, swords and staves; one depicted a man hanging by one foot, another showed a cadaver mounted on horseback, scything down a harvest of fleeing people. On another card, angels flanked a regal figure on a throne, while below them the dead rose from their coffins, naked and pink with life.

'These were painted in the seventeenth century,' the Barone said, his voice soft and hushed with respect. 'Although the designs date from much earlier. They look fragile, but they're not. Here, touch them for yourself.'

Brookes took the card nearest to him, the Six of Staves. It was surprisingly heavy, and felt stiff and brittle as glass. The back was blank, a pale rectangle the colour of old ivory smudged by time. Brookes rubbed his finger across it, and seemed to feel the touch of all those others who had held the card through the centuries. The idea gave him a queasy sensation, something dirty under his skin.

He dropped the card back onto the table. 'They're certainly very pretty objects,' he said, in the tone of a man who has little use for pretty objects. 'But if you're not intending to tell fortunes, what do you do with them?'

'Not tell fortunes exactly, no. The future is dependent on a great many factors already pre-existent. All the cards can do is elucidate some of the directions that the future might take. All of us carry truths of which we are unaware.'

The Barone gathered the cards into a pile and began shuffling them. A slow, quiet susurration. 'Would you care to try an experiment?' he asked.

Brookes refilled their glasses from the cognac bottle. He still felt a punchy combative energy in his blood, an alertness to attack. All this, he thought, could be a ruse to test his credibility, but the quiet of the castle seemed to breathe around them, waiting for him to agree.

'Some people object to the cards, you see. They find them . . . rather sacrilegious I suppose.'

Brookes grinned quickly. 'That doesn't bother me much,' he said.

'Good, then we shall begin. I would like you to shuffle the pack for yourself.'

He passed the cards to Brooke. They were so large that he found it hard to shuffle them, especially with one hand stiff and clumsy in bandages. They slid and skated and seemed to want to escape his fingers. When he had finished shuffling he placed the pack face down on the black silk.

'Now I want you to select three of the cards,' the Barone said. 'Cut the pack, and take the top three cards from the pile on your right.'

Brookes was beginning to feel slightly drunk. He had not tasted spirits for a long time, and the cognac was fierce inside him. He wanted to laugh at the ritual, but the Barone seemed to have conjured a solemn hush within the room. In the half-dark and the flickering fireglow it was difficult not to be unnerved, and he almost wished he could feel some inspiration, some sense of determined will. He cut the deck in the middle, slid the top three cards clear and sat back in the armchair.

'Well done,' the Barone said, scooping up the rest of the deck and laying it aside. 'Now arrange the cards before you in a line.'

He's taking this all completely seriously, Brookes thought. The last time he had seen the Tarot used there had been an atmosphere of barely repressed hilarity. *You should avoid travelling by water. Beware of women with red hair carrying axes. Somebody in your family is conspiring to murder you . . .*

Brookes laid out the cards.

One by one, the Barone turned them face up.

Five of Cups.

Knight of Swords.

The Tower.

'So?' Brookes said. 'Will I meet a tall dark stranger, or what?'

The Barone gave him a wry look and shook his head.

'The cards are read from left to right,' he said. 'The first card signifies the past, very interesting in your case. Particularly those influences from the past which bear upon you most strongly now . . .'

The card showed five heavy golden goblets against a murky brown

field: four upright, the fifth lying on its side. 'Five is a number associ-
ated with loss,' the Barone said, hushed. 'Something has been taken
from you. Perhaps something or someone close to you has gone, or
has been taken unjustly. Perhaps they have died or been killed. It is
the card of great regret.'

He's bluffing, Brookes thought. This is ridiculous. 'And the next?'

The second card depicted a knight in black armour on a caparisoned
horse, a broad sword in his hand. But he had placed it the wrong way
up – he reached out to correct it, and the Barone seized his hand.

'The Knight of Swords,' he said, 'signifies your current situation.
Your *present*, you might say. He is a figure of great courage and energy,
impetuous . . . a man of honour, a noble warrior. He brings great
change to everything around him. But if the card is reversed . . .'

'It means the opposite,' Brookes said. 'A coward, then. A liar.'

'Not the opposite, no. But the significance is negative. Reversed,
the knight is still strong and full of energy and courage, but he uses
his strength for ignoble purpose. He is perhaps dishonourable. A *mer-
cenario*, or a killer. He is the bringer of destruction.'

'Sounds like a thoroughly bad hat all round,' Brookes said, deliberately arch, and tried to laugh. But his throat was dry and his pulse
hammering – the room felt charged with electricity. He had chosen
the cards himself, and the Barone could not have guided him. 'What's
next?' he said.

But he could already see what was next: the image of a stone tower
struck and shattered by a blast from the sky. Two figures, one old
and the other young, tumbled from the collapsing battlements. He
remembered what the Baronessa had told him. *Leave as you would a
house on fire.*

'The third card relates to the future. It is perhaps something you
must overcome in order to reach your destination, or maybe an event

which you cannot avoid. Perhaps it is the final destination itself. The tower is being thrown down, you see: it is an image of ruin. But there is no need to read this as an actual tower. Some might relate it to pride or vanity, for example or, with Freud, the *ego*. We are humbled by the forces of the unseen.'

'Since I currently live in a tower, the meaning seems clear enough.'

The Barone swept the cards together again and began shuffling them back into the pack.

'You know,' Brookes said, 'a moment ago I thought the knight was supposed to be me. But it could just as well be you, couldn't it? That's your heraldic emblem, after all, a mounted knight with a sword?'

'Perhaps I am the knight, yes,' the Barone said. 'Perhaps it is you. Or perhaps it relates to some outside force that neither of us yet knows. What the cards tell us can be interpreted in many ways.'

A light tapping on the door then, and the Barone glanced up. He called out in Italian, and the door opened a crack. The face of the boy, Pietro, appeared in the gap, sullen and pale.

'*Papa,*' the boy said. '*Mamma dice che devi venire ora.*'

In the darkness beyond the door Brookes could make out the shapes of the others waiting – the Baronessa, Odetta and the doctor. The Barone wrapped the cards quickly in the black silk and placed them in their box.

'You must excuse me,' he said. 'I will return very shortly.'

As soon as the door was closed Brookes looked up at the clock in the corner. Eleven thirty exactly. He hadn't checked the time when the family had last disappeared like this, but surely it was close enough. He got up and went to the door: sounds of muffled whispering from the other side. The door had no lock, and he could have thrown it open if he wanted.

He had thought, that last time, that whatever the Barone and his family were going to do would happen in some deeper chamber of the castle – perhaps in the study where he now stood. But only the corridor lay between this and the family's living area. A secret door then? He tried to remember seeing some irregularity of the panelling when he passed along the corridor, but he had been too distracted by the pictures and the dancing candlelight to notice anything. Suddenly he felt disgusted; he was being drawn into their mystery despite himself.

Pacing back across the study, he tried to gauge its size relative to the dining room; it seemed much smaller, and was certainly narrower, but perhaps its depth was the same. A tiny chamber could lie behind it even so. In the far corner was a second door – Brookes took the lamp from the table and went to it. The door opened to his touch, the lamplight spilling into the room beyond. Book-spines lined the walls, some on shelves and others behind glass, old leather sloughing away from ribs of gummed paper. Beside the fireplace was an old chintz armchair with its horsehair stuffing spilling from a rent in the back. In the centre of the room was a billiards table, the baize discoloured by a spreading puddle of damp. In the far wall was yet another door – he was in a suite of interconnecting rooms.

There was no time to explore further. He closed the library door and returned to the study, dropping back into his chair beside the fire. The cards were in their box upon the table still. Brookes lifted the lid, and folded back the flap of black silk that covered them. He was almost certain there had been some trick: the Barone had switched the cards somehow, or arranged the deck so the right cards would be produced. He lifted the pack from the box – that cold and slightly unhealthy feeling again as he touched them, like the touch of dead flesh. Passing them between his fingers, he looked at the images again.

There were no duplicates, no fakes. He placed the cards back in their box and closed the lid.

The Barone returned, looking weary and little embarrassed.

'My apologies,' he said as he sat back down. 'A tedious business. I will explain some other time,' and he brushed the matter aside with his palm.

'Now,' he went on, 'I have a favour to ask. I know it must be rude to ask favours of guests, but something has occurred to me and you might be able to help.'

'Of course,' Brookes said, cautious again.

'What I would ask of you – please, feel free to say no – is this: would you perhaps like to teach my children to speak English?'

'What?' Brookes said. He had been expecting something less mundane.

'They know a little already, of course, although they are ashamed to use it in your presence! I have tried to teach them, but I find it hard to be both father and tutor. Their schooling, you see, has been rather interrupted.'

'But I don't know anything about teaching,' Brookes said. 'I don't know if I'd be able to do it.' He remembered squatting in a forest clearing surrounded by a ring of partisans, teaching them how to field-strip and clean a Sten and a German MG34; demonstrating how to fix detonators to sticks of gelignite, how to wrench a weapon from the hands of an opponent and turn it against him, how to disable a man with a knife-cut to the hamstring.

'It's really not so difficult, I'm sure,' the Barone said. 'We have some books here, some English books for children. Rather old now, of course, but all you need to do is to follow the words with them and be sure they understand.'

'It's important to you?' Brookes asked.

'Yes, it is. You may think that I live in complete isolation from the world, Captain, but even so I know the course that events must take. Perhaps there will be some miracle. Perhaps Herr Hitler will create his secret weapons at last and his fabulous Destiny will be realised.' The Barone paused, and Brookes caught the momentary flicker of buried emotion in the man's expression. Something else there, beneath the surface of calm assurance, which he was less able to control. It lasted only a second, then the Barone composed himself once again. 'But it is highly likely,' he said, 'that the English-speaking nations will win this war, and then they will determine the future of us all. My children must speak the language of the victors.'

'I'll do what I can,' Brookes said, after a grudging pause.

'Thank you, Captain.' The Barone reached out, as if to shake hands, but instead gripped Brookes' knee. 'I would appreciate it greatly,' he said.

6

'BROKE. YOUR NAME. Capitano Broke.'

'My name is Brookes.'

'Yes! My Papa say me. Francesco Broke.'

'Francis. Or Frank, if you prefer.'

'Franco. I like Franco.'

It was the second lesson. Odetta sat at the table, arms folded, wearing a thick jumper and a scarf. The room was an old nursery, only a short distance from Brookes' own chamber along the stone-paved corridor past the bathroom. In the corner was a mournful rocking horse with a broken runner. Several trunks with hinged lids held shabby toys and children's clothes, and hanging crooked on the wall was a big smoky oil painting of a country landscape with goatherds resting beside a stream.

The shutters were open to either side, the windows pouring watery daylight.

Pietro had not presented himself a second time. During the first lesson he sat thinly at the table in miserable distraction and refused to say a word in English; to his sister he had complained of the cold, of his boredom and hunger, of his dislike for this tall, gaunt foreigner in his ill-fitting clothes. Odetta, however, seemed to find the experience amusing.

She looked older than Brookes had thought the first time he had seen her, while her brother looked younger. Her lips were slightly chapped and her eyes bright.

'How . . . old . . . are you?' he asked, speaking with careful emphasis. She made a face at him. 'What age?' he said.

'I have seventy,' Odetta replied.

'Seven*teen*,' he corrected. '*I am seventeen years old.* Repeat.'

'I am seventeen years of old,' she said, her voice gruff, mimicking him. 'Yes Capitano!' She threw up her hand. A fascist salute.

'Let's look at the book again.'

He had found the books packed away in a box of dust among the rest of the nursery things. Some were in French, some were in pictures, only two were actually in English: an 1897 copy of *Grimm's Fairy Tales* and a book called *The Enchanted Castle* by E. Nesbit. The date on the inside cover was 1907.

Their progress during the first lesson had not been good. They had crawled laboriously through the opening pages of the Nesbit book, Odetta pronouncing the words with no sense of their meaning, pausing to roll her eyes or adjust her hair while her brother stared at the open page like an enemy and said nothing. Brookes had fought down the impulse to speak to them in Italian. Conscious of his own inadequacy as a teacher, he had felt language itself becoming slippery and uncertain. If it were a machine – an engine, or a gun, or a wireless set – he could strip it down to its components, explain each part and reassemble it in clear and logical sequence. But words were such devious and undisciplined things, obeying no rules but their own.

'We were here, I think,' Brookes said now, pointing to the paragraph he had marked. 'Read, please.'

Odetta took the book from him and stared at it. '*The nar-row pass-aidge. Ended in a roo-und. Ark all fring-ed with fernas. And cree-pairs. They pass-ed throff the ark . . .*'

'Through. They passed *through* the *arch*. Read on.'

'*Into a deep. Nar-row gulley woe, who . . . hose bank-ess were off. Ston moss cover-ed . . .*' She looked up, lips pursed, frowning. 'Why do we have to read this stuff?' she asked in Italian. 'I've read it before anyway, so I know the story. It's a book for children!'

'English,' he said. 'Speak English.' The raw scars on his hand itched and he rubbed at them, irritated.

Odetta leaned back in her chair, pushing the book away from her.

'*My name is Odetta . . .*' she began, sing-songing the words, '*I am seventeen. I live in Too-reen. I have many fri-ends. I like the music and the dancing and the colour of yellow and I like to riding the horses.*'

There had been youths of her age among the partisans, and some younger still, boys thrown into manhood by war. Homes destroyed, families murdered, they were wiry-tough and fearless soldiers. At night beside the campfires they liked to talk about the Germans and fascists they had killed, each sniper-shot and knife-thrust described, each death re-enacted.

Odetta yawned and tugged the sleeves of her jumper down over her hands. There was an oil heater placed beneath the table, clicking and ticking, but it did little to warm the room.

'Why do you pretend you can't speak Italian?' she said.

'English, please,' said Brookes. 'Speak in English.'

'Why, though? I know you understand me. You talked while you were sick, while I was looking after you, you talked a lot. In Italian. You speak fluently, don't you. Actually you have a sort of Florentine accent.'

Brookes felt very still and sober, his hands braced on the table before him. He stared down the length of the room. He had a sudden desire the slap the girl, hard across the face. The thought shamed him.

'Don't worry,' she said. 'Nobody else heard you. Only me. It's my secret, and I haven't told anyone else. Nobody can hear us now either, can they? Pietro's sulking in his room, Uncle Umberto's asleep or something, and Mamma and Papa . . . they're doing something, I suppose. It's just us.'

'I'm sorry,' he said, after a long pause. He spoke in Italian, and Odetta grinned, triumphant. 'I wasn't sure if I could trust you,' he said. 'Any of you, I mean. Sometimes people disclose more if they don't think you understand them.'

'And is that want you want? You want everybody to *disclose*?'

'I wanted to try and find out as much as I could, yes. From all of you.'

'Not from me,' Odetta said. 'I haven't anything to *disclose*.'

Brookes closed the book and laid it aside. There seemed little point in continuing with the lesson now. He felt stupidly relieved.

'Tell me about yourself,' he said. 'Do you like it here?' He waved a hand vaguely to indicate the castle around them. Odetta sucked her bottom lip.

'Not that much,' she said. 'I miss Turin. It's so quiet here, and I don't see my friends . . .'

'Your friends from school? Were you at school, *liceo* or something?'

'Oh no, that finished years ago,' she said. 'I mean, I had to leave . . . Papa decided to send me to a school in Switzerland instead, at Geneva. It wasn't really a school though, more like a holiday. Skiing, you know. Meeting boys . . .'

She gazed off around the room, feigning distraction. Through the open shutters were the scratchy trees, motionless in the mist. Brookes knew now why Odetta had seemed younger at first: she was not a child; she had simply not been allowed to grow up.

'How old are you anyway?' she said.

He hesitated again, then in his best British accent: '*I have thirty-three of the years.*'

She laughed, wrinkling her nose and showing her gums. It was a good laugh, a real one. Brookes had not heard genuine laughter for a long time. He grinned back at her.

'You're quite old,' she said. 'I thought so.'

'Thank you.'

He wished they had something to eat or drink, or some task to perform. A way of filling the space between them. He had always felt uncomfortable just passing time with others.

'Who's Carla?' she said.

'Who?' The room was suddenly hard and bright.

'Carla. You called me Carla when you came into the dining room that time and I dropped the tray.'

'She was a woman I used to know,' he said.

'Were you in love with her?'

Brookes swallowed. Coughed. 'Maybe I was,' he said. 'Perhaps, a little.' He couldn't decide whether he was lying.

'Did she look like me?' Odetta asked.

'Not really, no. No she didn't.'

'Oh. I thought maybe that was why you called me by her name . . . because you thought I was her . . .'

'I was confused. Ill, and feverish I think. I can't remember it clearly.'

He stood up, took his stick and limped the few paces to the window. He could not see the village from here, hidden by the forest or the slope of the mountain perhaps. The view held no signs of life; everything was motionless, floating in the mist which pressed up against the glass. There might have been nothing there at all, no world outside beyond the curtain of grey vapour and the ranks of trees. But the war was out there, and closing steadily. In his mind he saw the pummelled cities burning under aerial bombardment, heard the plunging blast of the mortar shells stepping closer, then stepping closer. It seemed to him then that this was the last place untouched by war, alone and unique. The castle shrugged off the world, too enrapt in its own mystery, the slow stone exhaustion of centuries.

So many years he had lived in war, learning to live by its logic. Positions to be taken, positions to be held. Positions surrounded, infiltrated, destroyed. He lived by attack and defence, concealment and ambush. If there was peace in this place, it was not his peace. He had no place here. He must go. *Leave as you would leave a house on fire.*

Behind him the girl stirred and shifted on her chair, the heater clicked and ticked.

'Is the lesson over then?' Odetta asked. Brookes looked at his watch.

'Yes, that's enough for today,' he said. He expected to hear her leaving, as she had left after the first of their lessons. But her brother had been with her then, and now she was alone. He wanted her to leave, but when he looked back and saw her, still sitting at the table, he was glad.

'It's so cold in here,' she said. Then, a moment later, 'Do you want me to show you around the castle?'

Despite the Barone's invitation, Brookes had been reluctant to explore the castle too thoroughly. He had paced the yard, swung his stick at the brambles in the overgrown and desolate stretch of garden below the chapel, but otherwise he had seen little of it. He did not want to become involved with the place; he did not want the family getting accustomed to his presence. All that would make it harder for him to leave, when the time came.

Now Odetta led him along narrow corridors, between plain damp walls bulging and sloughing plaster, through rooms of heaped furn-iture, sagging wardrobes and mould. The building seemed to stir as they passed, the inert fabric awakened by their presence – boards moaned beneath their feet, dust-motes eddied briefly; the walls themselves appeared to warp away from them slightly, resentful. Odetta moved quickly, light-footed, as if unwilling to offend the stillness, the dead air.

'How long have you been here?' he asked her.

'Oh, months. About six. Since the summer,' she said. 'I used to wander around more when we first arrived. But it was warmer then.'

'And before that? You were in Turin?'

'Before that . . . Turin, yes.' He noted her hesitation. 'You ask lots of questions don't you,' she said. 'Are you a spy?'

He put his hands in his pockets and made an offended expres-sion.

'Papa thinks you might be an English spy.'

'No, I'm not. Sorry.'

'Oh well . . . But if you were a spy, you wouldn't admit it, would you?'

They were in a small antechamber now. A heavy doorway was set into an arch, the keystone carved with the figure of a knight on horseback. A rather dwarfish knight, and very weathered. Brookes rubbed his thumb over the outline, smudging the figure with sooty black dust until it was indistinguishable.

'This leads to the great hall,' Odetta said, grasping the iron ring and turning it. 'It feels locked, but it's not. You just have to push it hard.'

Brookes set his good shoulder against the door and shoved.

'Again,' she said. 'Do it again.' Another shove and the door gave with a grate of old oak and a shriek of iron. Her arm was around his waist, her body pressed quickly against him. 'Don't fall!' she said.

He stepped away from her, across the threshold and into the hall.

The room was around fifty feet from end to end. To one side was a fireplace, large enough for a man to stand within it, and a minstrels' gallery of ornate old wood spanned the far wall. The noise of the opening door echoed, dust whirling in the light. As he crossed the hall Brookes thought he heard the echo of his own breathing.

'Brrr, so cold!' Odetta said, hugging herself, and stamped her feet.

Everything under dustsheets, soiled grey like dirty snow over a hilly landscape. A huge chandelier had been lowered from the ceiling to lie on the covered table, all the crystal beauty of its symmetry lost in glassy disarray. The whole room felt upside-down, somehow. Paintings had been removed from the walls and propped, their backs to the room – two rows of blank canvas rectangles. Odetta tilted one of them upright, the heavy gilt frame almost her own height, and stood on her toes to look down at the picture.

'Come and see this one,' she called to Brookes. 'It's my favourite. So ugly . . .'

Brookes took the painting from her and tilted it further back:

a full-length portrait of a man in eighteenth-century costume, wearing a full-bottomed powdered wig. A hunting dog cavorted at his feet.

'Look at him! He looks like he's sucking a lemon! Like an *Inglese!*'

They propped the painting carefully back against the wall. There were others: the pop-eyed and the haughty, in half-armour and frock coats, all alike under their smoky glaze.

'They're your ancestors,' Brookes said.

'So Papa says. They don't look much like anybody I know.'

'Your father's a very strange man.'

'Strange? I don't think so. He's changed since he came here though.' Brookes knew she was uncomfortable talking about him. 'He reads a lot, all the books in the library about the history of the Cavigliani family. I can never remember it all . . . the difference between the Guelfs and the Ghibellines, or why Count Somebody invaded the Grand Duchy of Wherever . . . Why we need to know all that I can't think.'

She led him on across the hall, through the draped furniture. Above the grand fireplace, the crest of the mounted knight gazed down at them. At the far end, beneath the minstrels' gallery, they entered a corridor lined with dark wood. Odetta slowed, then placed a hand on Brookes' arm. She took one long stride, then a short skip.

'You have to do it like that,' she said in a breathy whisper. 'The boards creak if you step in the wrong place!' Brookes followed, placing his feet where she had done.

'What would happen then?' he asked. She waited in the shadows, and his last step brought him up close, almost colliding with her.

'You go straight to hell!' she said, round-eyed.

At the far end of the corridor was another door; Odetta opened it, and a cold breeze swept in. Outside was the dank vaulted portico beneath the loggia.

'This way we can move around without crossing the yard,' she said, hushed. 'Sometimes people look out the windows, you know. They watch you pacing up and down out there all day long. I've seen you myself . . . You pause sometimes, don't you, and look around at the mountains.'

She was talking over her shoulder as they walked under the arches to a round half-tower – surely another spiral stair, Brookes guessed, probably one that led up to the panelled corridor outside the study.

'What is it you look for out there?' she asked. Brookes tensed slightly, but she was still smiling, her tone lightly flirtatious. She found it funny, that was all. 'You remind me of something, you know,' she said. 'Like a dog, sniffing the air. Like you can see or smell something that I can't. It makes me laugh sometimes, but it's strange.'

'It's just instinct,' he told her.

Past the tower they were out in the open, skirting the top end of the yard.

'We have to be quiet here,' Odetta whispered. 'Papa's rooms are just above us, and sometimes he leaves the windows open.'

Brookes exaggerated his step, walking high on his toes, and Odetta snorted with suppressed laughter.

'What about the Baronessa?'

'Oh no,' she said. 'Mamma's got her own rooms over the great hall.'

They had reached the edge of the yard. Before them was an area of bushes and long wet grass bounded by the high stone wall of the castle compound. Almost hidden by the bushes and the bulk of the keep was a last tower, low and round with a peaked roof.

'That's where I want to take you,' Odetta said, beginning to forge a path through the weeds and bramble bushes. 'Do you need help?'

Brookes shook his head but stumbled almost at once. Smiling, he made his way after her, leaning heavily on his stick. At the base of the tower broken stone steps mounted to an archway. Odetta had already skipped up the steps and stood poised in the opening, gazing back at him as he climbed towards her.

'This is where I saw you first.' She brushed her hair back behind her ears, waiting until he had drawn close to her. 'Come inside,' she said.

It was a circular chamber, the walls green with slimy moss and the floor damp. Several of the slates had fallen from the roof, and daylight squinted in from overhead. Odetta was sitting in a deep window alcove, where a vertical slot looked out towards the side of the mountain above the castle.

'You were out there,' she said, pointing. 'I had to stare a long time to be sure – there was a lot of mist that day. Then I thought you must be dead.'

Brookes leant into the alcove. Through the slot he saw the slope of the mountain rising from a wooded hollow below the castle. Odetta was pointing to a cleared area between the trees, where the grey rivulet of a mountain stream showed between rocks.

'You looked like a shipwrecked sailor,' she said, 'washed up on a deserted island. I was going to run out there myself and find you, but I met Uncle Umberto on the way, and he brought the others. They thought you might be dangerous, but we couldn't leave you lying there. We built a sort of stretcher and carried you inside. You seemed half dead, and nobody expected you to live, but we brought you back to life, didn't we?'

'I suppose you did.'

'Umberto didn't want me to see the surgery, but I insisted. I'd found you, after all. So I saw it all – I had to pass the dressings and instruments. I saw the bullet in your back. It's still there isn't it…?' She touched his back, very gently. He felt the pressure of her hand on his scarred flesh. 'Can you still feel it?'

'A little, yes, sometimes.' They were very close together in the window alcove. Her hand stroking his back. She looked very young.

'What were you doing in here, when you saw me?' he said, stepping away from the alcove and walking to the centre of the room. Rainwater dripped from the shattered slates above.

'I come here sometimes to be alone,' she said. 'It's very peaceful, don't you think? I don't suppose any of the others have even been in here. You wouldn't have a cigarette, would you?'

'No, sorry. Your father gave me some, but I left them in my room.'

'Shame,' she said. She was looking out of the window again now, and Brookes could see that she was shivering slightly and trying to hide it. The air was cold enough to fog their breath. It truly was a peaceful place, he thought; neglected, a little sepulchral. He pictured Odetta sitting there alone, cold in the dimness, waiting for life to find her.

'I'm afraid your brother doesn't like me much,' he said.

'He doesn't like your being here,' Odetta replied, staring out at the mountains. 'He thinks it's against the rules.'

'Your father's rules?'

'The rules that protect us. It's a sort of obsession of his, since Vittorio died. Since we came here.' There was a catch in her voice, and she kept her face turned away as she spoke. She sounded less like a child now.

'Everything is so different here,' she said. Her voice was as cold as the stones around her. 'Even the trees look different. Not like home at all. I sometimes think, you know, that the old life is still out there somewhere, waiting for me. Turin, and my friends . . . just sort of frozen in time, waiting for me to come back. But other times I can forget about it completely. It's odd, don't you think?'

Brookes shrugged, already moving towards the door.

'Soon the snow will come down from the mountains,' she said quietly, as if to herself. 'Then we'll be buried here.'

They were halfway to the vaulted portico beneath the loggia when they saw the man. He was a ragged shape in the middle distance, a blown black scrap running between the ruined chapel and the side of the keep. Odetta had clearly noticed him, but was pretending she had not.

'There's a man there,' said Brookes, 'didn't you see him?' The man had vanished now, around the back of the sheds.

'Oh . . . yes,' Odetta said, still not looking. They walked on into the passageway. 'It was just somebody from the village. They come up here sometimes and take things from the sheds. There are some old tools and things in there. Bits of firewood.'

'Don't you mind?'

She shrugged. 'We can't really stop them. The gates are broken and don't close properly.'

'But they could come up here in the night and rob you, surely?' He was only half serious and she knew it.

'They don't come at night,' she said. 'They think the castle's haunted. There are ghosts, they say.'

'And aren't you afraid of the ghosts too?'

'No,' she said. 'We are the ghosts.'

They were outside the door to the great hall now.

'Where is the village?' Brookes asked. 'I've never seen it.'

Odetta turned to face him. 'You can see it from my room,' she said. 'I live up in the corner tower. Do you want to have a look?'

Brookes caught her quick glances of complicity as they climbed the creaking stairs, the finger raised to her lips as they passed the first landing and the door of her uncle's room; she was breaking the rules, and wanted him to know it. Limping heavily on his left leg, he played along, creasing his brow and moving with deliberate stealth. This kind of game might have irritated him, but he was surprised to find that it did not.

Odetta opened what appeared to be the door of a cupboard. Inside was another, much narrower, flight of stairs that rose upwards again between the partition walls of attics. The room at the top was small and square, a turret chamber with a high sloping ceiling and dormer windows on two sides. There was a bed piled with blankets and quilts, a desk and side table cluttered with bottles and mirrors, clothes draped over chairs and heaped inside open suitcases, everything dusty and in disarray. Here, Brookes thought, were the contents of several rooms compressed into one. The girl was clearly used to having servants clean and tidy for her. In the corner beside the door stood another of the stuffed animals – a rangy dog, stiffly posed with raised forepaw. Odetta patted its shabby head as she passed.

'This is Benson,' she said. 'Don't worry – he doesn't bite.' She opened the window and leant out. 'Over there. Can you see it between the trees?'

Brookes joined her at the window. Below them the valley soared away, forested slopes falling to either side into a trench of mist. He looked down, and saw the road leading from the castle gates and curling between the trees. Far below, held in the hazy cleft of the valley, was the string of tiny grey houses. Smoke was rising from one of the chimneys.

'We don't really see the people from the village very often,' Odetta said. 'They're just peasant types.'

Brookes leaned a little further into the window and angled his gaze

over the valley towards the opposite slopes. Almost above the height
of the castle was a cluster of stone cottages.

'Who lives there?' he asked.

'Oh, nobody, probably,' Odetta said. She leaned closer in beside
him, their arms touching, and looked out across the valley. 'It's a
lovely view when the fog clears,' she said. 'Oh, look!'

High above the misty gulf of the valley a bird was circling – a
hawk or a falcon, Brookes thought. Some big heraldic predator, glid-
ing through the unseen topography of the air. Both of them watched
it until it passed from sight.

'I wish I was like that,' Odetta said. 'I wish I was free.'

'You are free,' Brookes told her. She shook her head, curls bouncing.

'I'm not,' she said. 'We're . . . we have to stay here, don't we.
Because of the war.'

She wanted to say more, it seemed to Brookes, but could not. Sad-
eyed she stared out into the valley.

'Don't tell anybody I brought you up here,' she said abruptly.
'You're not supposed to come up here. You're not supposed to look
out of the windows, if they knew they'd kill me. Promise me.'

'I promise,' he said.

Brookes lay awake, listening hard into the silence and silence. Through
the familiar sounds of the castle around him – the rattle of a shutter
in the wind, the steady creak and tap of old beams overhead – he
hunted for the other sound, the new sound that had snatched him
back from the edge of sleep. Then, as his eyes adjusted and the faint
shapes around him gained form, he heard it: something like a mosquito's
whine, a strange high singing that came and went. Music, he realised.

Sitting up, he trained his ears to the sound, trying to determine
where it came from. Somewhere deeper in the castle, he guessed.

The shapes of the room were clear to him as he stood up and pulled on his coat. Two steps from the door he paused, hearing the music again, rising and falling in the steady whisper of near-silence that surrounded it. He took the knife from the bedside table and slipped it into his coat pocket.

Dropping down the stairs, he guided himself along the corridor at the bottom. A bitter cold, so cold his teeth ached, and he pulled the coat tighter around him. He moved quickly without his stick; no need to feign a limp in the dark. He had left his boots back in his room and paced soundlessly in his socks. The knife hung cold and sharp in his pocket.

Through the fractured shadows of the nursery and the rooms beyond he passed sure and silent, the whitewashed walls pale and insubstantial in the dark. Cold breezes rushed at ankle-height over the bare floor-boards. He was disembodied now, a floating consciousness probing the margins of the spaces around him. Smells guided him – wood-rot and mouldy plaster, camphor and dust, the swift steely breaths of the night outside. The castle unknotted itself from darkness before him, ravelling back behind him as he passed.

Ahead, a floorboard cracked and he stopped, back in his body once more, one hand reaching out to the flaking plaster to steady himself. Staring, eyes narrowed, he tried to pick out movement but saw nothing. Doors to his left, leading to narrow rooms filled with cupboards and shelves, old wardrobes packed with old, mothballed clothes. He felt sweat prickle on his brow, the sensation of another presence, unknown and unseen – a tremor in the air, like walking into a room moments after another person has left.

But then he heard the music again, clearer and more distinct now. Nothing he could identify, it swam in and out of the range of his hearing. Pushing away from the wall, Brookes moved on along the corridor and up a short flight of steps. The door to the great hall opened silently to his touch – he had only pulled it partway closed when he returned from Odetta's room. The vast hall was deep with moving shadows and frosted moonlight; through the tall arched windows the night sky was filled with falling snow. Brookes brushed the table as he passed, and the hanging teardrops of the fallen chandelier chimed briefly. He was halfway to the far door when he halted. Standing still, he felt again the swift cold apprehension that somebody was close to him, a tightness at the nape of his neck. Don't move, he thought. Become shadow.

His eardrums grew tight as he listened, as if the pressure in the hall was increasing. He moved only his eyes, seeing the room in negative, silver on black, searching out the flicker of movement, of enemy life. The feeling ebbed into the silence. Brookes eased himself forward again, one long pace at a time. An owl cried outside, and he almost laughed with relief.

Along the corridor, careful to avoid the creaking floorboards, he scaled the wooden stairs to the first landing, then crept quietly on through the distances of the castle. The dining-room was bright to his night-sharpened eyes, a dull glow from the embers of the fire lighting the haze of smoke above the snuffed candles on the table. Plates, pots and glasses still uncleared. He had not eaten with the family that night. Quickly he checked his watch in the low firelight – not yet twelve. He had thought it was much later.

Wind heaved at the shutters, and he heard the music again, singing from the dark. He placed it now – not from deeper in the castle, not from inside the castle at all but from outside, from the valley below, carried on the night breeze.

Leaving the dining room, Brookes stared down the panelled corridor. Lamp light showed beneath the closed door of the study at the far end, winking a morse of orange reflections from the glass of the framed prints on the walls. He could hear them talking behind the study door, the low stir of voices. Hardly breathing, he felt his way along the corridor, tapping with the tip of the knife. There were no hollow panels, no concealed openings. Back again, he stepped through the arch into the barrel of the spiral stairs. Cold air funnelled down from above – an open window up there somewhere. He began to climb, feeling his way around the curve of the steps above, gritty dust beneath his fingers. Two turns of the stair and moonlight flooded him. He was in a tiny turret, cobwebs and the smell of dry bird droppings, slot embrasures to either side.

Leaning across the worn stone of the sill, Brookes looked down over the rooftops and the valley beyond. Clouds raced, chasing a gorgonzola moon. At first the far side of the valley was dark, no sound but the rush and scythe of the cold wind. Snow flurried, already settling on the far slopes and the cracked tiles of the roof below him. Brookes tasted it in his mouth. There was no music now, but he knew where it must have been coming from. The little group of cottages on the far side of the valley which he had seen from Odetta's room was invisible, but he could guess the position. As he stared, a light suddenly appeared, small and distant. A pinprick in the vast darkness of mountains and valley – maybe a single bulb or an electric torch shining from a window.

He felt the cold on his face as he stood watching, willing something else to happen. The light did not waver. How many people over there? A wireless, electricity, warmth of human life. He remembered the Barone's warning to him after dinner on that first evening. *Do not show yourself at the windows.*

A minute passed, maybe two, then the far light winked out. Brookes remained at the embrasure, hunched into the collar of his coat. Blown snow flecked his shoulders and clung to his unshaven jaw. Then, shrugging off the chill, he turned from the window and groped his way back down the stairs.

Voices echoed along the panelled corridor, and light spilled from the dining room. He slid himself silently into the angle behind the open door.

Through the crack between door and frame he saw the room, and the figures beside the table lit by the glow of a paraffin lamp. The Barone had his back turned, but Odetta was clearly visible, her eyes red; the Baronessa stood slightly to one side, hands raised and calming. At the edge of the lamp's glow was Pietro, staring at the floor, sullen as usual. The scene was composed, stilled and held in the amber light, and Brookes squinted into the crack of the door, holding his breath, listening.

'I know you did,' the Barone said. His voice was no longer smooth and subtle – no longer the measured tone of a hypnotist. It cracked at the edges of the words.

This is important! What did you tell him?'

'Nothing!' Odetta shouted. 'I told him nothing!'

Then an exchange too hushed for Brookes to make out, the Barone whispering harshly, threatening. He pressed himself into the angle behind the door, staring into the light from the dining room.

'Liar!' the girl cried out again. 'You're a liar!'

The blow sounded like a pistol shot – sudden and swift, a crack across the cheek that staggered the girl backwards. The Baronessa had already grabbed her husband by the arm.

'No, no,' she was saying. '*Basta!* Stop this now.'

Odetta dropped her hands from her face. She glanced up at her father once, then ran from the room. For a moment the Baronessa paused, still gripping her husband by the wrist, then turned and followed.

Pietro slid off his stool like a shadow and followed her, with a last long glance at his father. Brookes stepped back smartly into the arch of the stairwell as the Barone approached with the lamplight spilling from his hand. The light passed close before moving away down the corridor to be swallowed by the darkness.

Brookes waited in the archway, blinking away the afterimage of the lamp. The whole exchange had taken only seconds. It was a performance, he thought, staged for his benefit. He was supposed to witness this – but none of the family could have known he was there watching them. Now the tableau was broken up, the figures dispersed, he could almost believe he had imagined it. But in that brief glimpse as the light passed, he had clearly seen the Barone's face wet with tears, his expression washed by more than anger alone. The slightest echo of the raised voices lingered, and somewhere far away a door slammed.

7

OUTSIDE THE CASTLE the valley was muffled with snow, white under a white sky. Clear in the cold air came the sound of a church bell. An Italian sound, Brookes thought, that flat black clang, quite different to the sharp ringing of northern Europe. Sunday then; he pictured the people going to church, tiny figures threading the valley paths through the heaped snow. He imagined the church itself, small and blunt with its campanile slender against the massive flanks of the mountains, the warmth inside heavy with incense and the smell of damp clothes. Heat of bodies, murmur of Latin, the slow steady whisper of ritual.

The Middle Ages, the Barone had said, did not feel so distant here, and for the first time Brookes began to understand what he meant.

Even the sound of the bell, tolling sad and flat in the muffling snow, seemed an echo of the past. For so long he had lived in war, now he felt adrift without it. The world and its conflicts gave something to push against, or something to be carried by; without it there were only individuals, defenceless against themselves.

Brookes had little idea of the exact date. He estimated that he must have been in the castle for three weeks, maybe a month including his period of feverish sedation. That would make it early December. But he could not be sure, and he had seen no calendar anywhere in the castle. To ask something as obvious as the day or the date might be taken as a sign of weakness, a reversal in the obscure game the Barone seemed determined to play. Neither would Brookes ask him to explain the light in the cottage on the far side of the valley, or the scene that he had witnessed in the dining room. He would guard his suspicion, give his host no further opportunity for evasion and denial. Odetta might be different, more pliable perhaps, but he would wait his chance.

He saw little of any of them even so. Ranging through the castle, he would sometimes catch a flicker of movement in an arched doorway, or on the landing of an upper stairway; something that might have been a figure, or perhaps just a drape shifting in the breeze. He sensed their presence around him, soaking into the ancient atmosphere of the castle itself, the grim spirit of the place. Only with a sudden step, a quick look back, would he catch sight of the boy, Pietro, stalking along behind him. He suspected there were other watchers as well – other eyes studying him from the high windows around the courtyard, from the bends of crooked corridors, across the depths of shadowed rooms.

In the library Brookes circled the stained billiards table, scanning the ranks of books ranged along the shelves. The room was damp and

dim, the titles difficult to make out. Some volumes carried no titles
– all were smudged with dust and worn by hands. In several places
books had been removed, bare tracks left in the dust of empty shelves
where they had been dragged free and never returned. But there
seemed no order to any of it, no way of telling what had been taken,
or why. There were books on ancient history, etymology, ornithology,
ethnography; a massive crumbling book on phrenology, pages of faded
etchings spilling from a burst spine. The paradise of a nineteenth-
century autodidact. Brookes was searching for maps, anything that
would show him the position of the castle, the surrounding valleys,
the roads and the towns. He found nothing.

The inner door, the one that led to the Barone's private chambers,
was closed. Brookes tried not to glance at it as he paced the room,
but still half expected it to open suddenly, the Barone emerging like a
carved figurine on an astronomical clock. There would be no chance
encounters, no unguarded moments.

A tall slim volume bound in bristly brown leather proved to be a
handwritten monograph on the history of the castle. Brookes took it and
went to the armchair beside the dead fire, easing himself down onto the
tired springs and matted horsehair. He flicked through the book, heavy
old pages releasing their scents of dry wood and moth-husks. There
should surely be a plan of the castle itself, if not of its surroundings. In
all his wanderings Brookes had yet to determine the exact dimensions
of the castle's interior – chambers multiplied, corridors veered at odd
angles, windows gave onto strange perspectives of the inner courtyard
or near-identical views of the mountains outside.

Following the Spanish occupation of the mid-sixteenth century, the
south-west wing was extensively rebuilt by Barone Federico Cavigliano.
In particular, the ceiling of the great hall, previously damaged by fire,
was remodelled and the suite of rooms above it completely renovated.

The new panelled ceiling of the hall was further beautified with in-laid panelling and several fine decorative pieces by the master painter Giancarlo Serafino of Novara. These pieces can still admired today. The great fireplace was also replaced, and the gallery at the upper end of the hall installed . . .

Brookes glanced up from the page, quickly alert. He was staring at the door to the Barone's chambers. A faint breeze had passed, that was all. The slow inhalation of the castle itself. Thumbing through the rest of the book, he found no plans, no illustrations at all. Then he noticed the stubs of the cut pages, the missing leaves that did not interrupt the flow of the text. There had been pictures, clearly, probably plans, but somebody had sliced them out of the book.

Replacing the volume on the shelves, he moved through the other books, holding them balanced by the spines and letting them fall open to the cut pages. A book on folklore customs of Upper Piemonte and Lombardia. A book on the castles of northern Italy. A book on the geology of the mountain valleys. In every one, every map, every plan, everything that could give shape and form to the outside world, a sense of direction and place, had been expunged. The castle and the land that surrounded it was a void, unmapped and diffuse.

Brookes picked up the walking stick and hefted it thoughtfully, slapping the worn handle into his palm. If the Barone himself had removed the maps, then he truly intended to make leaving the castle difficult. But if not the Barone, then who? He gave a quick irritated shrug, pulling the overcoat back over his shoulders.

Probing ahead of him with the walking stick, the soft creak and yield of snow beneath his boots, Brookes moved across the yard. There had been a fresh fall in the night, the blankness of the snow crossed by two lines of footprints, coming and going. He had heard the voices of the men from the village at first light as they came up to the castle for firewood. Now he saw that several of the sheds around the base of the keep had been ripped open – doors hung on their twine, sealed into oblique angles by the drifting snow, and inside the emptiness gaped black. On this side of the castle there was less shelter from the wind off the mountains, and the snow was sculpted into billowing curves around the base of the walls. A spume of dry powder blew from the white-capped roofs.

To the right of the keep was a larger building, double wooden gates padlocked shut. Brookes stood close against the gates and pressed his eye to the gap between them. A spear of diagonal light crossed the space inside, curving over the polished flank of a heavy automobile.

Around the corner he hauled his boots through the deep drifts against the walls. Kneeling in the snow, he cupped his hands around his face and started though the dirty panes of a low window. The car threw back its curves from the darkness, gleaming.

'Lancia Astura,' he breathed at the glass. '1936 model.'

Stepping from the shelter of the garage wall into the bladed wind, he saw a figure waiting beside the locked doors. It was the Barone, dressed in heavy tweed and carrying a shovel. For a moment he was too startled to speak – the man seemed to have risen from the ground, from the unmarked snow, silent and sudden as an apparition.

Like two walkers on a country path, they waited until only a few steps separated them before either spoke.

'Good morning,' Brookes said.

'Isn't it?' the Barone replied. He wore an alpine hat with a feather in it. 'You were admiring my motor car, I think.'

'Beautiful machine you've got in there,' Brookes said, nodding at the garage door. Even now that he could make out the Barone's footprints in the snow, the shock of unease had not left him. The man must have sprinted across the yard, fast and silent, to appear so suddenly.

'And you'd like to see it better, I expect?' the Barone said. 'First, though, I must clear this snow from around the doors. If you'll excuse me . . .'

The Barone bent and swung the shovel, but Brookes caught his arm. 'Let me do that,' he said.

'Are you sure? Perhaps the exertion is not good for you?'

Brookes took the shovel from him and began digging at the bank of snow. Heat bloomed through his muscles.

'In fact, you should not be wandering about here in this weather at all,' the Barone was saying as he watched Brookes working. 'It's good to see you're recovering so well from your injuries, but you'll certainly take a fever, I think, and my brother will be very angry!'

Brookes smiled, trying to imagine the doctor being *very angry*. He could picture the man in his previous life, a most considerate gynaecologist to the wealthy women of Turin; picture him washing his hands, raising an eyebrow, executing a courteous little half-bow as he showed the lady to the door. But the doctor was far too fastidious, too coldly remote from the world, to be angry. In a way Brookes missed his daily visits – his wounds had healed well enough now not to need regular inspection. Something in the doctor's sense of passive indignity was very genuine. He had a thin skin, and the world wounded him. There was no guile in the man at all.

Not so the Barone, who glittered with it.

The blade of the shovel rang on stone. When the Barone dragged back the door, light flooded into the garage, forming the black shape of the car out of the darkness.

Inside was engine-scent, greased metal and oil. The Barone took a drum of liquid from the corner beside the doors and unscrewed the car's radiator cap. The sweet alcohol smell of methanol antifreeze rose as he poured – less a smell, Brookes thought, than a taste: raw spirits flavouring the air. He felt them on his tongue.

'I have to run the engine a little as well,' the Barone said, 'to charge the battery.'

'You're leaving here some time soon?' Brookes asked.

'Oh no. But if ever we should need to go . . .'

Brookes nodded, walking around the rear of the car. The far end of the garage was a workroom, benches along either wall covered with objects blurred into anonymity by thick dust. There were coils of brass and copper wire, heaps of old corks, a set of porcelain insulators; the valve panel of a dismantled wireless and a collection of clockmaker's tools. On a shelf above the bench was a row of big glass valves of various sizes, and at the far end, in a small case almost sealed with dirt, were the gutted remains of a 1927 Marconiphone crystal receiver set.

Brookes picked up a few of the things, dropping them nonchalantly back onto the bench. Black grease coated his fingers. He wiped them on a bit of ragged cloth as he walked back to join the Barone.

'I've been meaning to ask you,' the Barone said, putting the cap back on the radiator, 'how the English lessons are proceeding? I'm sorry Pietro has not been very enthusiastic. I would have made him attend, but my wife is a little soft on the boy. Odetta, though. How are her studies?'

'Her studies?' Brookes said. The Barone glanced up at him and nodded; nothing in his expression, or the tone of his question, seemed unnatural. Nothing suggested that the scene Brookes had witnessed in the dining room had taken place at all.

'Well . . . She tries to understand.'

'Good. That she tries is the important thing. She is a very

impressionable girl, my daughter. Sometimes her imagination distracts her.' Then, as if a thought struck him, he paused in his work and frowned. 'I hope she has not been at all disrespectful to you?'

'No, not at all.'

'Good. If she tells you anything that seems unusual, I suggest you ignore it. Anything, you could say . . . *far-fetched*.' He enunciated the phrase fastidiously.

Brookes paused, cloth in hand. He considered asking how Odetta was supposed to communicate these *far-fetched* things. 'Tell me, Barone,' he asked, 'are there any of your family I should actually trust?'

The Barone smiled, wide-eyed. 'You can trust me!' he said.

He opened the door and got into the car. The ignition coughed, then the engine came to life, a great bass roar, and in that noise Brookes found a key to the present again. Here he was, in the twentieth century. Exhaust smoke rolled and hung in the cold air, and he breathed the smell of it gratefully. After a few plunges of the accelerator the Barone left the car idling.

'Get in,' he called, leaning across to open the passenger door. 'It's warmer inside, and I have a flask of coffee.'

Brookes swung himself down into the car, into its walnut and chrome, its soft black leather upholstery, the deep detonating vibration of the engine. Warm air spilled over him from the dashboard vents.

Once he was seated and the doors closed, the Barone unscrewed the cap of his silver flask. 'I only have the one cup,' he explained, 'so I hope you don't mind sharing.'

The coffee was hot and bitter and acrid, heavily laced with brandy. For a while they drank in silence, passing the cup between them.

'My daughter, incidentally,' the Barone said, 'informs me that you are quite capable of speaking Italian.'

'She told you, then.'

'Of course she told me, Captain.' The Barone had assumed a grave manner. 'She is my daughter. Her loyalties lie with me.'

There was a lengthy pause. The switch in mood was baffling, but Brookes allowed himself no sign of uneasiness. All the pleasantries that had passed between them had been leading up to this.

'I'm sorry if I misled you,' he said, in Italian.

The Barone smiled thinly. 'Then if you'll permit me, I shall speak in my own language from now on,' he said. 'Much as I enjoy the practice, I do find English lacks a certain expressivity. And may I commend you on your excellent pronunciation, by the way?'

'When I first came here,' Brookes said, 'I knew nothing about you. I thought it better . . .'

The Barone held up a palm, cutting him off. 'Please, no need for apologies,' he said. 'I understand, in fact. You have your duties, and I have mine. Both of us are . . . *bound*. Have a cigarette.'

Once again Brookes noticed how different the Barone sounded when he spoke Italian. There was none of the stiffness and hauteur of his English speech. And yet there was still something unnatural about the way he presented himself, a chameleonic quality that the change of language could not disguise.

'Your wife, I believe,' he said, as he lit his cigarette, 'understands English too.'

'She's an educated woman,' the Barone answered. 'And she understands more than she lets on. About a lot of things. She cares very deeply, though. With her current condition it's sometimes hard to judge, but truly she cares about her family. Family, Captain, is the most sacred thing, for both of us.'

'I wouldn't know much about it, I'm afraid,' Brookes replied. Smoke swirled against the windscreen glass, lit by the glare of snow outside.

'Of course, your erased past,' the Barone said. 'You never had a family?'

'My parents are both dead,' Brookes said. 'They'd lived apart for many years.'

'A terrible thing,' the Barone said, shaking his head. 'How did they die, if you don't mind my asking?'

'My father drank himself to death,' Brookes said, raising his brandy-laden cup.

'Ah. And your mother?'

'Suicide,' Brookes told him. Paused a moment. 'She sat in her car with the engine running and a hosepipe connected to the exhaust.'

The Barone stared into his lap for a moment, fingers interlaced. Then he looked across at Brookes, frowning. Brookes sat stone-faced.

'I'm very sorry to hear that,' the Barone said. His tone was one of rebuke. Bad taste. But the mood did not last, and Brookes caught his hidden look of amusement in the rear-view mirror.

'I hope you know,' he said, with fresh enthusiasm, 'how pleased we all are to have you staying here with us.'

'You are?' said Brookes, dubious.

'Of course! It gets so stale, you know, having the same people around one all the time. Your presence has enlived us all immensely! And perhaps now you no longer have to pretend not to understand us, you might like to participate a little more.'

'Participate?' Brookes asked. For a moment he thought he'd misunderstood.

'Yes, with the family. Participation is the root of civil society, is it not? And perhaps we constitute a form of society here, cut off from the world, don't you think?'

'I wouldn't like to impose on you. As I've said . . .'

The Barone broke in again, his tone final. 'Whatever you wish,' he said. 'You are free to do whatever you wish.'

Some suggestion, Brookes thought, in the Barone's words, and he waited for more, some further hint or insinuation, but none came. Speaking in Italian again, he was aware of the subtleties that could slip his comprehension. He had never felt less certain of his fluency – as if they were speaking some other language, not Italian but a private code of suggestion and evasion. The Barone, meanwhile, had turned to the dashboard and was tapping at the dials, fiddling with the vent knobs.

'Why don't you actually drive somewhere?' Brookes said. 'The roads aren't too deep in snow. Better than just sitting here running the engine . . .'

'You think it's safe for you to leave the castle?' the Barone replied, incredulous.

Brookes shrugged, nonplussed.

'You feel claustrophobic?' the Barone said, then nodded slightly. Less a question than a confirmation. 'I understand. But you must not be seen outside the gates!'

'And what about you?' Brookes replied. 'Can you be seen outside the gates? Or are you hiding as well?' He knew his irritation was obvious; he meant it to be. He had the sudden urge to seize the Barone – hit him maybe – burst the courteous facade and grasp something real inside. He took a long breath and held it.

Abruptly the Barone shut off the engine.

'That's enough, I think,' he said, and opened the car door.

8

THEY FOUND THE dead man early the next day. Brookes was in his room when he heard Odetta's scream, the single high wail cutting through the thin morning air. Outside, they were already waiting for him, poised at the top of the ramp that dropped to the gatehouse, the Barone and the doctor breathless after running, their coats unbuttoned.

'There's a man down there,' Odetta said, pointing. As Brookes approached her she reached out suddenly and clasped his arm. They had been waiting for him to take responsibility, and their relief was obvious. Brookes walked slowly down the ramp into the deep blue shadow of the gates. He heard the others following him, their boots creaking on the iced cobbles.

The body lay between the arches of the gatehouse, on its back with its arms twisted out, a crumpled shape against a background of glaring white snow. He had clearly been dead for some time. The blood on his face looked glassy and black. At the bottom of the ramp, keeping their distance, Umberto and the Barone stood looking at the corpse with expressions of frank distaste. Odetta stood back against the wall, pressing her hands over her nose and mouth. It occurred to Brookes that she had probably never seen a corpse before.

'Well, he's certainly dead,' Umberto said.

Brookes approached and dropped to one knee, carefully lifting the lapel of the jacket.

'What are you doing?' the Barone called. He sounded slightly disgusted, as if Brookes were disturbing the body somehow. As if he was robbing the corpse.

'Searching for documents,' Brookes replied. 'Don't you want to know who this man is?' But he found nothing in the pockets, somebody had already taken anything the man might once have carried. One of the eyes was gummed closed, the other half open, and he remembered Carla lying dead in the ferns. There was no smell of decomposition, but Odetta was still holding her nose. Brookes looked back at them gathered just outside the inner arch of the gatehouse. They would have looked at him like that, when they found him out on the mountainside. The dead man even resembled him superficially: younger, but with similar features; the shared look of men whose lives had run in parallel. When he reached beneath the body the discovery jolted him. The coincidence was almost uncanny.

'He was shot in the back,' Brookes said. 'There's congealed blood under his clothes. I'd say the body lay in snow for some time, then was dragged up the hill.'

'The people from the village,' the Barone said. 'They must have found him and brought him here. They must have intended us to . . . dispose of him in some way. They didn't want a stranger buried on their land, so they passed the bad luck to us.'

Outside the gates, Brookes could see tracks in the snow, the blood-streaked rut the body had left as it was dragged. He stood up and gripped the corpse beneath the arms, lifting it. He felt the ache in his muscles; the body was heavy with death, head lolling, stiff-necked.

'Help me, one of you,' Brookes said. Neither the Barone nor his brother took a step forward, both of them pale and still. 'Or do you want to just leave him here to rot?' Odetta shifted against the wall, as if she might step forward, but her father sharply ordered her back.

The Barone circled the body before stooping to take hold of its ankles, flinching at the touch of the dead flesh. Between them they lifted it again, the corpse sagging unnaturally, then stumbled up the ramp with the weight slung between them while Umberto hurried to fetch the shovels. Halfway up, Brookes paused for the Barone to get his breath.

'Do the partisans know you're here?' he asked.

The Barone shook his head.

They buried the dead man in the overgrown garden behind the rear wall of the ruined chapel, scraping a shallow grave in the stony soil. Odetta stood at the balustrade watching them. Their breath came in short white bursts as they dug. The dead man lying beside the grave looked younger, barely out of his teens.

'He might have been a civilian,' the Barone said. 'A villager in a discarded army jacket, perhaps?'

Brookes shook his head. Stones rattled as he flung them from the spade. 'Look at his hands. They're smooth, not weathered like a field worker. He was a student or a city clerk. He probably joined the partisans fairly recently.'

The Barone grounded his shovel, his throat contracting with a dry heave of nausea. Brookes wondered what they would have done if he himself had been dead when they found him. Would they have managed to bury him, or just tried to ignore him, as they ignored so much of what happened outside their walls?

There were no pieties, no words of ceremony as the earth was flung over the corpse and heavy stones from the wall piled on top. Odetta lingered at the balustrade, watching the end of the burial, but once it was done she departed with the others, and not a word was said. They left Brookes alone beside the mound of stones, leaning on his shovel.

The muscles of his arms and back ached, but he felt the first tremors of warm nervous energy spreading through him. He stared up at the mountains, at the massive walls of snow and rock high overhead, and realised for the first time the risk of remaining in the castle, both to the family and to himself. It was as if his presence was drawing the war towards them. Soon other men would come; not dead men stripped of identity but living ones, soldiers with guns in their hands. He remembered the Barone and his brother waiting above the gatehouse, immobilised by shock. The sight of death, the presence of it, had ruptured something, just briefly. When Odetta grasped his arm, the expression on her face had been clear. She had known that her family were powerless against the world outside.

As he climbed back up to the courtyard, heavy-footed through the snow, Brookes fought to calm himself, not to break into a run. The insubstantial fears that had shadowed him fell away as he moved. He knew now that the longer he stayed at the castle, the more the family would come to rely on him, the more they would expect him to act as a shield between themselves and the outside world. The effort of carrying the corpse had tired him, but he knew he was capable of more. Tonight, he thought – he would leave tonight, and be long gone before anyone missed him. Passing the chapel he caught a flicker of movement. Pietro stood in the shadow of the ruined doorway, watching him. He retreated as Brookes approached, stepping carefully backwards. When he looked at the boy's face Brookes saw no sign of recognition – he was as blank as the corpse, as cold and alien. But his lips were moving, shaping silent words. An incantation, a spell to ward off nameless terrors.

Brookes turned his back on the boy and marched away across the snow towards his room. Only when he reached the steps and glanced across the courtyard did he see the Barone, crouched beside the well scrubbing his hands from a bucket of ice-cold water.

In the gulley of the castle gate the ice was thick and glassy under a coating of snow. Total darkness too, and Brookes picked his way slowly and carefully. As he eyes adjusted he saw the snow as a dull blue glow; then he was under the gatehouse and his footsteps rang on the exposed paving.

Beyond the shelter of the gates lay a landscape fantastic in moonlight, billowing white and unstable. Snow had drifted thick against the castle wall, and he walked heavily though it, lifting his knees with every stride. The snow was loud, groaning and crunching. He tightened the scarf around his neck, pulling it up to cover his nose and mouth.

He wanted to run, putting distance between himself and any thought of retreat back to the warmth and relative safety of the tower room – but walked steadily, conserving his strength, careful of ice underfoot. He aimed to reach the bottom of the valley by dawn, hopefully find the railway and jump a train heading south. He carried a canvas bag hoisted high on his shoulders, a small rucksack he had found in one of the wardrobes, relic of Baronial hiking holidays. Inside, a change of warm clothing, two blankets, packets of dried fruit and cooked rice he'd smuggled from the kitchen; also cigarettes and matches and his sharpened table knife.

That evening he had eaten dinner with the family again, a last meal, and a comparatively unpretentious one this time – the Baronessa had given up her evening gown and pearls, and sat at the table in her woolly cardigan. He had wanted to say something to them before he left, something that they might remember later, when they discovered him gone, and take as a goodbye. But he left the room quietly, speechless, almost embarrassed. He was deserting them, and he could not let them know that.

Perhaps, he thought, he should remember them as they appeared during that last meal: the Barone composed and dignified at the far end of the table, his wife's cool elegance, the doctor's polite enquiries about his health, commiserations for the cold, the discomfort and the poor food. But he was outside the castle now, he had left the gates. Better to forget them completely. Instead he pictured a map, a network of avenues opening before him.

Scrambling, feeling his way ahead, he began edging down the slope. Trees crackled and hissed, and somewhere the loaded branch of a conifer bent and released its snow with a muffled swish and thud. He had passed halfway down the slope when he paused to look back – the castle bulked black against the ragged clouds, lightless and solitary. Again, for a moment, he felt the urge to turn back.

'Go to hell,' he said, and started onwards again.

Kicking a path through virgin drifts, falling forward once to sprawl in snow that felt almost warm to his numbed hands, Brookes traversed the slope, dropping steadily towards the stream at the bottom of the valley. Rock and shattered stone ground loudly underfoot. Below him he could see the road curving down from the castle, a swoop of snow clear and smooth in the moonlight – his tracks would be visible if he walked there, and he kept to the broken slopes above it. A short distance further and he saw the low humped bridge that crossed the stream, carrying a branch of the road across the valley and up to the scattered cottages on the far side. Brookes kept moving, parallel to the road as the valley narrowed between the flanks of the mountains.

The wind was stronger here. He shivered, feeling the cold working deep into his body and the heavy beat of his blood. He was moving faster, leaping the deeper drifts, the long skirts of the overcoat flapping around his legs. Several times he stopped and held himself motionless, listening into the steady boom and whine of the wind. Snow kicked up in sharp flurries, chaffing his face. The wind moved the forest, swaying and creaking the trees towards him. The broken slopes, the implacable crags and the massed trees were forming an army against him, maneuvering to bar his way. Brookes shuddered, gritting his teeth against the fantasy, then strode forward again. He mumbled scraps of music to himself, little catches and snatches of half-remembered tunes to the rhythm of his steps.

'*Bah-ba-da-da-dah all dressed up to go dreaming,*' he muttered, just under his breath, the words ballooning out in mist ahead of him, '*now don't tell me I'm wrong . . . dah-da-da-dah-da-da . . . I want you to know . . . not just because there's moonlight . . . but moonlight becomes you so!*'

The noise of the wind was in his ears, and the trees rattled at him from the darkness. When he glanced back, the castle was no longer in sight. He pushed on, into the vortex of blown snowflakes. Singing louder now, his breath punching.

'*Ah, some like a night at the movies, some like a dance or a show! Some are content with an evening spent . . . home by the radio.*' Marching as he sang, his feet slipping sometimes, bounding across the snow-filled crevices – '*But whenever I have an evening to spend, just give me one like this . . . da da doo . . . can't think of anyone as lovely as you . . . catching a breath of moonlight . . .*'

He wanted to shout, just to impose his voice on the emptiness around him. He kicked at the snow, and the wind caught it. '*He blows it boogie-rhythm, eight to the bar!*' he sang out loud, dancing a few steps forward, '*he can't blow a note without the bass and guitar . . . da da dah!*'

Then stopped, braced against the slope of the hill with the snow swirling around him, his voice faltering. Slender trees pressed close to his left, and the ground fell away towards the stream to his right. Wind, strong and vicious, howled in his face, and there was no sign of the village. Ahead of him was a gulf of darkness where the vivid snow vanished. He reached out with the stick, prodding for solid ground, and found nothing – he had marched to the lip of a rocky precipice hanging over the valley. Three more steps and he would have pitched himself over the edge.

Brookes sat, then slid down into the lee of a black boulder. He was exhausted, his leg locked stiffly with pain and the wound in his back throbbing. Sheltered from the wind, he fumbled through his pockets for a cigarette. Behind him the trees cracked and heaved, shedding their snow. '*Damn stupid . . . fucking idiot . . .*' he mumbled under his breath. It took several attempts to light the cigarette, then he lay back in the shelter of the rock. He had no idea how far he had walked, or in which direction. Surely he should have reached the village by now, but in the blizzard he could see nothing. His footsteps in the deep snow behind him were already being erased by the wind.

He was lying in much the same position as the frozen corpse that he had buried behind the ruined chapel. The man must have lain like this as the life ebbed from him. Cold was striking into his bones. He saw other nights ahead of him, nights of heatless solitude, hungry in forests and holes in the mountains. He saw himself wandering without a map, creeping into villages at dusk to steal food, avoiding the roads and the daylight, a fugitive in the dead of winter. Shivering, aching with emptiness, he knew he had misjudged his strength badly, and the failure was cruel. He felt the urge to sleep, to relax into the warm snow; he fought it, blinking and shrugging himself awake. Already he knew that he could not continue.

Too dark to check the time by his watch. He sat huddled into his coat waiting for the wind to die down. An indeterminate time passed before he stirred from the shelter of the rock and found the wind had dropped and the sky above was clearer, showing a few stars. He began to pick his way back along the slope, retracing his route. After a short distance he rounded a spur of the mountain and saw the castle up above him, much closer than he would have guessed – all his scrambling over the rocks had carried him less than a mile from the gates.

With the castle in sight ahead of him, he found the going much easier, even though most of it was uphill. He had reached the stony slope below the drive when he heard the distant swell of music on the breeze, the high waft of trumpets, clarinets, violins . . . For a moment his numbed mind could not connect the sensation – he thought the music was in his own head, an echo of his singing. Then he saw the light appear amongst the cottages on the far side of the valley: the same light, the same distant open window that he had seen from the turret.

Climbing, sliding a little, he gained the shelter of a tree jutting from the hillside and fell against its trunk. The moonlight was brighter now through the moving scraps of cloud, and Brookes checked his watch: eleven twenty-five. It had been barely more than an hour since he left the castle gates. Cursing under his breath, he crawled down into the nest of frosted bracken around the base of the tree. He leaned back and gazed upwards, waiting, counting the seconds, the fatigue and the pain forgotten now. The moment must surely have come and gone. There was no music any more, only the night, the wind and the whirling snow.

From the cottage on the far side of the valley the light was a single point, unmoving and bright, just as it had been when he watched from the turret. The face of the castle was dark – Brookes scanned it, picking out the narrow windows on the ground floor, then the larger ones above. There were the two big windows of the dining room, then to the left he saw the balcony. It was a small stone projection with a balustrade, and he might have missed it in the bulk of the castle. But then, as he stared at it, an answering light appeared.

A door had been opened – the door at the end of the panelled corridor between the dining room and the study – and the light came from a paraffin lantern propped on the balustrade. Brookes edged closer, hugging the cold bark of the tree as the bracken crackled around him. The lamplight flickered and a figure stepped out onto the balcony, a man in a heavy coat. Then the light swung upwards, shining directly on the man's face, and Brookes recognised the Barone. He stood with the lamp lighting his face for a few seconds, then stepped back. Next came the Baronessa; she also lifted the lamp to her face. At this distance, Brookes could not make out her expression. The Baronessa retreated, and one by one the rest of the family stepped to the balustrade: first Odetta, then Pietro, and lastly the doctor.

Each of them held the lamp to their face, illuminating themselves to the watchers across the valley. Brookes had thought they must be signalling, but now he knew otherwise. He glanced back towards the cottages – too far away and too dark to make out the flash of binocular lenses, but he was sure the watchers must be using them. Even at this distance, he could distinguish only smudges of faces he knew well, vague in the lamplight. He was still looking back across the valley when the far light winked out. A moment later the lamp was drawn back inside the castle and the door to the balcony closed.

Brookes lay against the tree, the cold burning through his clothes. He waited a long time, tired, conscious of his defeat. The castle was drawing him back. He hauled himself upright and began the slow scramble towards the gates. He was returning, and nobody would even notice that he had left.

9

DAYS OF CEASELESS snow, winter's walls piling steadily around the castle and its stump of rock. Under the piled roofs and the eaves hung with icicles, the chambers were solid with frozen silence. Draughts swooped in the empty corridors. The days passed, one into the next, and Brookes tried to count them as they went, brief episodes between slow dawn and plunging dusk. On those evenings he ate with the family the silences were oppressive. Brookes knew now that it was not reserve that kept them from speaking freely, nor the weariness of boredom. None wanted to begin a conversation that might end in truth. Any meaningful word could destroy the spell that held them.

In grey light through the ice-rimed window, he sat hunched over the table in his room. Spread before him were the parts for an improvised

wireless set, some of them already soldered together with the tip of a
knife heated in the fire to melt the flux. He wore fingerless mittens,
but his hands were numb and his fingers cramped, working a tiny brass
screw into its socket. He blew on his fingertips, gripped the screwdriver
and turned it, grinding splinters from the metal.

Brookes had gathered what he needed in several night trips to the
garage. The valve-board, transformers and variable condenser were all
assembled now, a mismatched array spread out like a circuit diagram
on the tabletop, all wired in sequence to the instrument panel of the
old Marconiphone set, with an earth lead clamped to a water pipe
down near the floor. With his knife he had bored a hole through the
window frame for the aerial wire, which snaked from the tuning coil
to hang suspended on a bracket outside, twisting in the breeze. He
tried to remember the best transmission times for the big European
stations – he didn't trust the makeshift aerial to pick up any but the
strongest signals. The last connection fixed tight, he sat back, clapping
warmth into his hands. Beneath the table was the car battery from
the big Lancia, wired to the radio. Brookes lit a cigarette to reward
himself for his labours.

Three hours later, in the gloom of early dusk, he was bent over
the green glow of the tuning dial. The headphones hissed in his ears,
a surf of empty noise as he moved the dial slowly, listening hard for
the sound to thicken into speech. Vague echoes and crackles, at one
point a voice submerged in static. He moved the dial slowly back
and forth across the frequencies. A whining came through the hiss,
then a percussive crackle. He turned the dial, fingers just brushing
the bakelite, and heard music. Chanting perhaps, something choral,
he could not be sure.

Then, rising up sudden and clear from the ether, the voices of
men joined in song. He recognised the tune, but could not place it

at first. He leant closer to the set, breath held tight, gently bringing the sound into focus. A touch, and it was clear to him. The voices were ruby and glowing.

Stille nacht, heilige nacht
Alles schlaeft, einsam wacht
Nur des Kanzler truer hut
Wacht zu Deutschlands Gedeihengut
Immer fur uns bedacht
Immer fur uns bedacht.

His finger moved the dial, and the carol bled away into the hail of static. Further, through the grunts and whistles of lost stations, unformed traces of life somewhere up in the evening sky, he caught a last crackle before another voice filled the headphones – a voice familiar as rain and red postboxes.

. . . sad and anxious thoughts will be continually with the millions of loved ones who are suffering hardship and misery and risking their very lives to preserve for all mankind the fruits of Christ's teachings and the foundations of civilisation itself . . .

He turned the dial and brought the voice into clarity, sharp as if the speaker sat beside him.

The prayers of good men and women all over the world have been answered. The tide of battle has turned, slowly but inexorably, against those who sought to destroy civilisation. On this Christmas day we cannot yet foretell when our victory will come. Yet it will come, and soon. Our enemies still fight fanatically, but they themselves know that they and their evil works are doomed to a sure and certain destruction . . .

The end of December then. He had been at the castle for nearly two months. How was that possible? He flicked off the radio, trying to determine it – the weeks he had spent here unawares, the year almost done. And neither the Barone nor his family seemed to know or care.

'Merry Christmas,' he said to himself as he removed the headphones.

A morning in early January, and Brookes found the boy playing in the snowy courtyard. Under the grey sky Pietro was dashing clumsily back and forth, dwarfish in his bulky clothes and fur hat. The drifts rose almost to the eaves of the low sheds around the keep, igloo buildings in a smooth white terrain. Against the door of the garage Pietro had propped a board with a face roughly chalked upon it, a circle with dabs for eyes and nose. The board and the door behind it were already starred with shattered snowballs, and as Brookes watched, the boy bent mid-stride to scoop up another. Still running, he passed the board and pounced back, ambushing his target. The ball struck, thudding against the board and showering snow.

'Ha!' Pietro shouted, flinging up his arms. 'Ha! Got you!'

Standing at the head of the steps outside the servants' wing, leaning on the wooden rail, Brookes watched the boy. Pietro was engrossed, his face red between the ear flaps of his hat, panting as he ran heavy-legged in his big boots. Already he had kicked dark paths across the centre of the yard. Strange to see the boy so unaware, so prepossessed – Brookes had become used to his silent presence, the slight figure tracking him through the castle, waiting on the stairs outside his room and fleeing at his approach.

The steps a smooth white ramp, Brookes descended carefully, driving his heels deep to find a grip. He paced quietly across the yard until he stood near the boy. Pietro was stooped, intent and oblivious. Brookes gathered up a handful of snow, packing it between his cupped hands.

As the boy drew back his arm, Brookes lobbed the ball, arcing it high across the yard to smack against the garage door just above the target, a white starburst. Pietro dropped his arm and turned.

'Hey!' he shouted: surprise or accusation. Then he spun around again, off balance, and flung his own ball. It thudded into the target and Brookes clapped. He was crouched over, packing together another ball, when a lump of snow struck him on the shoulder, icy shards spraying the back of his neck and tumbling down inside his collar.

'Ha! Got you!'

Brookes straightened at once, caught the boy's brief grin. Then he was running, bounding though the snow at a tangent to the wall of the garage with the ice tickling his spine. After ten strides he turned and hurled the ball – it went wide, but the boy still ran to avoid it.

Now they were both running, dodging as they tried to outflank each other. Brookes felt the burn of the wound in his back, the slivers of ice melting against it. He was panting laughter. In places the drifts were knee-deep, Brookes and the boy stumbling and catching themselves, running backwards, arms wheeling. Twice Pietro fell on his face, but both times he leapt up again, breathless and determined. A snowball exploded off Brookes' knee and he let out a mock howl of outrage.

'Ha!' the boy shouted again, but when Brookes turned to snatch up another missile he saw the Baronessa standing on the steps from the loggia.

'Pietro!' she called, arms folded. 'Pietro, what are you doing out here? You know you're not allowed to play here, go inside at once!'

The boy stared back at her, a huge snowball clasped in both hands. The Baronessa took three more steps down the stairs.

Brookes tossed his ball lightly, intending that she dodge it, but the Baronessa was looking at her son and not at him: the snow burst against her upper arm, showering powder. She stared down at the patch of white on her sleeve; then Pietro threw the snowball that he had been clasping, and it shattered on the stone stair rail.

'How dare you!' the Baronessa said, open mouthed. 'You . . . *villains!*' The boy was laughing, raucous and mocking. She stooped down, knees together, and grabbed a handful of snow – Brookes and Pietro were already running.

Brookes glanced back as he neared the sheds and saw her coming after him, the snowball canted back in one hand and the other clasping her coat closed. She threw it, and he stumbled backwards and dropped to sit heavily in a deep drift as the ball curved away overhead and struck the wall behind him. The Baronessa laughed, pointing at him, her face flushed bright.

'That's what you get for playing boys' games!' she cried. Over near the garage, Pietro was already crouched in a rut, gathering more snow. Brookes scooped up a light handful and flung it back at the Baronessa, but it broke up in the air and cascaded over her.

Then something struck him in the face, driving packed ice into his nose and mouth. Dazed, he felt one half of his head numbed, and when he opened his eyes there was blood spotted on the snow. Beside his knee he saw a round black stone.

The Baronessa was already running towards him as he got to his feet clasping his face. Blood was streaming from his nose, and he could feel the bruise rising under his fingers. He held up his free hand to her.

'I'm fine,' he said, 'don't worry.'

But then a second ball hit him on the shin, and this time the stone broke from the concealing snow and skittered away between his feet.

'Pietro!' the Baronessa shouted, 'Pietro, what are you doing?'

Blood warm and wet between his fingers, Brookes took his hand from his face to see the boy running back along the far wall of the yard towards the steps. The Baronessa called out to him again. 'Pietro! Come back here at once!'

'That's not my name!' the boy screamed. 'Leave me alone!' Stumbling with his arms out for balance, he crossed the yard and leapt up the stairway to the loggia.

Brookes crouched, the snow between his knees spattered red. He scooped a handful of it and pressed it to his cheek.

'Ow,' he said. 'Bloody hell!'

The Baronessa crouched beside him, taking his hand and drawing it from his face.

'There's a cut there,' she said, 'and your nose is bleeding too.' She steadied him as he got to his feet. 'You have to come inside,' she said. 'I've got hot water on the stove.'

She took his arm and escorted him back across the yard.

'I'm sorry,' she said. 'I don't know why he did that. I don't know what he was thinking . . .'

'Don't worry,' Brookes said. 'I'm not hurt.' The pain had shocked him, but it was easing now, and his pride welling back. But he allowed her to lead him, unprotesting, her hands clasping his arm. Up the steps and across the loggia, they kicked the snow from their boots and went into the scullery room.

Brookes dragged off his coat and jacket and sat on a straight-backed chair beside the fire while Teresa poured hot water into a dish and took a wad of clean cotton from the shelf. Then she squatted in front to him, wiping the blood from his face with the damp cloth.

'I'm so sorry,' she said, 'I don't know what to say. I'll make sure he apologises to you.'

'Really, don't worry. It can't be easy for the boy being stuck in this place, surrounded by snow. No friends, you know.'

Pale sun came obliquely through the dusty windows, lighting her face as she wiped his lips with the damp cotton. The neck of her blouse was open, framing a string of pearls, the line of her collarbone where it caught the light.

'Why don't you let him play outside?' Brookes asked. She paused for just a moment.

'Oh, it's better not to,' she said. 'We try to be as unobtrusive as possible. And it might be dangerous. He might injure himself.' But her expression was guarded, uncertain, and she would not meet his eye. Brookes thought of the stone cottages on the far side of the valley, and the nightly ritual with the lamp. The watchers could not possibly see into the castle yard, but perhaps the Barone and his wife thought it best not to risk even that.

'I heard you, from in here,' the Baronessa said, taking his hand again and raising it to his face, 'just hold that there, that's right . . . I was about to start preparing lunch, and I heard the shouts and I didn't know what was happening . . .'

She had been scared – her face told Brookes that. Her shoulders hunched slightly, a shudder running through her body, and he remembered the Barone telling him about his wife's instability. But the idea that the woman was unbalanced, mentally unsound, seemed even less credible now than it had done at the time.

'What are you frightened of?' he asked. His head was tipped back with the wad of cotton pressed to his cheek.

'Frightened? No, I . . . well, you never know. You don't have children do you, Captain Brookes?'

'No.'

She stood up and tossed the handful of bloody rags onto the fire.

They took a short flight of stone steps that rose from the loggia. The Baronessa went ahead, leading Brookes up into a long gallery with windows down one wall and doors on the other: this was the suite of rooms above the great hall, he realised. The Baronessa's private quarters, and those of her son. Faded rugs of Chinese design covered the floor, and there were hunting trophies, old and mouldering like those in the Barone's study, jutting horns and antlers from the walls. Towards the end of the gallery stood a suit of armour. The Baronessa was banging on one of the doors, rattling the handle.

'Open the door this instant! Pietro, come out at once!'

Brookes walked further down the gallery. At the far end he could see two doors, one opened slightly. The Baronessa's own rooms, he guessed. The armour stood against one wall, dented and coated in black paint, the pieces wired together. One gauntlet gripped an upright halberd – Brookes imagined that the blade might fall if he tried to walk any further.

'Pietro, come out and say sorry to the Captain!'

The door opened suddenly, Pietro's face, vicious with indignation, glaring though the gap. Behind the boy, the room was a wreckage of books and strewn papers, blankets heaped on a narrow bed. Boxes and furniture were stacked around the door, as if the boy had tried to barricade himself in. A sour, airless smell came from inside.

'That was a beastly thing you did,' the Baronessa said. 'Why would you do such a thing? Speak!'

The boy glared, looking at neither his mother nor Brookes. His mouth was a tight slot as he spoke. 'He's not allowed to be here,' he said. 'It's against the rules. He has to go!'

'Don't be ridiculous! Where do you get these ideas? And how dare you speak to me like that!' But Brookes could see that the boy's words had needled her – the Baronessa raised her hand, trembling.

'Say you're sorry for what you did,' she told the boy, her voice taut with threat. Pietro's face fell, his eyes half closed, and when he spoke his lips barely moved.

'I'm sorry for what I did.'

'Don't tell me, tell him. Tell our guest.' But she was softening already – she felt the boy's sense of injustice. Pietro looked up at Brookes, staring at him, savage.

'I'm sorry I hit you with a snowball,' he said.

Teresa pulled her blow at the last minute, but the slap was still loud on the boy's cheek. His expression did not change; he dropped his gaze to the carpet.

'Stay in your room until your father calls for you,' the Baronessa said. The boy nodded and the door closed.

They were back in the loggia before she spoke again, and her voice was thin with anger and recrimination. 'He's such a stupid boy sometimes,' she said. 'He does such stupid things. He'll apologise to you properly later, I know he will.'

She led him back into the warmth of the scullery, and they sat beside the fire. The Baronessa lit a cigarette, then passed the packet. Her hands trembled slightly. Brookes noticed the chilblains on her fingers.

'I don't believe I did that,' she said quietly. 'I never hit them, never. But he . . .' she shook her head, resigned.

'Don't blame him,' Brookes said. 'He's only young. I suppose he's been taught to hate the English, after all.'

'It's hard to avoid,' the Baronessa said, and shrugged. 'He lives in a sort of dream, you see. These ideas he has, about rules and punishments. I fear for him. Ever since my eldest son died . . . ever since he was killed.'

'I suppose Pietro must be upset to have missed Christmas too.'

Her face was blank with surprised incomprehension. Brookes laughed lightly.

'You forgot about it as well?' he said. 'Nearly a week ago now. It's the New Year, don't you know? It's 1945. Soon it'll be . . . what? Epiphany?'

The Baronessa folded her arms, shivering slightly.

'We have so little idea of time here. It feels better for the children not to know anything. Please tell them nothing about it.'

They sat a while in silence, smoking. Then the Baronessa laughed quietly to herself.

'It's funny,' she said. 'When I first saw you both out there, running about in the snow, I thought . . . silly of me, but I thought you might have become friends. *How lovely*, I thought.' She laughed again, sad and tired.

'Maybe we were, for a little while. Something like friends. Partners.'

'Until I came out and spoiled everything.'

She looked at him now, a searching expression, like she was trying to read him. She had a slight squint, Brookes noticed; eyesight not so sharp.

'You know, I still can't quite believe in you,' she said. 'I can't quite believe the way you just appeared on that mountain.'

'You think I came here on purpose?'

'Not came. *Were sent*, perhaps. Maybe not willingly. Maybe not in any way you were aware of.' She paused, that long and seeking stare. 'Who are you, Captain?' she said. 'Where do you come from, really?'

Uncomfortable under her levelled scrutiny, Brookes found it hard to speak.

'From England,' he said with a shrug. 'From far away. And to be honest, I have no idea what I'm doing in this place either.'

'You hold yourself so tightly,' the Baronessa said, frowning. 'So tightly, like you don't want anything to slip out. You don't want to show human weakness, do you.'

'I could say the same about you, Teresa.'

'But I'm not afraid to confess my fear.'

'It's not an easy thing for a man to confess.' They had moved closer as they spoke, into the warmth of the fire, their voices quiet now, complicit.

'You remember what I said?' she asked him. 'About leaving?'

'How could I forget? And as soon as I can, I will.'

'It may be too late already,' the Baronessa said, almost a whisper, and turned back to the fire again. 'What's he been saying to you? My husband?'

'Quite a lot, but not much that makes any sense. Games and suggestions. He seems . . . superstitious. I think he's trying to confuse me. Actually I was hoping that you might be more direct.'

'In what way?'

'Perhaps you might tell me more about your situation,' Brookes said. 'About why you're here, and why you can't seem to leave. You're being watched, aren't you? That cottage on the far side of the valley . . . and every night . . .' he paused. The Baronessa did not look at him, but her face was closed now, a barrier fallen. The warmth of the room dropped with it.

'There are some things we choose not to discuss,' she said. 'Please respect that.'

Brookes waited a moment, hoping for some sign that her resolve would fail. Then he nodded. 'Very well,' he said, and stood up to leave. At the door he halted and turned to her again.

'Just one other thing,' he said. 'Why did your son say that his name wasn't Pietro?'

'Oh, that . . .' She looked lost for a moment, hugging herself. 'I don't know. As I say, he comes out with such stupid things sometimes. You know what children are like.'

'No,' said Brookes. 'No, I don't.'

10

THROUGH THE WIRELESS headphones the world came to him, bringing its news of destruction. Easing the tuning knob as the signal faded, bringing the voices back into definition, Brookes closed his eyes and concentrated. The BBC: the globular vowels of Old England.

It was disclosed officially last night that the American First Army has launched a new offensive against the northern flank of the enemy salient in the Ardennes. Great armoured battles are still being fought in the vicinity of Bastogne, but Supreme Headquarters have stated that despite a heavy snowstorm the American forces have advanced three and a half miles into the salient, and continue to make strong headway in the face of fierce German resistance . . .

He imagined those to whom this news might mean something: crouched as he crouched over radio sets all across Europe, listening to these distant echoes of a faraway war. Clipped voices that could not hope to summon the carnage.

On the eastern front, the outlines of the great battle of Budapest are becoming clearer as the pall of smoke thickens over the Hungarian capital. The Russians report major penetrations on the eastern bank of the Danube, and one Russian commandant has declared that a considerable part of the city is now in the hands of the Red Army . . .

As he moved across the airwaves he noted down the frequencies, scratching the numbers in pencil on the tabletop: BBC, Radio Londra, Radio Roma, Radio Fascista Repubblicana (the voice of 'the divine Wanda Osiris' singing *Che Successo alle Copacabana?* between the propaganda bulletins); Soldatensender Sudfront; American Forces Radio, the skirl and clash of a swing band filling the headphones now, horns and piano riding the steady hiss of background noise. Glenn Miller maybe, or the Benny Goodman Orchestra. Brookes nodded along to the beat, tapped the pencil to the syncopated rhythm. But the news stations pulled him back. The steady demand of now.

In southern England yesterday, schoolchildren were among the victims when a public library was destroyed by a direct hit from a V-bomb. The bodies of two girls, aged eleven and twelve, were recovered from the rubble. Another flying bomb struck a hospital, killing the medical officer and three others, while a third demolished a block of flats. Fire broke out and rescue men worked beneath the searchlights and in dense smoke to recover the trapped and injured . . .

Meditating, his head dropped into the folds of the scarf that wrapped his neck. In his ears the noises whined and crackled, seeming to advance and recede through a hail of interference, a steady rush of distance.

Meanwhile, in Italy bad weather is continuing to cause difficulties for our troops, slowing the advance of the Americans in the Apennines and

the British Eighth Army along the Senio river. Battling through the heavy
snow, the Canadian Corps have consolidated their positions north east of
Bagnacavallo, ready to resume their offensive towards the industrial centre
of Ferrara as soon as weather conditions permit . . .

The Apennines, the Senio – two-hundred miles to the south, and
the armies had not moved for months now. The war went on. Brookes
flipped the switch, and the noise cut off with a pop.

If his days were monochrome, his nights were vivid with dreams.
Fantasies of entrapment and frustrated escape; in his sleeping mind
Brookes blundered through the snow again, blizzard-wrapped and
lost. He found the castle transmogrified, warped into a labyrinth of
dungeons and windy turrets; through tortuous stone passages he wan-
dered, and every wall yielded to his touch, swinging back to reveal a
further place beyond. Somewhere in the maze Carla was waiting for
him, and if he could find her he would be saved. But every chamber,
every twisting staircase carried him deeper, and below him was an
engine throbbing, a great generator powering not heat and light but
cold and darkness. He heard the sound of it, faint at first but growing
louder, and his eyes were filled with dust and cobwebs.

'Don't worry, they won't find you here,' the Baronessa said. Brookes
sensed her standing close to him in the shadows. He felt her smooth
hands on his face, her palms against his cheeks. Her voice breathed
in his ear. 'They can't get you here,' she said. 'There's no way in or
out!'

But then he was alone with a weight bearing down upon him, and
realised where he truly lay – in the shallow grave behind the ruined
chapel, with heavy stones piled over his corpse.

He woke suddenly in the hard light of dawn, shocked from sleep;
the sound that had entered his dreams was still there, distant but

clearer now and growing steadily louder. He shook himself upright, the dream fading from him, and the cold rang in his ears.

Fumbling, still half asleep, he cracked open the inner shutters, pulled them back and leaned into the embrasure of the window. The noise came chopping through the snow and the stillness of the morning, shifting in pitch as the engines raced on the icy roads. Angling his view from the side of the window, Brookes saw the three motorcycles as they turned onto the road leading up to the castle gates. Three black machines, each with a sidecar, throwing a mist of snow from chained tyres. They skated and veered as they took the corner onto the final slope.

For a moment he could not react, his mind slowed and dulled by sleep. He tried to remember his last talk with the Barone – what had he said? Was there anything to suggest a betrayal? But the bikes racing on the winter road looked so sinister in their intent that Brookes could not believe the Barone himself had called them.

Stumbling into wakefulness, he pulled on his coat and boots, then grabbed the knife before running downstairs and out onto the steps. The Baronessa was coming across the yard in her rubber boots. She saw him and waved, flapping her hand intently. She was mouthing something – *Go back! Go back!* – then stabbing a finger at the doorway behind him. Brookes retreated inside again just as the first motorcycle roared beneath the arches of the gatehouse, the noise of the engines exploding into the closed quiet of the courtyard. He reached the window of the old nursery in time to see the three machines come swerving up from the gatehouse ramp, past the shapeless drifts around the ruined chapel.

Five men in camouflaged weatherproof capes: three on the bikes and two riding in the sidecars. All the men were armed, and two of the sidecars had machineguns mounted. Brookes gripped his

knife tightly, the blade dull and spotted with tarnish. It felt completely useless.

The bikes halted, engines still barking and whining. Along corridors
and up steps, he reached the heavy door of the great hall and shoved
it open. The windows here were too high to see the yard, and he ran
light-footed across the floor through the sheeted furniture. Up the
stairs three at a time, he crossed the landing and came to a skating
halt in the scullery, hurling himself down onto a pile of rice sacks
beneath the window. The scullery window was frosted and opaque,
but one clear pane gave a view out onto the loggia and the courtyard
below: the frozen well, the stone angel white-cowled, and the three
figures following the Baronessa back towards the steps.

The man walking in the centre was clearly the leader. He strutted,
sure of himself, throwing off his cape and handing it to the man
beside him. While the other two carried Beretta machine-carbines, this
man wore only a pistol holstered at his belt. Stocky, powerful, built
like a labourer, he had a square unsmiling face and blunt features.
Beneath the cape he wore the same black rollneck jumper as the other
two, the same grey-green army trousers and heavy boots. All three
wore peaked black field-caps of German pattern, and as they moved
closer Brookes could make out their shiny metal cap badges: a skull
with a knife between its teeth.

Lying on the sacks, he felt something clenching inside him. His
breath was short and stabbed his throat. He had known danger many
times, but this was a new kind of fear – the dread of something he
barely understood, something that could fracture the world. He had
become slack, he realised suddenly. His old reflexes, the smooth impregnable shell of his fearlessness, were lost to him. He was exposed.

Now another figure entered the frame of vision: the Barone, walking along the loggia to the head of the steps. Briefly he passed in front

of the window, too swift for Brookes to make out his expression; nor could he tell anything from his posture as he walked halfway down the steps and stopped. The Barone waited, upright and unmoved, for the three soldiers to approach him. Then he threw his arms out wide.

The leader stepped up to him, and the two men embraced.

Their words were dulled by the thick glass of the window. Crouching down lower on the heap of sacks, Brookes pressed himself into the corner of the room, one eye watching through the clear pane as the Barone and the commander walked together up the steps to the loggia. At the top they passed directly in front of the window – they were in silhouette against the light of the courtyard, but Brookes caught their smiles as they moved into the shadow.

Directly below, he could see the two remaining men waiting at the bottom of the steps. In different circumstances, the contrast between them could have been comical: the first was a giant, with the heavy black beard and creased scowl of a barbarian chieftain. His cape was thrown open, and he wore an eight-inch hunting knife and a pair of German stick grenades thrust beneath his belt. The second was only a boy, his cap too large and falling over his ears. Beneath the cap brim was the face of a vicious child. He looked about fifteen years old, but he lounged over the stone balustrade smoking a cigarette and caressing the stock of his gun.

The Baronessa appeared in the loggia again and went back down the steps, wrapped in an overcoat and carrying a tray with glasses and a bottle. The two soldiers tipped back spirits and blew steam from their mouths. From the scullery window Brookes could not hear what they were saying – he sat forward, pressing his face to the pane. The vicious child laughed, throwing back his head. He held the gun in the crook of the arm, pointing at the Baronessa's belly. Still grinning, he lowered the angle of the barrel, jutting it towards her loins. His friend was laughing too, great silent shrugs. The Baronessa was trying to smile, but Brookes could see that she was clumsy with fear. When she bent to place the tray and the bottle on the step, the boy swung his foot lightly, catching her on the rump. Without a word, she turned and ran up the steps. As she approached the scullery door Brookes threw himself back down onto the sacks, out of sight of the window.

The door shuddered as she came inside and set the tray down on the edge of the sink, the streak of dirty snow marking the skirt of her coat. Then she froze, staring back over her shoulder at Brookes.

'*What are you doing in here?*' Her whisper almost silent. Brookes raised a finger to his lips, then nudged the door closed with his foot.

From somewhere deeper inside the building he heard the Barone's voice, then the other man, the commander, speaking. The voices passed outside, onto the loggia. Brookes stayed down, flat on the rice sacks; the Baronessa was still beside the sink, white-faced, fingering the neck of her blouse.

The voices passed the window.

'We'll certainly do anything and everything we can,' the Barone said.

'You be sure of it, all of you,' the commander replied, his voice surprisingly high and nasal, bronchial-sounding. 'Remember . . .' and they moved away down the steps again to the yard.

Two more minutes until Brookes heard the cough and snarl of the motorcycle engines. The noise echoed back off the walls of the castle, growing deep and resonant as the three machines dropped into the ramp leading down to the gatehouse. Then they were outside and moving away down the road into the valley. For a long time afterwards Brookes could hear the noise clear and distinct, a roar fading to an insect whine through the massed trees. In the castle the silence was cavernous, stillness falling gradually as dust settles back over a room.

They were gathered in the dining room, the Barone and his wife, Odetta and the doctor. Brookes pulled out a chair and sat, composed and calm. Odetta left the room at once, and the Baronessa shot a pointed glance at her husband before following.

'Who were your charming visitors?'

'Nobody you need concern yourself with,' the Barone said. 'They are gone now, and will not return for some time. As you see, this is a great relief for us.'

'I'm sure I recognised that big chap with the beard,' Brookes said, scratching his chin. 'I must have seen his picture in the newspapers somewhere. A famous murderer, perhaps?'

The Barone failed to look amused. 'I'm sure in your ramblings about the mountains,' he said, 'you must have seen a lot of strange people.'

'I did. And many of them told me about the Black Brigades. Fascist paramilitaries, aren't they? I hear they enjoy stringing up children with piano wire. An uncompromising message to the partisans, supposedly. Are they friends of yours?'

The Barone took some time before replying. He looked, Brookes realised, tired, and far less assured than he had ever seen him before. 'The gentleman I was speaking with,' he said, 'was Comandante Attilio Battista. He commands the Black Brigade in this district. They're very powerful, and it is best to treat them with courtesy, I find. They visited us here several times, back in the summer and autumn, but I didn't expect them today. Apparently there's been a lot of partisan activity in the neighbouring valleys – bombings and several attacks on police posts. Assassinations of public officials, that sort of thing.' His voice was thin with distaste.

'The Comandante wished to know if I'd seen anything of the perpetrators. They like to check on everybody. But, as I say, now they've gone and I don't expect to hear from them again for some time.'

'If they'd seen you, they would have killed you,' the Baronessa said, coming back into the room. She brought coffee, four cups on a tray.

'Killed all of us, more likely,' said the doctor. 'They're savages. Released convicts and psychopaths with fanatics to lead them.'

The Barone looked at his brother, a muscle working in his jaw. 'We shouldn't be so quick to judge,' he said quietly. 'What do we know of what happens out there?'

'We know more than enough already, surely,' said the Baronessa, quieter still.

The silence in the room stretched tight, as if each dreaded the sound of the motorcycles once more. The four of them sipped their coffee. Nobody would look at Brookes.

'The Comandante told me some interesting things,' the Barone said at last.

'Don't . . .' the Baronessa said abruptly.

'Some interesting things.'

Draining the last of her coffee, the Baronessa got up and walked out of the room. Her husband watched her go, circling his thumbs idly.

'What things?' Brookes asked.

'He told me that there's an Englishman, a fugitive, believed to be in these mountains,' the Barone said. 'A soldier, it seems. A sergeant, to be precise, called Farrell, or something similar. This Englishman is an engineer, and was working with one of the partisan groups. The partisans believe he betrayed them, giving away their position to the Republican forces. Now they want to find this man and exact their version of justice. Needless to say, Battista and his men would also like to find him.'

'It sounds unlikely,' Brookes said. 'Why would an Englishman betray the partisans?'

'Ah, well, that's the interesting thing. The Comandante believes, as indeed the partisans appear to believe, that it was a deliberate act by the English. They and their American friends fear that the partisans are becoming too strong a force. Perhaps they suspect that their command has been taken over by Communists, and of course these Communists will oppose Allied government after the fall of Mussolini. Battista tells me that the English refused to supply the partisans in their . . . *liberated zone* in Ossola. Now they're actively trying to undermine the partisan formations.'

'Utter rubbish. That's Fascist propaganda, surely you couldn't believe otherwise?'

The Barone raised his hands and shrugged. 'In our current state, what can one believe?'

'Better to believe nothing,' the doctor muttered. He was staring hotly at Brookes.

'And so you suspect I might be this man Farrell?' Brookes said.

'No, not at all. Your name is Brookes, is it not? And you're a captain, not a sergeant. In fact, the name of this man is probably not Farrell either! My memory for English names is very bad. So many of them sound alike.'

'While we're on the subject of names,' Brookes said, 'I might ask about your son's.'

'Pietro? Why, his name is Pietro, of course!'

'He has another name,' the doctor said quickly. He looked at the Barone, then back at Brookes. 'Yes, another name, which he prefers. It was what his brother called him.'

The picture on the sideboard – the smiling youth. Vittorio, Brookes remembered.

'Zach,' the doctor said. 'He likes to be called Zach. Sometimes he won't respond to Pietro at all . . . I think his brother took the name from a comic book, perhaps . . .'

'He's a very strange boy, my son,' the Barone said wearily. Then he clapped his hands together. 'If you'll excuse me, Captain, I really must go and lie down for a while. I slept very badly last night.' Walking around the table, he let his palm fall heavily onto Brookes' shoulder.

'Now you see,' he said, 'how dangerous it is for you to leave this place?'

Beneath the arches of the gatehouse, Brookes stared into the night, into the wind's razors and knives, into the depths of the valley under the shredded sky. Flurries of snow came eddying from the castle roofs above him. The tracks left by the motorcycles were still visible here, crisscross lines of grey slush on the black paving, but outside on the road the wind had smoothed them into soft furrows.

The Comandante and his paramilitaries could return at any time. They could return in greater force, search the castle, root him out. Once he had been their equal, as savage as them, but he was weak and alone. Healing but not healed, he felt that weakness as never before. If not Battista, then the partisans, the militia, the Germans . . . The safety which he had once assumed was no longer here. Beyond the castle gates, the whole world wanted him dead. And the castle was open to his enemies.

Shivering now, Brookes threw his weight against one of the big ironbound gates, trying to heave it closed. Stone hard, stone weight, the massive door would not shift. Brookes shoved, then dragged at it. The hinges were broken, the gate wedged back against the wall.

'*Fuck*,' he said through his teeth. He slammed his fist against the studded wood. Pain lanced his arm and he reeled back. He plunged his grazed knuckles into the snow, then stuck his hand beneath the lapel of his coat.

Stamping beneath the arch, hugging his injured hand, Brookes breathed deeply. Already the drifts in the valley were becoming too deep even for Battista and his motorcycles. This at least, Brookes thought, was a cause for hope. He gazed at the swarming sky and hoped for a snowstorm heavy enough to erase everything, white out the world and all its crimes. He would be safe here until the thaw. Long enough to recover, to make himself fitter and stronger; to regain control and be rid of this alien feeling, this powerlessness.

Squinting into the dark, he tried to make out the shapes of the buildings high on the far side of the valley, but he could see nothing. He had no idea of the time – his watch had stopped and in all the day's disruptions he had not thought to wind it – but the hour of the family's ritual with the lamp on the balcony must be approaching. And now at last he could guess its purpose, and who it was that lived in the cottage on the far hillside. He could guess who had broken the gates, cut the telephone line, shut off the electricity. The Barone and his family, he knew, were just as much prisoners here as he was himself. He could almost laugh.

11

BEFORE HE REACHED the stairs he knew that somebody was in his room. He had left a lamp burning in there when he went out to the gatehouse, and the light shining down into the stairwell shifted slightly as a figure passed before it. The slightest creak of a floorboard. He sat carefully on the bottom step, unlaced his boots and pulled them off, then removed his coat. Silently he climbed. The stairs curved and the light grew, and he could hear the quiet hiss of the radio.

Odetta was beside the table with her back to the door, wearing the headphones. The dials glowed green, and Brookes could make out the steady pop and fizz of music, of big band swing. The girl was dancing, hands clasping the phones to her head, shoulders bobbing, hips swaying, her feet pacing short steps side to side, almost in time with the rhythm. Her skirt swung as she swayed, and she whispered a low wordless music.

Brookes stood braced in the doorway watching her. For a moment he thought her unaware, artlessly clumsy and lost in her enjoyment, but then her attitude changed. She did not turn, but something in her movement became deliberate and controlled. She knew he was there watching her. She went on dancing. Finally she turned, grinning, and feigned a gasp of surprise.

'Oh!' she said, pulling off the headphones and dropping them clattering to the tabletop. 'You crept up on me!'

Brookes shook his head, shrugging himself away from the door and across the room. He picked up the headphones, put them on; the music was sudden and strident, blaring clarinets and saxophones, snapping snares. He took them off again.

'I'm so sorry!' Odetta said, hands clasped before her, not looking sorry at all. 'I came looking for you, and found your radio. I didn't mean to be nosy. It's so wonderful to hear music again.'

'Listen if you like,' Brookes said. He crossed to the fireplace and squatted before it; he had stacked a pile of kindling in the grate earlier, bits of splinted wood, torn paper and rags. He struck a match and lit the fire, then raised his cracked hands to the flame. The graze on his knuckles was not too bad, scabbed already. Dirt was dug in under his nails. Behind him Odetta snapped off the radio.

'Don't be mean,' she said. 'I came here to be friendly. I thought you might like some company. I'd like some company too.' She crouched down beside him, then settled herself to sit on the floor beside the fire. Brookes tried to relax, tried not to find her presence too deliberate.

'So you like American music?' he asked her, trying for a neutral tone.

'Mmm, very much,' she said, the dance in her eyes still. He noticed her scent, distinct and softly spiced. 'We're not supposed to like it though. We weren't even allowed to listen to it, but we did anyway. I used to like the American films too. Everything American.'

'What's your favourite film?'

She paused a moment, considering, sly. '*Wizard of Oz!*' she said. 'Even if I had to watch it in English. That was illegal too.'

Brookes smiled, feeding bits of broken wood to the fire. Only conversation, he thought. There was nothing more to it than that.

'Who were those men who came today?' he asked her.

'Papa told you who they were,' she replied. 'I hate them. Soldiers frighten me.'

'Don't I frighten you then?'

She frowned, thinking about it. 'No,' she said. 'No, you don't.'

'But I thought they were supposed to be on your side. The Black Brigades.'

'I'm not on anybody's side. And they're worse than the Germans.'

'You hate the Germans too?'

'Of course I do!' she said with sudden clean anger. 'The Germans killed my brother!' Then caught herself, gnawing at the side of her cheek.

'Your father told me,' he said slowly, 'that your brother died in North Africa.'

'Did he? I don't know why he would say that. But I'd rather not talk about it.'

Brookes got up and crossed the room. Odetta was quiet for a while. He took the water jug from the table and drank deeply, the cold tightening his throat.

'What kind of soldier are you anyway?' she asked. Brookes shrugged, unsure how to answer.

'I used to see soldiers often, in Turin,' she went on, gazing into the fire. 'They were home on leave, I suppose. I didn't like them. But you're very different, aren't you. You don't have a uniform.'

'I used to have one.'

'Yes, but it's more than that. Like you carry the war inside you.' She was looking back at him now, over her shoulder, studying him. 'It makes me trust you, I don't know why. I know I shouldn't.'

'Nobody should trust anybody,' he said. He turned down the lamp, and the firelight cast his moving shadow around the curved walls.

'Don't you have any brothers or sisters?' Odetta asked.

'No, I don't have any family.'

'No parents either?'

'Both dead a long time ago.'

'What about a wife?' she said. 'Were you ever married? Or engaged?'

'I had a fiancée once,' Brookes said. 'But I never married.' He kept on pacing, slower now. The room was close and getting warmer although the gales blew snow against the shutters. He felt an obscure sense of entrapment.

'Was that Carla? You told me about her.'

'No, Carla was somebody else.'

'Was she blonde then, Carla? I used to think that all English women had blonde hair. Like Jean Harlow.'

'She wasn't blonde, no, but she wasn't English either. And neither is Jean Harlow.'

Odetta curled herself up off the floor and went to the bed. She sat on the edge of the mattress, perched, nervous-looking.

'Back home in Turin, I had some *boyfriends*' – she used the English word – 'but they were just kids. Just silly boys from rich families.' She sat still for a moment, then began clumsily dragging her jumper off over her head.

'What are you doing?'

'Too warm,' she said, her voice muffled by the jumper's tight wool-len neck. Her face appeared, hair pulled up and then falling back to her shoulders, and she threw the jumper aside. 'That's better.'

Brookes kept pacing, the door to the fireplace and back. He scratched the back of his neck. He stuck his hands in his pockets. He was aware how he must look – stupidly ill at ease. Odetta had taken her shoes off and was lying on the bed, legs stretched out in thick black stockings. She wore a blouse, pink, flower patterned, with a frill down the front. Her fingers were idly picking at the buttons.

'What do you do,' she asked, 'if you want to kiss somebody but you don't know if they want to be kissed?'

'Depends,' Brookes said. 'Somebody once told me that a woman will always forgive a man for trying to kiss her, but will never forgive him for not trying.'

'And what about a man? Do they forgive?'

His breath was tight in his throat. He stopped pacing and stood in the middle of the room. From the corner of his eye he could see her legs stretched out straight on the bed.

'Did your father send you here?' he asked her, but quietly, too quietly for her to hear. Her questioning face, anxiously impatient. In that expression he had his answer; this had been her own inspiration. How long, he thought, had she considered this? How long had she dared herself? Her single-mindedness was unnerving.

He took two paces across the floor, then raised a knee and knelt on the side of the mattress. Odetta reached out and touched his thigh, circling her hand around his leg, slight pressure drawing him towards her. The suddenness of his desire was a revelation to him.

Brookes threw off his jacket, shed his sweater, then sat beside her.

'What are you doing?' he said quietly, deep in his throat. She rose to meet him, her arms circling his neck and dragging him down.

Then he was beside her on the bed, embracing the softness of her body, the wetness of her mouth against his. Hungry, he sucked at her bottom lip, then kissed her cheek and the line of her jaw. Her arms were still locked around him, gripping tight; he could feel her breathing, the rapid rise and fall of her ribcage as she lay beneath him.

She drew her face aside, trembling, as he started unbuttoning her blouse. The frill of pink cloth parted to reveal the smoothness of skin tight across her clavicles, the flesh of her throat and the curve of her breast beneath. Blood hammered in his head.

There was a slim gold chain around her neck, a crucifix lying on her chest. His hands paused, clenched at the opening of her blouse. Carla had worn a necklace just like that. The tiny figure of the dying Christ glinted cold against her warm flesh. Odetta opened her eyes and stared up at him. Just for a moment he saw her face, eyes closed and lips parted, and suddenly it was the terrible image of Carla's face, crossed by the shadow of the ferns. She touched the gold cross.

'Don't you like it?' she whispered, her voice trembling. 'Are you . . . are you a *vampiro?*' She smiled wanly, trying to laugh. 'I'll take it off . . .'

She lifted the gold chain, but Brookes stopped her. He was hot, breathing hard, and felt sick.

'No,' he said. 'No, we can't do this.'

He hauled himself violently away from her and sat on the edge of the bed. Odetta was dragged up with him. She fell against his chest, her arms still clasped around his neck.

'You can't!' she said, and he felt her body tremble against him. 'Please don't. Don't leave me.'

His body was all bone and sinew, every muscle taut; he was conscious of his hard hands, bruising her soft flesh.

'I don't want you to leave,' she said again, and he turned back to her, gentler now. He held her as the nausea rocked him, and he felt the wetness of her tears. 'I'm sorry,' she said. Her skirt was rucked up around her waist, and he carefully pulled the hem down to cover her thigh. He could hardly bear to touch her now, his own body so filled with deathly horror that he repulsed himself.

'I just wanted . . .' she was saying, 'I just wanted to feel something. I wanted to know what it's like. I'm so lonely here and there's nothing . . . nothing else but this and it's never going to end, we're never going to escape from here, this is everything and I hate it. I hate it.'

'Odetta,' he said. 'Odetta please. Lie down. Lie down now.' He was stroking her back, awkwardly, his hand like a tool. Gradually he eased her down, drawing her arms from his neck until she lay flat. She rolled away from him then, over onto her side with her face turned to the wall, weeping quietly.

'I don't want to hurt you,' he said.

'It always hurts, doesn't it?'

'That wasn't what I meant. You're seventeen. You're a child, you don't know anything.' He was being cruel. He intended to be. He wanted to drive her from the room. Instead she lay still and silent on the bed, her legs drawn up.

'How am I supposed to know anything,' she said, her voice muffled by the quilt, 'if there's nobody to teach me?'

Brookes stood abruptly. He went to the table and took another drink of water. He lit a cigarette with an angry flourish.

'I'm sorry,' he said. 'I can't be your teacher today.'

Odetta said nothing, and for a few minutes there was silence. Then she shifted suddenly, swinging herself off the bed. She snatched up her jumper and took her shoes from the floor. Her hair fell forward to cover her face, and she did not look at Brookes.

'Goodnight,' she said curtly, then marched out of the room, banging the door behind her. Brookes dragged the chair nearer the fire and sat down, the cigarette burning between his lips.

On the bed he lay still, feeling the warmth of her body from the quilt. He had not thought about what he was doing. About what he had done to her. At the time, he thought he was protecting her from himself. Without thinking, he had acted carelessly, and now his only ally had been turned against him.

'Stupid,' he said.

He rolled onto his side, lying where Odetta had lain, the quilt a little damp from her tears. Extinguishing the lamp, he pulled the quilt over him and hoped for sleep. The fire, unfed, had burned down to a throbbing glow. Instead of sleep, another sensation came over him, a restless tenderness, something close to desire but abstract. He thought of Carla, and of Odetta, and the two women blurred into a single person. He felt a sense of precarious lightness, a stalking and intangible feeling of loss. Lying on his back, then on his side, he listened to the wind at the shutters and sensed the great cold world outside. He threw off the quilt and stood up.

When he opened the door the blast of air from the steps chilled him, waking him instantly like a splash of iced water. He felt his way down and through the nursery, his skin alive to the night. Up the passage he found the door to the great hall still wide open where Odetta had passed through, the huge room beyond vaulted with shadow. Then the stairs, each tread a groan beneath him, and he reached her door. It was not bolted.

A confusion of tumbled shapes in the dark, clothes thrown on the floor, over chairs, heaped in profusion. Brookes stood beside the narrow bed, the quilts and covers so thick he could see nothing of the body within. He let the coat fall from his shoulders then took off his trousers and shirt, stooped to remove his socks, and stood in his underclothes. She was watching him now, her eyes bright over the top of the quilt. He raised the covers, and the bed opened to warmth and soft scent. He climbed in beside her.

'You're cold,' she said, whispering, as she moved to give him room on the narrow mattress. The covers buried them, and she lay turned to the wall with the curve of her back towards him. She was wearing a nightgown of thin satin, and her body felt coated with smooth liquid. Shivering, he bound himself close to her, one arm across her body, stealing her warmth. She took his hand and pressed it to her breast, and he felt the swell of her nipple through the fabric.

For a long time they lay like that, twined together and motionless. He could feel the tension in her body, the speed of her heart. He remembered Carla, under the ferns, the doubled S of them. He put the thought from his mind. No thought now. He was beyond thinking. Instead he felt only the luxury of the moment, sinking into it warm and secure. He could have remained like that all night, wanting nothing else but this touch, this shared and secret warmth. But she was moving now, shifting awkward and nervous under the covers, wriggling herself around to face him. He stroked the furrow of her spine, lazily down to the curve of her hips, the rise of her buttocks. His fingers touched bare flesh beneath the nightgown's hem.

'I'm not in love with you,' she whispered. 'I'm not a child.'

Their lips met, and slowly she relaxed against him, opening her body in little shudders with every breath. Her arms were around him, and she slid one leg across his hips, clasping him. She touched the wound in his back and he flinched. Suddenly then she pressed her head against his, almost aggressive, rubbing her cheeks and her mouth across his face, through the rasp of his stubble. Then she pulled back and stared at him a moment, their faces a span apart in darkness, a bewildered gleam in her eyes.

'You want this?' he said, the words in a breath, almost a gasp. He felt her nodding, the hair moving against his face. He pressed himself into the hollow of her, his knee between her legs, his palm grasping her thigh, his hard penis against her belly, but she rolled away.

'Not like that,' she whispered, quick and scared. She was face down now, stretched along the bed. He climbed across her, the covers lifting heavy on his shoulders, and a draught of cold air rushed between their bodies. Then he pressed her beneath his weight, pinning her down, and she was breathing hard through her nose, fast tremulous breaths. Blind under the covers, he dragged up her nightgown, felt the glaze of sweat on her thighs as he parted her legs. She grabbed his hand and clung to it, her shoulders rigid. With the first thrust he pierced her, the slight soft resistance and then the give, and a jolt went through her. She sobbed once, quick and muffled by the pillow. She squeezed his hand tight.

There was no disorientation on waking; such a natural sensation to ease from sleep into that soft warmth. Brookes lay quietly with his eyes open to a grey pre-dawn light, and Odetta slept in his arms. Her face was childishly round, pouting, a slight frown between her eyebrows, one hand lightly curled at his chest as if she had tried to grab him in her sleep. One of his arms was trapped beneath her. He gazed at her face, her innocent eyelids, and wanted to kiss her but feared she might wake. He shifted slightly, closed his arms around her, then tried to sleep again.

A song was running through his mind, surfacing from dreams. He hummed it to himself, hearing the words sung by a multitude. *Bella ciao bella ciao bella ciao ciao ciao!* . . . They were in a clearing of the forest, gathered around a fire, and one of the partisans had a guitar and another a violin. The song was played fast, and some of the younger men were trying to dance like Cossacks, hopping and tumbling as the rest all clapped time. Brookes sat at the edge of the gathering, Carla lying against his chest, and he felt the rhythm through her body as she sang over the thrum and squall of the music.

'Viva Staline!' A man was shouting hoarsely, raising a bottle into the firelight. Applause and cheers, the tumbled dancers rolling on the turf, howling laughter.

'Viva la Armata Rossa! Viva la Unione Sovietica!'

A volley of cheering, raised cups, raised rifles. Carla raised her fist in salute.

'Viva viva viva,' Brookes said quietly, clapping his palm against Carla's thigh, smiling to himself as the guitarist started strumming the chords of *La Bandiera Rossa*.

Eyes open, he awoke to a sudden apprehension. Light came from the uncovered window, lining the room with pearl. Brookes shifted as the cramps wracked him, drawing his dead arm gently from beneath the girl's body. Sliding from the covers, he stood up and went to the window: smoky grey dawn outside, the snow hanging in the air and massing on the piled forest. He looked back at the bed – Odetta stirred slightly, let out a sleepy snore, muttered something under her breath.

'*Fuck*,' Brookes whispered. '*What have I done?*' His head was aching.

Quickly now, stiff and mechanical, he snatched his clothes from the floor and pulled them on, shuddering with the certainty of his error. He stood with his hands on his head, fingers digging into his scalp, into the pain in his skull. He would not look again at Odetta – he was out the door and creeping down the stairs as he pulled on his jacket. To be caught now, he thought. *Idiot!*

At the bottom of the stairs he slipped through into the great hall. A mirror just inside the door framed his face for a moment, harried and malevolent. He wanted only to leave, to escape this place, run through the snow and the depths of the forest and get himself far away. Pulling the lapels of the coat tight around him he paced down the hall, between the ranks of reversed canvases. He almost made it to the door.

'Franco!' she called, her voice carrying an echo. He turned to look back, and saw her standing on the wooden gallery at the far end of the hall, wrapped in a blanket, hair a mess of untidy curls. 'Where are you going?'

He walked a few steps back towards her, shivering in his jacket. Odetta's face was sleepy and baffled. 'To my own room,' he said. 'It's better.'

'You're not leaving?'

'No, I'm not leaving.'

She looked at him for a few moments. Then she blew him a kiss.

12

THE WINDOWS OF the bathroom were blanked with snow. Brookes stood shirtless in hard morning cold, braces dangling, chin lathered, stropping a straight razor on a leather belt. The small basin of luke-warm water stood on the wash-stand before him. He breathed on the mirror, then rubbed at the glass with a rag and saw his reflection through the frost.

Dinner the evening before had been an ordeal. Clearly the people from the village no longer brought their offering of fresh food – the single pot held a watery broth, a selection of burnt vegetables floating on a surface layered with oil. The Baronessa apologised; the fire had been too hot, she explained.

'You seem restless, Captain,' the Barone had said down the length of the table. 'Are you feeling well?'

'Not quite, no,' Brookes told him. 'Bit of a cold again I think.' The doctor placed a palm against his forehead and pronounced that he had a temperature. 'I believe you've taken a fever,' he said. 'Too much wandering about outside, no? Too much running in the snow!'

And Brookes had felt dazed and unkempt, as if he really did have a fever – he wanted to drink a great deal, glass after glass, become drunk and not care any longer what they thought of him. The tense sober quiet around the table seemed ice thin, and he longed to shout or sing or pound the tabletop with his spoon. Odetta sat curled over her dish, hair screening her face, flicking glances hot with complicity at Brookes every time she raised her head. He had been glad to escape early to his room.

Now, raising the blade, he began to scrape the hollow of his jaw. He paused, black-flecked suds sliding along the razor and dripping into the basin beneath. Outside, footsteps moved past the bathroom door and up onto the spiral steps. Brookes heard them echo. Too late now to try and catch the visitor before they reached his room; he flicked the blade, spraying foam across the mirror, then wiped his face and pulled his shirt back on.

He was thinking it might be Odetta waiting for him as he jogged up the stairs. Instead he saw the doctor, hovering in the doorway. Doctor Umberto, come with his thermometer and his brisk bedside manner to check on the invalid. Brookes came up behind him silently, planting his hands on the doctor's shoulders, surprising him. Umberto spun round, clear of Brookes' grip. The wireless set lay spread on the table beneath the window.

'What is *this?*' the doctor said, pointing. His voice was panicked. 'This is no good, you cannot have it! This is forbidden!'

'Forbidden by whom?' Brookes asked. He shoved the doctor forward into the room and closed the door, leaning back against it to seal the exit. Umberto stared at the wireless, shaking his head, fingers working at his lapels.

'That's a car battery!' he declared, pointing again, his finger weaving in accusation. 'That's *our* car battery!'

'I borrowed it,' Brookes told him. 'Don't worry, I can put it back easily enough.'

'But . . .' the doctor fell silent, his arguments dying in his mouth. 'I must tell my brother about this . . .' He was red in the face, embarrassed by himself, close to tears. The mere breath of violence and his resolve had collapsed.

'Better not. Why don't you sit down?'

Mutely, the doctor did as Brookes had told him, falling into the chair with his head in his hands.

'Now,' Brookes said, seating himself on the edge of the bed, 'perhaps you can help me understand a few things. You don't need to speak, just nod if I'm right.'

The doctor stared up at him from between his hands.

'Somebody, or some organisation perhaps, is forcing you to remain here in this castle. That same person forbids you to have a radio or telephone, forbids you any but the most essential contacts with the outside world. Am I right so far?'

The doctor nodded slowly, sadly.

'Whoever this is has a spy of some sort in the cottage on the far side of the valley, keeping watch over you. Every night you show yourselves at the balcony facing the cottage, so the watchers can be sure you're all still here. Right?'

Again the doctor nodded. 'Sometimes we don't have to,' he said. 'If the snow's too heavy. It's only when they shine a light first. They told us that.'

'And this person is Comandante Attilio Battista, or somebody senior to him in the Black Brigades, yes?'

For a moment it seemed the doctor would not respond, then he nodded once. 'Yes, it's him,' he said.

'Why?' Brookes asked, leaning closer.

'I cannot tell you!'

'Why?' Stronger this time, with an edge. It was easy.

The doctor flinched back in the chair, his face falling. 'Are you threatening me?' he asked, fearful but with a slow curiosity. Brookes understood that the man had been threatened many times before.

'No,' he said. 'I'm just asking you.' He sighed and threw himself back to lie on the bed. He could hear the doctor exhaling, breathing slowly, steadying his nerves.

'I'm sorry,' Umberto said. 'I promised I would say nothing about these things. But you seem to have guessed most of it already.'

'You want something from me,' Brookes said. 'You want to use me. For what? Do you want me to protect you? Am I to fight off Battista and his men for you?'

The doctor coughed a quick laugh. 'Oh no, no,' he said. 'That would hardly be a fair contest, would it, eh?'

'Then I'm mystified.' The chair creaked as the doctor stood up.

'You must understand that he would kill us, *he would kill us* if he knew . . . It's amusing, but when you first came here I even believed that you were a spy! For *him!* I saw the bullet in your back, I cut away the flesh and dressed the wound with my own hand and still I believed . . . I thought that was something Battista could be capable of. I never wanted you here. I never trusted you. I see I was right.'

He was stepping away, moving steadily closer to the door.

'I won't tell my brother about this,' he said, gesturing lightly, dismissively, at the wireless. 'But please, be more discreet. Please do not ask us questions we cannot afford to answer. That is the price of your safety.'

He stood beside the door now, waiting for Brookes to speak. Brookes lay silent on the bed.

'What have you learned on your device?' the doctor asked, his tone softer now and less scared. 'What's happening out there, really?'

'The Reds have taken Warsaw,' Brookes told him. 'They'll be at the German border within two weeks. The Americans should break through to the Rhine soon afterwards. In Italy, nothing. More bombing raids – Genoa, Milan, Verona . . . but the armies aren't moving.'

'So it goes on,' the doctor said sadly, bemused. 'So it still goes on.'

'Not for long,' Brookes said. But the doctor had already left the room.

Hours before his next visitor. A light knock at the door, and Brookes sat up in bed.

'Come in,' he called. It was Odetta, carrying a tray.

'Hello,' she said, a little shy. 'Because you're sick I thought I'd bring your food for you.'

'I'm not sick.'

'Well, I didn't think so, but we have to pretend don't we.' She sat on the bed in her coat and scarf, balancing the tray across his knees. Rice broth again. He set it aside on the table.

'Lovely day today,' she said, staring about the room. 'Clear. And it's stopped snowing.' She unwrapped the scarf and took off her coat.

'Your uncle came to see me,' Brookes said.

'Yes, Mamma told him to come. She was very concerned. *You must go and see the Captain.* Uncle didn't want to . . .'

'What did he say?'

'Oh, he thinks you need to rest a little more.'

She pulled up the covers and crawled beneath, bulky in layered woollens, shoving up close to him with her head nestled into his shoulder. Her clothes were cold and damp against him.

'I like it that you're a Captain,' she said, snuggling. '*Capitano Franco. Capitano mio . . .*' Clumsy beneath the covers, all shoulders and elbows, she began struggling out of her jumper. Brookes lay still, passive. Odetta took her clothes off and tossed them from the bed – jumpers and skirt, stockings, blouse, underwear, all flung and scattered across the bedroom floor.

'This is dangerous,' said Brookes. 'Somebody might come to check on me.'

'They won't. They're all *hibernating!*'

Naked, she embraced him again, the warmth between them. She slid her hand under his vest, fingers spread across his skin. He told himself that he didn't want this, but it was too easy to just lie back and let it happen.

'I like this part here,' she said, spanning the muscle of his shoulder with her spread hand. 'And I like this.' Her fingers gripped his bicep. Her lips on his skin. He ran his hand through her hair, feeling the heavy softness of curls. The weight of her body against his flank, and of her thigh as she moved across him.

'I don't think we should . . .' he said. 'I don't have any . . .' he couldn't remember the word in Italian, 'any *gloves . . .* any *protectives.*'

'Don't worry. Do what you did before.'

He didn't do anything before. He didn't care then. She was on top of him, straddling his body, her breasts pressed against him and her breath hot in his ear.

'I'm not scared any more,' she whispered.

Afternoon ebbed into evening, and they lay together with the covers up to their chins, sharing a cigarette. Smoke curled and spilled in the brittle air above the bed. Brookes had dragged the wireless set to the edge of the table so the cord of the earphones would reach them – they had a phone each, and listened to the high swoon of the American dance music she loved. The reception was poor, distorted voices cutting into the music, strange whines and blizzards of static, and he kept having to reach out to adjust the tuning. Odetta shifted her body in time to the music, jogging the covers, grinning. She was glowing. She was hot with happiness.

If I could protect that, he thought. He squeezed his encircling arm tighter. If I could hold that and keep it safe. She turned her head and lay with her face close against him, her nose pressed against his, her eyes staring into his eyes, so close her eyelashes brushed him when she blinked. Where did it come from, he thought, this tenderness, this gentleness that possessed him now? No training had given him this, no learned reflexes of attack or defence. Something innate then, something truly of himself. Or perhaps those ghosts inside him, all the grey phantoms of the men he had been, sloughed identities not cast away but consumed, all of them lost now far from human warmth, far from love, but reaching upwards and outwards, towards the light.

But still the conditioning was there; the steel voice telling him to close himself off, cauterise emotion before it could flow. Deny this, the voice told him, and he felt a fist closing around his heart. It was almost a pain, almost a physical pain. In her eyes he saw himself reflected, a dark miniature, his true self staring back at him. She could have unravelled him like fraying wool, if only she'd known which strand to grasp.

The fire was burning low, and Odetta leapt quickly from the bed and dashed across the room, high on her toes. Naked she stooped over the fire, flinging on sticks, then smartly, giggling, ran back to the bed. Brookes raised the covers and she slid in beside him, already shivering, the soft dark down raised on her goosepimpled forearms. She burrowed against him. The slight creak of a floorboard, from outside – maybe someone stepping back from the door . . . Brookes smiled at his own instinctive alertness. It was the wind, he said to himself. The wind, or the sigh of an old building.

'Where's your brother?' he said, drowsily.

'Pietro? He's in his room. Designing weapons, if you really want to know.'

'Weapons?' Brookes said. 'What for?'

'To defend Italy, I suppose,' she said. She pressed against him, gripping his shoulders, mock-fierce. 'To defend us against you! Giant guns and curly swords and things. He draws them for hours and hours. It's a sort of hobby. Actually he's just miserable because he never got to be in the Balilla and fire real guns. You know what that is? The Balilla?'

'Fascist Boy Scouts?'

'Right. He was in the Children of the Wolf, but he really wanted to join the Balilla afterwards and wear the uniforms and do rifle drills. But it was too late . . .'

'And you? You had to join as well?'

'Oh yes.' She laughed, settling herself against his shoulder again. 'I was in the Little Italians. But I never got to join the Young Italians because . . . well, for the same reason. It was fun. We marched around a lot and did gymnastics and sang all the proper songs, you know.'

She pushed her hair back and scrambled up to sit, drawing the covers to her shoulders. A suppressed giggle, a faint blush, then she sang, clear and high:

We are the golden dawn
Alive in the rising sun's rays
And in our little hearts, burning with love
We pray God Save The Duce Always!

She glanced at him, half mocking, half proud. Brookes shrugged
and gestured for her to continue. Odetta coughed, then threw back
her head and sang out the chorus:

Ready at your signal, Duce, Yes!
For Italy and the King!
Beautiful Italy, our native soil
We love you, the children sing!

'You think it's silly don't you,' she said, embarrassed now. 'Mamma
doesn't like me singing it either. Do you think she heard?'

He shook his head, smiling. 'No, but you sang it well.'

But she was frowning, drawing her body into a defensive crouch,
fiddling with her hair. 'I miss those days,' she said, and there was a
catch in her voice, as if just for a moment she might cry. 'Everything
was better then. Before . . . There's not even a king any more is
there.'

'There is a king,' Brookes said. 'But he's in the south. He's on the
side of the Allies now.'

'I don't care where he is,' Odetta said. 'It doesn't matter who wins
the war. Italy will lose. We'll lose.'

She slid down beneath the blankets again. For a few moments they
lay in silence, the radio hissing to itself on the table.

'You called your father a liar,' he said to her. 'Why did you do
that?'

'He told you?' She raised herself on one elbow, mouth slightly open, her face flushed.

'No, I saw it. You called him a liar and he hit you.'

She was trying to appear amused, but her expression still showed surprise. Fear as well, perhaps. 'So you *are* a spy!' she said. 'Or maybe . . . maybe you turn into a bat at night and fly around, spying on people?'

'Why did you call him a liar?'

Odetta shrugged heavily, turning her head from him. Beneath the covers her foot jerked compulsively. 'I don't know,' she said.

'There wasn't a reason? There looked like there was a reason.'

'We're all liars,' she said with sullen pique. 'Even you, you're a liar too aren't you? Sneaking about spying on people, telling lies about yourself. I won't tell you why I said it. I can't remember.'

She glared up at the ceiling, still blushing furiously. Brookes knew that there was no point in pressing further.

'You're right,' he said. 'It was a lie, about what I was doing before I came here. But I said it to protect you, not myself.'

Her interest was awake now, drawing her out of her hunch. She gazed at him, eyes questioning.

'I'm not an escaped prisoner of war. I was a liaison officer, working for British military intelligence. I was parachuted into the mountains to link up with the partisans. I stayed with them for almost a year.'

'With the partisans?' she said. 'Did you fight with them too?'

'Some of the time, yes. Mostly I was communicating between them and my superiors, and instructing them in demolitions. Sabotage. That was what I was trained to do.'

'And did you . . . kill a lot of men?'

'Some men. Yes, I've killed. But it was necessary, you understand.'

Her expression now was unguessable – trying to decide

whether to believe him, perhaps; whether to feel the privilege of confidence or the insult of not being trusted before. She shuddered, rolled to lie face down on the mattress with the covers bunched over her.

'I hate violence,' she said.

And he nodded, about to reply, then caught himself. No point in pretending, he thought. Six months ago, even two months ago, he knew what he would have said. *I love it.* Said it not only for the shock, but because it was true. Now, though, he no longer knew what he thought. No longer knew what to think.

'Have you ever killed a woman?' she asked.

Brookes swallowed, shook his head only to clear the thought. 'Let's not talk about these things,' he said. 'Better not.'

'But you want to go back, don't you. You want to leave us and go back to your war.'

'I have to,' he said.

'No. You don't. Nobody does.'

Then she took his hand, squeezing his fingers into the warm dampness of her palm.

'I don't want you to go.'

He kissed her, his arms around her, holding her close. Slowly she relaxed against him. Stay like this, he thought. It was almost a prayer; as close to a prayer as he would ever allow himself. An impossible request, to an impossible God – stay like this, don't let the next thing happen. But the next thing would happen, and soon, and there was nothing he could do to hold it from them.

He was leaning from the window of his bedroom the next day, adjusting the wireless aerial, when he heard the first scream. Late afternoon, the light already fading and everything granular and gritty with coming dusk. Brookes paused on the iced window ledge, then heard the scream again. Birds wheeled and battered the sky.

Down the stairs, he came out onto the steps above the yard at a run. The snow was trodden smooth and glassy and he spilled over at once as his boots slipped from beneath him, slamming down hard on his back. Raising his head, he saw the two figures at the top of the courtyard, struggling and frantic in the waste of snow. The Barone dragged his daughter by the wrists, and she fought against him.

'Leave me alone!' she shouted, her voice ragged. He tugged at her and she staggered. She must have been in the round tower when he found her. Her secret retreat.

'What have you done?' the Barone cried, 'what have you done?' His words too were frayed with tears, both voices carrying oddly, clear in the thin air. Brookes scrambled to his feet, gripping the rail at the top of the steps. The Baronessa was coming from the main building now, bounding across the snow with her coat flapping.

'I don't care! Get off me! Leave me alone!' Odetta screamed. She was on her knees, her father trying to haul her upright. He let out a wordless cry, a terrible echoing wail – his wife reached him then, a confusion of dark shapes as they met. Brookes was halfway across the yard when another body collided with him – the doctor, grappling him a halt.

'Please go back,' Umberto said with urgent emphasis. 'This is none of your concern.' His grip was surprisingly strong. At the far end of the yard Pietro stood to one side, hands in his pockets, impassively watching his family's grief.

Tracing his palm along the wall, Brookes moved quietly down the passage from the scullery towards the open door of the dining room. Warmth met him, and he paced closer until he could see them sitting before the fire. The Barone was in his armchair, Odetta kneeling beside him. His embrace enclosed her. Neither said anything; the Barone caressed his daughter's head, then bent to kiss her hair.

'You like to creep about like a thief, don't you.'

Brookes turned sharply, his back to the wall. The Baronessa stood behind him in the shadowed passage.

'Or are you a thief?' she said, her whisper taut with anger. 'You've stolen something from us, after all.'

'Not stolen,' Brookes said. 'Received.'

'This wasn't supposed to happen.' He could barely see her in the darkness.

'Then what was *supposed* to happen?' he asked.

She turned and walked away from him. Brookes followed, down the passage and out onto the landing. Last faint light of day, and she faced him again; still the mask of courtly indifference, eyebrows arched in cold disdain.

'She was only doing what she thought he wanted. What she thought my husband wanted. We discuss you, you see. We discuss you, and she overheard.'

Teresa moved closer, and Brookes took a step back. He felt the wall behind him, one of the hanging pictures shifting as his shoulder pressed against it. The Baronessa moved closer still, a wild gleam in her eyes. Brookes saw the tension in her, the urge to strike him barely restrained. He felt the blow already.

'This is a game,' she said. 'But you don't know the rules.'

Suddenly she shot out a hand and gripped his face, fingers digging into his cheek, thumb pinching his jaw. Brookes seized her wrist but she clung tight. Behind his shoulder glass popped in a picture frame.

'*Bastardo!*' she said, through her teeth and he flinched. 'Coward! Now you'll try and run away, won't you?'

She released him suddenly, shoving his head aside. Brookes tasted blood from a bitten lip. Teresa was breathing deeply, flushed with desperate energy, a kind of reckless, excited rage. Brookes remained leaning, refusing to act – he put his hands in his pockets, his own convulsive anger held tight.

'You don't understand,' she said. 'You were supposed to take me. That was his idea.'

The woman before him towered in her rage, her slight and shadowed body huge with condemnation. He refused to buckle, to let the shock register – he found her eyes in the shadow and held her gaze.

'Your family is disgusting,' he said.

'We're all disgusting, yes. So are you, Captain Brookes. Because you're a part of us now. I told you to leave when you could.'

Shoving himself from the wall, he closed with her in a single stride, a hand at her throat and the other clasping her upper arm. Tendons in her neck cabled taut; he felt the rapid pulse under his hand, the flutter of breath. They moved together, steps forward and back – a dance of slow restrained aggression.

'So tell me the rules,' he said. 'Tell me everything.'

The Baronessa smiled slowly, her body relaxing, and he let his arm slacken. She grabbed the lapel of his coat, darting forward to kiss him hard and sudden on the mouth.

'I'll be waiting for you tonight,' she said, her voice metallic, strange. 'I'll leave the door unlocked.'

13

A TALL OVAL mirror reflected the scene in fireglow and candlelight. The silvered glass was cobwebbed by age, by two or three centuries of reflected images: dress suits and evening gowns, medalled and ribboned uniforms, winking jewellery. The room was a stage set in amber and smoky red. The deep bed and the draperies – satin and polish, walls papered with something embossed and tactile. A classy sort of brothel perhaps, or somebody's notion of one anyway. Brookes watched himself sitting in an ornate chair, tensed and uneasy in his layered stevedore's woollens, and felt as out of place as a machinegun in a ladies' dress shop.

What would it cost him to belong? Who must he become, he wondered, to inhabit the oval of the mirror as the mirror itself required?

A certainty of distinction, centuries of lineage, an ease with luxury he did not possess. But he would never want that. He had never been at home in comfort – puritan disdain ran in his blood, the anarchic levelling urge to destroy, to kick and shatter the mirror pane, rip down the drapes, burn the bed. He would turn all the palaces of the world into pigsties. He thought of the soldiers, hundreds of thousands of them shivering in their foxholes that night on the Gothic Line: Americans and Germans, British and Italian, Indians and Poles and Canadians, all of them alike under the freezing blizzards. Which of them would not trade places with him, here with the blaze of the log fire, the warmth of the room in the icy night, the air heavy with a woman's scent? And now he saw the Baronessa, slowly emerging from the shadows outside the fire's flicker. She walked up to stand behind him, red silk sheathing her, and placed her hands on his shoulders.

'You kept me waiting,' she said.

He had almost not come at all. For hours anger had kept him in his room, seething alone and determined to remain that way. But to live in the castle in solitude, in combative disapproval, in ignorance, would be intolerable. Odetta was untouchable. Escape in the snow and cold was impossible. He had no choice. The game urged him onwards.

In the long gallery leading to the Baronessa's room he had delayed further, walking so very slowly beneath the mounted animal heads. Passing the standing suit of armour he tested the edge of the raised halberd and found it was blunt.

He walked in on her without knocking. Teresa was sitting at her dressing table on the far side of the room. The red silk gown, the pearls, the earrings: a priestess at her altar. She was writing a letter, or pretending to write one. As he sat down he caught her crafty dab of fresh scent, her quick determined squint into the small mirror before her.

'There's some food on the table there,' she said as she stood behind him. 'I thought you might be hungry.'

Fruit in a dish, a plate of rice mash. He shook his head. 'I'm not,' he said.

The Baronessa shrugged. Her hands lay on his shoulders, and she squeezed lightly.

'So this is all your husband's idea?' Brookes asked, addressing her reflection.

'Not any more. It's mine now. Do you like it?'

'What happened between you two? You have separate rooms, you can hardly bear to speak to each other. He forced you to come here?'

'My husband,' she said, stooping over him to whisper, 'is the Devil.'

'Why are you really here? Why did you leave Turin?'

Her hands moved to his neck, the exposed skin. 'Are you here to interrogate me, Captain?'

'I shouldn't have to.'

'But is that what they trained you to do, in your army? Interrogate people, torture people? Make them confess? I've known men like you. You like to use people, don't you.' He watched her smudged face in the mirror, her impassive mask. Then he felt the prick of sharp steel against his skin and saw in the reflection the thick hairpin she held against his throat.

'Never touch my daughter again,' she said, slow and controlled. 'If you touch her, I'll kill you.'

He let his head drop back, exposing the column of his throat. She cupped his chin, drawing him back against her belly while the pin traced a line across his jugular.

'Perhaps I should kill you now and be done with it.'

'Go on then,' he said. 'Redeem the honour of your family.' He gazed up at her, blinking. The silk gown hung open slightly, and beneath it she was naked.

'Honour?' she said. 'We lost all that months before you came here.'

The pin had drawn blood; Brookes could feel the beaded wetness of it. Still he didn't move, kept his hands in his lap – but he wanted to reach up to her. He felt for her, in the crisis of her position, and wanted to tell her how unnecessary it was. As if the words, the touch of his hand, could banish this shoddy fantasy and return the real woman, the Teresa he had spoken to that day at the well, and later in the scullery. But the room held only the contrived certainties of a prearranged seduction.

Keeping the pin pressed to his neck, Teresa circled him, silk hissing around her legs. With one fluid motion she straddled his lap, facing him. Brookes forced himself to breathe. Thoughts, sluggish and disconnected, coiled in his skull. He felt her weight and her feverish warmth. The pin fell, point first, and Brookes heard it spike the floor beside him.

'Tell me the truth,' he said. 'About this place.'

'There is no truth about this place,' she said, easing forwards against his body. 'It's all . . .' kissing the line of his jaw, 'an illusion. Can't you tell?'

'You don't feel very illusory.' He clasped her thighs beneath the silk.

'I am . . .' breathing in his ear, her arms snaking around his neck. 'I was sacrificed for an illusion, after all . . . an illusion of safety . . .'

Arms linked beneath her, he heaved himself up and carried her across the room. He felt himself divided: one self, the real self perhaps, left sitting in the mirror's reflection observing the scene, while some disconnected double bore the woman towards the bed. He was a voyeur, spying on himself, or on some character that looked like him in a threadbare erotic show. Halfway to the bed Teresa started giggling. He threw her down into the depths of the mattress, and the springs banged and squealed.

Laughing, eyes pressed shut, she lay on her back as Brookes stripped her of the gown. 'Oh!' she cried. 'You made such a noise! You actually *growled*, like a . . . just like an *animal!*' Her long fingers were pressed to her chest, which rose and fell with sobs of laughter, and the pearls rolled against her collarbone. Gulping a long sigh, she opened her eyes and looked at him.

'How ridiculous we are!' she said. 'Isn't this ridiculous? You must think I'm insane!'

Brookes stood beside the bed, pulling off his clothes. Naked, he sat down at her side. Her mascara was smudged, and he wiped her cheek with his thumb.

'I'm sorry,' she said. 'I haven't slept in weeks. It feels like that . . . Oh, these things are never easy! I'm nervous, isn't it stupid?' Slowly he ran his fingernail down her body, from her neck over her breastbone and the arch of her ribcage to the soft plain of her belly. A brief thin line, white on her pale skin.

'You're quite fascinating, you know,' Teresa said, recovered now and watching him intently. 'I don't know if you intend to be.' With a quizzical frown, lips pursed, she placed her palm against his chest, flat and splayed, pressing the muscle.

'What are you doing?' he asked.

'Trying to find your heart,' she said. 'Trying to find if you have one. Or if you're just an empty shell.'

He stretched himself on the bed beside her.

'Sometimes,' she said, speaking to the ceiling, or the pillow, 'we think that if we do the worst things, it'll make everything else better.

As if we can reach a balance somehow. Or maybe just a point of saturation. I don't feel . . .'

'Shhh,' he said, touching her lips. He drew her into an embrace. For a while they lay like that, bound together, shared breath on skin.

'Make love to me then,' she said, her mouth against his shoulder. 'And perhaps afterwards I can sleep.'

Sleep she did, but Brookes could not. He was used to hard beds, or none at all, but the mattress was absurdly soft. He became queasy in its yielding depths, half smothered by piled quilts.

Things became clearer to him as he lay thinking. She had been punishing her husband, or punishing herself; or perhaps merely placing herself between him and her daughter. Tawdry, maybe, but acceptable, he thought. Immediately afterwards, lying in the groaning trough of the bed with Teresa's body beneath him, he had relaxed down onto her filled with slow sad release. There was sweat between her breasts, and his balls ached, and he kissed the tendons of her throat and tried to kiss her lips. She turned her head and shoved him away. As soon as she was free of him she rolled over onto her side, a sleepy moan in her throat. The mattress bulged a ridge between their bodies.

For a while he lay listening to her breathing. He wanted a cigarette, and needed to piss. Throwing back the quilts, he felt the cold air on his skin and was refreshed by it. Teresa shifted and mumbled, the mattress creaking beneath her. Brookes got up and paced quietly across the room. He opened the door of the huge armoire and gazed at the ranks of dresses – the blue silk gown from the night of his first dinner, others in satin, chiffon, lace. Running his fingers through their scented whisper, he tried to imagine the life that Teresa must once have led. A world where these silks and flounces, smooth furs and cut silver buckles had a place. Had she dressed that way on their first meeting just to show what she was capable of? And did she, Brookes wondered, dress so sumptuously when Comandante Battista paid his visits too?

He took a cigarette from the pocket of his coat. In a small wooden locker beneath the washstand he found a tin chamber pot. Standing naked in the middle of the room, he lit the cigarette and held the chamber pot as he pissed into it. With the cigarette between his lips, the gush and the spatter, he felt a sudden uplift of cocksure arrogance. If he shifted his hips he could piss on the carpet . . . The mood passed quickly, and he shuddered with the cold. Carefully he replaced the pot beneath the washstand, stubbed out the cigarette after two more drags, then lifted a quilt from the bed. Lying on the hard floor, he rolled the quilt around him. A little later he heard a steady dry creaking. Teresa was grinding her teeth in her sleep.

Snapping out of a light doze, Brookes sat up. Teresa stood beside the bed. Slow and assured, she crossed the floor, her naked body a lean white shape in the darkness. Casting aside the quilt, Brookes whispered her name, then again, louder, but she seemed not to hear.

She reached the dressing table and knelt down, then dropped forward onto her hands and knees. Brookes was crawling towards her, not making a sound. As he drew near, Teresa rocked back onto her haunches, then forward again, banging the top of her head against the drawer of the dressing table.

'Teresa?' he said urgently, not whispering now.

Again she rocked back, and again forward, her head thudding, moving with the animal automatism of sleep, the conviction of dream. Brookes crouched beside her, unnerved, his hand poised to touch but not wanting to touch, not wanting to wake her to the awareness of what she was doing. Lightly, as lightly as he could, he took her shoulders. Her muscles were tight and there was a convulsive strength in her movements. He pressed harder, trying to ease her away, to absorb some of the force of her blows – abruptly she stopped and rocked back onto her haunches again.

'Teresa, go back to bed now,' he whispered, hoping that somehow she would hear and understand. Her body was shaking, but her face was as blank and peaceful as a sleeper. She swayed from his grip and stood up. Brookes stood beside her, keeping his touch light on her shoulder, trying to guide her back across the room.

'What have you done?' she said. Her voice rose slow and clotted from deep inside her, out of the fog of dreams, and she barely moved her lips. 'What have you done?'

Breathing quickly, fighting the urge to grapple her and force her back into bed, Brookes stepped away. Teresa wheeled in the centre of the room, looking as if she would topple at any moment, a strange low sound coming from her.

'You trapped us like this,' she said, speaking with slurred emphasis. 'You cursed us.' Suddenly she shouted, shockingly loud. '*Pezzo di merda!* It was you!'

Her arm flailed out, catching Brookes on the shoulder. He snatched for her wrist, but she was attacking him now, flaming with blurred energy, striking at his face.

'Bastard! You bastard! For your . . . pride, your reputation . . . And are you sorry? You . . . *worthless* . . . I *despise* you.' There was horror in her voice.

Brookes backed away from her steadily, taking the blows on his shoulders and chest. He knew that to wake her now could be disastrous. Steadily he stepped back and back as she came at him, hoping not to stumble against anything – she wore a ring on her left hand with a stone that cut him, but he did not flinch.

As swiftly as it had begun, the rage left her. Teresa stood swaying like a limp puppet, legs trembling beneath her, and now he guided her. Meekly she turned and went back to the bed, clambering beneath the quilts. Just as he thought she was safe, she lurched back upright, eyes wide and staring at him.

'Who are you?' she demanded, her voice clear and sharp. 'What are you doing here?'

'Just a dream,' Brookes said, smoothing her arms down to sides. 'Don't worry, just a dream.' And she closed her eyes and yawned back into sleep.

14

HE WAS UP early the next morning, leaving the Baronessa sleeping. A bright day, the sky luminous with early light, and out in the yard he stamped across the snow to the sheds around the base of the keep. Twitchy with sleeplessness, smouldering with sour adrenaline, he hauled free one of the big beams that had collapsed from the roof, then hefted it over his shoulder. Leaving it propped against the coping of the well, he climbed to the loggia and went inside. There would surely be a saw or an axe somewhere in the building, but Brookes wasn't sure where to look. Nobody to ask, of course.

Down the wooden stairs, he went exploring into the dusty gloom of the old kitchen beneath the dining hall. Scant light through the barred windows showed him heavy bench tables, stone vaulting overhead and a big bow saw with a cruelly serrated blade slung over two hooks. Then, as his eyes adjusted to the dark, he saw the sacks of grain and rice piled under the table; the grimy earthenware jars along the shelves; the wooden crate of apples in straw and the preserved meat slung from the overhead beams, great knuckles of ham and smoked sausage in mottled grey strings.

Brookes took a knife from the table, wiped it on his trouser leg, then reached down a sausage and pared away the greasy hide. Breakfast, he thought. None of the meats had been touched, and he had eaten nothing of the sort the whole time he had been at the castle. He cut slices of the sausage and sat on the table's edge chewing, the taste almost unbearably rich. Two slices, three, then he cut a hunk of the sausage, took an apple and the saw and went back outside.

Coat off, jacket off, he stood in his shirt with the sleeves rolled, sawing the beam with long hard strokes. The exercise was instantly invigorating; he felt the strength in his arm, the action of the muscles in his back. He broke a sweat, and enjoyed the cool breeze on his brow. Forward and back, the teeth of the saw biting and cutting, shooting a plume of bright orange sawdust forward into the snow with every stroke; the sound of it, the fresh cut smell, the heat in his body were all a delight. His chest was bruised but he ignored the ache.

After cutting half of the beam Brookes broke from his work and dropped the pail down the well. He heard the crack, and when he drew it up there were shards of ice in the water. He drank from cupped hands. When he glanced up, Odetta was watching him from the arches of the loggia. He splashed his face from the bucket and when he looked back the girl was gone. Chewing another slice of the salami, then biting a chunk of apple, he began sawing again. The sawn lumps of wood dropped and rolled in the snow.

'What are you doing, Captain?'

Brookes paused, then lifted the sawblade from the cut. The Barone stood on the steps above him, dressed in his tweed hiking clothes and feathered hat.

'Cutting firewood,' Brookes said. 'We use a lot of it, and we've almost run out.'

'That looks like a beam from the shed roof,' the Barone said.

'The villagers come up and take it, why shouldn't you do the same?'

'Yes, yes, Captain, but we can hardly stop them can we? I would prefer, however, if you did not. Would you pull the castle down around our ears?'

'Better than freezing to death,' Brookes said. 'Besides, I needed the exercise.'

'Exercise, yes,' the Barone said. He stepped carefully down to Brookes, nudging a lump of cut wood aside with the toe of his boot. 'Exercise is very important.'

Brookes slid the blade into the cut and drew back the bow of the saw. Before he could press the stroke, the Barone placed his bare hand on the wood, beneath the blade's jagged teeth. The slightest pressure on the saw now would cut him; a stroke would take off his fingers.

'I seem to have placed myself in your power, Captain.'

Brookes stood with muscles locked, the big saw drawn back. He was breathing hard from the exertion of the work.

'You may think,' the Barone went on, in a cool and level tone, 'that you have mastery over me now. But you must understand that sometimes passivity is a sign of the greater strength.'

Brookes met his eye, the acid penetration of his gaze. 'All that you have,' the Barone said, 'all that you have done is a gift from me. I still control you, Captain Brookes. I have given you the power to hurt me, and to hurt my family, but that is my will. The power you now have is like the power of children over things they do not understand. The power of a tyrant. That is all I have to say to you.'

He withdrew his hand and walked calmly away towards the loggia. Brookes eased the saw forward, and the teeth clicked and jumped against the wood.

Three pots of water had boiled over the fire, but the bath was still only warm, blood temperature. Brookes lay stretched in the tub, his knees jutting up. He slid back, dropping his shoulders beneath the surface, then the sudsy water closed over his head and roared in his ears.

He lay still like that, eyes closed, imagining himself in deep water, totally submerged and far from land. Small bright thoughts rose to the surface of his consciousness and dissolved. He felt alone, enclosed by liquid, heedless and careless. He could let himself drift, let his body sink deeper and deeper away from the light and the material world, away from reality and into abstraction. It was a comforting thought, and he watched it dissolve.

Surging upright again, released into air, he sat back in the tub as the water slopped and swilled around him. Teresa was standing in the doorway of the small bathroom, her weight on one leg, arms folded and head cocked to one side, watching him.

'You have a lot of scars,' she said. 'I never noticed.'

She seated herself on the rim of the tub, legs crossed, rather dainty as she looked down at him, studying his body. Brookes saw himself as she did – the length of him stretched beneath the water, his narrow hips and the white cage of his chest. She reached down and stirred the water around his penis with her fingertips. A wry half smile.

'What happened there?' she asked, nodding at his bruised chest. He told her, and for a moment she was silent. Only her hands moved, nervously twisting the rings on her fingers. 'I'm sorry,' she said at last.

'I haven't done that for a long time . . . the sleepwalking. Not since we came here. I had no idea. I'm sorry.'

'You talked,' Brookes told her.

'Did I? How strange. I wonder what I can have said?' Her tone was still light, but her eyes were glittering.

He wouldn't tell her exactly what she'd said, the bitter words she'd used. Better she didn't know. He looked at her again and saw she was crying silently, trying to cover her face.

'Forgive me,' Teresa said, sniffing and wiping her cheek. She composed herself, sitting up straight on the edge of the bath, very proper now. 'It's strange,' she said, her voice catching. 'You're only the second man I've ever slept with. After him.'

She paused.

'*Donc, qu'allez-vous faire, maintenant?*' she said, bolder now. Switching language had given her assurance.

'*Je ne sais pas,*' Brookes replied. The bathwater was getting rapidly colder, and he raised himself to a squat and reached out for the towel.

'You can't build a wall around yourself, Captain Brookes.' Teresa picked up the towel, held it outstretched as he stood with the water spilling from him, then wrapped it around his body.

'It seems, *Madame*, I have no choice in my actions at all.'

She rubbed his shoulders lightly through the towel. 'You can help us,' she said. 'I need you to help us.'

'How can I, if you won't tell me why you need help?'

'You'll know,' the Baronessa said. 'When the time comes, you'll know.' But she seemed uncertain even as she said it. In her eyes, Brookes saw the anxious look of faith.

'This bathroom's very shabby,' she said, glancing around at the bare walls and grubby linoleum. 'I have one in my suite you can use in future.'

'*Merci bien*,' he said. She touched his face, tracing his jaw with her thumb.

'Dinner will be served at nine, as usual,' she said. 'Everything proper, you know. Everything in its place.'

He took the best suit from the wardrobe, black wool by Caraceni in an early 1930s cut. He wore a grey polo-necked jumper and patent leather shoes that pinched his toes as he walked. They were all waiting for him in the dining room, not seated at the table but standing together by the window. Brookes walked into the firelight, noticing the hush as they stopped talking about him. He walked towards his own chair, then paused. Instead he went to the far end of the table and took the seat beside the fire. The Barone's chair. The Barone shrugged lightly, nodded, and led the family to the table.

This time the doctor served, ladling out the watery rice gruel. Brookes took half a salami wrapped in oilcloth from his pocket and began slicing it into a dish.

'I found this in the kitchen downstairs,' he said. 'Perhaps you might like some?'

They gazed at him, watching him cut the meat.

'It's bad,' Teresa said. 'Rotten.'

'It's smoked meat, it doesn't go rotten.'

'Seriously, Captain,' the doctor said. 'There are rats in the kitchens. All the preserved meats down there are bad. You really shouldn't eat it.'

Brookes took a slice of salami and began chewing it slowly.

'Nobody? Ah well then . . .'

A chair scraped back, and Odetta walked down the line of the table. Looking Brookes in the eye, she took a slice of the salami. She slipped it into her mouth. As she turned her shadow fell across him, hiding him from the others, and she quickly tossed a folded piece of paper into his lap. Then she went back to her seat and sat down again. The doctor gave a low groan of disdain.

'You must be careful, Captain, if you wish to leave us once the snow has cleared,' he said. 'Food poisoning is a serious matter, no?'

Brookes smiled tightly. Beneath the table he caught Odetta's folded note as it slid from his lap and transferred it quickly to his trouser pocket.

'I don't think the Captain has any intention of leaving us,' the Barone said quietly. Down at the far end of the long table, he was almost consumed by the shadows.

'I want to leave,' Pietro said suddenly. The boy spoke so seldom that for a moment everyone stared at him.

'We all want to leave, darling,' the Baronessa said. 'But we can't, can we. Now eat your rice.'

'No!' the boy cried, flinging down his spoon. He stood up, chair squealing, and ran from the room. The Barone exhaled loudly and raised his hands.

'He'll be back soon enough,' the doctor said. 'Best just ignore him.'

'Yes, of course,' said Odetta quickly, eagerly. 'After all, we're all having such a lovely time . . .'

'Odetta, *basta*,' her father said sternly. But before he could speak again the girl went on.

'Such a lovely time, I feel like singing! Who knows a song we could all sing?'

'Be quiet!' Teresa said. Odetta ignored her. The girl's face was alight, eyes gleaming as she drew herself upright. A swift current of alarm circled the table: Brookes saw them all tensed and suddenly alert.

'I know a good song! We can sing it together!' Odetta gulped, a little breathless, then began to sing. A high quaver – it took Brookes a moment to recognize it. *Giovinezza.* The anthem of the old days of fascism.

> *Youth, youth*
> *The springtime of beauty!*
> *Through the struggles of life*
> *Your song rings out!*

'Shut up!' Teresa shouted, leaping up from her chair. 'Shut up now! Why do you have to sing that diabolical rubbish?' She was livid, her throat taut – if she was any closer to her daughter she would certainly have struck her. Odetta paused, her mouth still open for the next verse. Slowly, carefully, she eased herself back from the table.

'You used to like me singing it, Mamma,' she said in a small voice.

The Barone was leaning forward heavily, primed to address them both, when a heavy pulse of noise came from outside, rattling the shutters. All heads turned to the windows.

'Thunder?' said the Baronessa, her voice yielding.

The sound came again, maybe closer – a low distant detonation.

'No. Bombs,' Brookes said. He stood and quickly snuffed the candles. Smoke curled upwards in the silence, then they heard the faint popping of gunfire carried on the wind.

'The bridge at Rocca Pietra,' the Barone said. 'Down at the bottom of the valley.'

A minute passed in heartbeats. Through the long silence they heard the noises of the building around them, the castle's slow shift and creak – the whine of an icebound shutter, the rattle of a loose tile on the portico, the steady drip of water melting down the chimney-back and the fire's snap and hiss.

'Mamma, they were shooting.' Pietro stood in the doorway, perched on the edge of the light.

'We know,' Teresa said. 'We heard them. But they've gone now.' She stirred the ladle in the big pot. A scrape of iron.

'A little more risotto, Captain?' she said.

Back in the bedroom, Brookes sat beside the fire. He would be alone for some time, he knew – he had left the family in the dining room, and they would be attending to their nightly ritual with the lamp on the balcony. For a while he just stared into the flames, trying to deny his own curiosity. Whatever Odetta's note said, he was sure he didn't want to know. He drew the paper from his pocket slowly, unfolded it just a little and glanced at the first line.

C'era una volta. Once upon a time. A fairy story then, Brookes thought with slight surprise. He heard her saying it, as she had in their lessons together. A *ferry tell.* Then he unfolded the paper fully and read. *Il Castello Incantanto,* it was called. Of course.

Once upon a time, there was an old castle high in the mountains. It was a strange place, forgotten by the world. In the castle lived a family, and they were forgotten by the world as well. One day a wolf came to the castle, dressed like a man. The daughter of the family found the wolf outside and, taking pity on him, brought him in and looked after him. The family welcomed the wolf, although they could never trust him because of his sharp teeth and savage ways. But when the daughter looked at the wolf she was fascinated, and forgot those things, and because she wanted to escape from the castle, and did not want to be forgotten by the world, she came to love the wolf and trust him in everything. But the wolf betrayed her. The daughter was angry and very sad, but she realised that the wolf had no choice, because he was only a stupid animal and had no human feelings. Then she pitied him again, because even though the wolf believed that he was free and could do whatever he wanted, the daughter knew he was a prisoner just like her.

That was everything at first glance, a cramped little scrawl in sloping handwriting. Then Brookes saw the extra line, written along the very bottom of the paper.

P.S. I am going to have a baby.

He crumpled the paper into his fist. A stab of anger, then a rush of shame. He could not believe it, willed it to be untrue. It was a trick, he thought, a trap to hold him. For a moment he wished she were there before him – he wanted to knock her to the floor. He crushed the balled paper against his forehead, cursing his own stupidity. His body was tight and hot with hatred now: hatred for her, for Odetta and her whole family, then hatred for himself. How could he have done this?

He remembered that last afternoon they spent together, huddled up warm in his bed. The tenderness he felt for her then, the desire to hold the harm of the world from her. But he was wrong. All along he had been wrong – he was the harm of the world. It was in him.

'The less you have to do with me,' he said, 'the better for you. Better if you never see me again . . .'

He wanted to run at once, escape this place, but the snow was piled against the windows and the world outside was dark and frozen. The hunters out there in the forests were faster and more deadly than he could hope to be. Nothing to be done but clear his mind and wait.

A shiver ran through him, up his spine and into the skull, and he stared down at the paper crushed in his hand. He relaxed his grip and the paper opened, an angular flower. Then a flick of his hand, and the note fell into the burning coals of the fireplace. Smoke curled pale around the edges, then a blue flame sprang up, lifting the paper slightly before consuming it, until only a dust of soft black ash remained.

15

SLOWLY THE TEMPERATURE edged upwards, bringing the seeping fog of an early thaw. Rain fell, rotting the snow in the courtyard, exposing patches of gravel and mud, and all through the castle was the sound of water, snow-melt from the roofs slipping and dripping. Every corridor had its puddled bucket, its soggy wads of old newsprint.

Brookes sat in the Baronessa's suite, beside the fire. Feeding chunks of cut wood to the blaze, he relaxed in a creaking cane armchair. He leafed through her magazine collection: *Paris Vogue*, *Bellezza*, *Illustrazione Italiana* – all the fashions of years past, the airy news and commentary of a lost, pre-war age. The best piece amongst all the magazine articles was a photo essay showing pictures of some place in the Himalayas – Tibet, maybe, or Nepal, Brookes didn't bother reading the captions. Instead he gazed at the pictures: the high immaculate mountains and huddled villages, prayer-flags in proud monochrome against a clear grey sky, natives in traditional costume carrying improbable loads. He imagined himself going to the place one day and visiting those villages, meeting those people; other mountains far from the war, far away across the Hindu Kush and the plains of the Ganges. With Odetta perhaps, or Teresa. Or with Carla. All of them brightly smiling in the clear clean air. All of it a fantasy, dreamy in firelight.

He saw nothing of Odetta herself. The family no longer gathered for meals together, or did so without inviting him to join them. The Baronessa came and went, seemingly busy with her chores or perhaps just escaping his presence. Her attitude to Brookes was contradictory and unguessable. At times she was capable of an almost prim politeness, the perfect hostess. At others she seemed violently offended by the sight of him, turning her back sharply if he approached her or tried to speak, pulling away from his touch. She would spend hours sitting at her dressing table playing Patience, the crisp slap of the cards on the polished wood punctuating the silence. If her attitude was intended to drive him away, it often worked; Brookes would take himself off to his old room in the tower to sit shivering in solitude, communing with the wireless, before creeping back to the warmth of her bedroom after dark.

Sometimes, though, she showed a different face. She brought wine from the cellars and they would sit drinking it together by the fire, lounging in the cane armchairs smoking cigarettes. In moods like these Teresa became talkative, describing with loving detail her previous life in Turin – the servants and the polished automobiles, the dinner parties and the balls. Meals were recounted in all their particulars, course by succulent course, costumes summoned in dressmaker's detail. Skiing holidays and seaside excursions with the Prince of This or the Duke of That were recollected with extraordinary clarity. Once, transported by the memories, Teresa took one of her dresses from the armoire and put it on. Brookes fumbled with the intricacies of the back fastenings while she preened, then sat back to watch as she promenaded the room in her silks and furs.

He suspected there was more to all this than memory alone. Often Teresa's words would fall hollow and her expression grow distant. As yet another ambassador bent to kiss her hand, another champagne fountain collapsed into glorious foaming ruin, the stories came to seem as fantastical as Brookes' own notions of running away to Tibet. This was not the Baronessa's past, but rather an alternative present she was describing, a perfect world of ease and refinement that perhaps she had never truly known.

At night they slept together in the huge bed. Brookes had grown used to the heavings of the soft mattress, and even come to enjoy the maternal hug of its luxury, but still he would wake suddenly in the empty hours, alert and agitated. He thought often about Odetta, wondered what she'd been doing and what she would tell him when they met. All his life he had moved through the world without leaving a trace, and now he was trapped, rooted here. All the bonds he had sloughed off and now here he was, bound up in a family's anguish.

Some nights Brookes and the Baronessa climbed beneath the covers chaste and distant as the long-married, slept their separate sleeps with the bed rising like dough between them. Teresa always wore her jewellery: the pearls at her throat, the bracelets around her wrists seemed to him a kind of armour, a last line of defence, as if she refused to show herself to him completely naked. It annoyed him at first, but he grew used to it. When they made love it was by a blind and unspoken consent, and in this also the Baronessa was changeable. Sometimes she submitted to him dumbly, lying almost motionless and without a sound, then pushing him roughly, impatiently, from her when he was done. But sometimes also she surprised him with a wild angry passion, pinning him to the mattress and riding him, crying out. Afterwards they would lie together, sweaty warm beneath the covers, and he held her as she wept against his chest.

She did not walk in her sleep again, but often she would mumble or call out, or grind her teeth. Once Brookes was startled awake as she threw her arm across him, fingers feeling for his face. 'Ettore,' she said, the name clear. And again, 'Ettore!'

He caught her hand and rolled across the swaying mattress to her side, but she had relaxed back into sleep again. In the morning he said nothing about it.

Another night, Brookes woke suddenly to the certain knowledge that there was somebody else in the room. He sat up, blinking, but could see nothing. There was the sense of another body, a disturbance in the air, almost the after-image of a figure printed in the darkness. Brookes held his breath, listening, tensed to leap up from the bed at the slightest sound. No sound came, and he glared into the solid shadow of the bedroom until his eyes ached.

He lay sleepless until daylight, and then spent the next two nights in his old room. He returned, and nothing was said. Nothing was ever discussed. He felt increasingly that he, and all of the family, were living inside a bubble. Every day it grew thinner and less stable. But still nothing was said.

Clashes on a large scale are still taking place between workers in northern Italian munitions factories and the German authorities. Information is available of the systematic dismantling of Italian factories by the Germans, who are concentrating machinery and tools at Bolzano before removing them to Germany. The full might of Allied air power is being turned against the supply and communication routes of the enemy leading out of northern Italy, in order that any attempt at German withdrawal may be made as costly as possible.

In the tower room, Brookes sat at the radio. The signal was bad, distorted by rain and the swinging of the aerial in the wind. Finger on the tuner, baring his teeth at the bursts of interference, Brookes listened hard into the volume of background noise.

Operations on the western front are now dominated by the advance of the American First and Third Armies on the heels of von Rundstedt's retreat from the Ardennes. In spite of the veil of military security, it is evident that some of the most dramatic events of the whole allied offensive are occurring west of the Rhine, upon which armoured columns like steel fingers of an all-powerful hand are closing in swift manoeuvres that have utterly confounded the enemy. Late intelligence tonight states that British and Canadian troops under General Crerar's command are engaged in fierce fighting in Xanten.

Meanwhile British and American bombers have struck one of their most powerful blows at Dresden, now a vital centre for controlling the German defences against Russian forces advancing from the east. In two attacks on Tuesday night the RAF sent 800 aircraft to the city, showering it with 650,000 incendiaries together with 8,000 pounds of high explosive and hundreds of 4000-pound bombs. The night assault was followed by day attacks, in which American bombers took part . . .

He moved the tuning dial and the voice vanished into static hiss. Brookes had seen photographs of Dresden in one of the Baronessa's illustrated magazines, one of the later ones, dated shortly after the Axis pact. *Our Shared Fascist Culture.* Narrow streets of gingerbread houses, tall spires and steeples over cobblestone squares. He tried to imagine what 650,000 incendiary bombs would do to a city like that. High explosive death. Steel and fire death; the annihilation of bodies. The wastage of bodies. He was numbed by the thought of it, but his hands gripped the edge of the table tight.

What did they feel, in England, when they heard this news? What did the soldiers on the front lines feel, in the Ardennes and the Apennines? Was there righteousness, justified vengeance, celebration? Was there remorse? Or do they feel as I feel, Brookes thought. Cold desolate anger, and the nausea of horror. Such a vast volume of death that no one life could count for anything now. All of them – the Barone, Teresa and Odetta, Umberto, Pietro – could die and still it would count for nothing. A single life seemed a faint and insubstantial thing, when so many could be extinguished in a single blow. Carla's death, his own death, meant nothing at all.

He moved the dial again, bringing the voice back through the hiss. *Marshall Stalin has announced that Russian forces are now driving deeply into Brandenberg from the frontier west and southwest of Pozan. A German report last night indicated that Russian tanks were less than 45 miles from Berlin. According to a broadcaster of the German Overseas News Agency, millions of German refugees, some of them in columns thirty or forty miles long, are streaming westwards away from the advancing Red Army. Marshall Stalin, in the order of the day addressed to Marshalls Konev and Zhukov, last night stated . . .*

He turned off the radio and removed the headphones, wishing to hear no more. The silence was sudden and total. He became aware of the pulse in his ears, the slight creak of the chair beneath him as he moved. He reached beneath the table and disconnected the leads to the car battery. Then he put on his coat, hefted the heavy battery and started back to the garage.

Brookes stood at the far end of the great hall with his back to the door, squeezing an old tennis ball of putty-coloured rubber in his right hand. All the furniture, the hooded chairs and draped tables, he had shifted to the centre and piled around the lowered chandelier, leaving a broad cleared space. He took ten paces down the length of the room, then spun on his heel and hurled the ball. It hit the panelling above the door and rebounded at an angle, and he was already running to grab it.

He threw again, then snatched the ball from the air. Again, and he leapt to catch it just before it reached the floor. The noise boomed in the empty space behind him: the thud of the ball against the wood panels, the scuff and stamp of his bare feet on the paving, and he felt the angry energy rushing through his body. Still he was not fast enough – once or twice he missed his catch, and the ball bounced off the floor and skittered away into the dusty far corners. He ran to fetch it, swearing viciously, then threw from a distance, lobbing high over the piled furniture. He felt the world around him spinning at great speed, out of any human control, and himself caught at the axis of its whirl. He wanted to fracture the stillness that held him.

Breathing hard, sweat breaking as the unaccustomed exercise sped his pulse and tightened his muscles, he threw at the corner and the ball deflected from one wall to the next. He ran and caught it at full stretch. He felt the strength of his body returning, the speed of his reflexes increasing.

The ball struck the panels high and bounded up in an arc. Brookes ran back, eyes tracking it as it passed overhead. It came down behind him, bounced off the floor and he lunged to catch it. The ball skipped from his fingers and up onto the table to roll finally to a halt in the rattling glass of the chandelier. Reaching in through the spinning crystals to retrieve the ball, Brookes saw Odetta standing on the minstrels' gallery at the far end of the hall.

'Be careful,' she called to him, then stepped back into the archway behind her. Brookes heard her feet on the stairs, then she appeared again at the far end of the hall, walking towards him. 'You might break something,' she said. She circled the heap of furniture and advanced into the cleared space.

'Don't worry,' Brookes said. 'I'm a good shot.' He flung the ball, and it boomed against the side wall, inches from one of the tall windows. Odetta stood still, watching him. His next throw came back at a wide angle; he saw the girl move and stamped to a halt moments before colliding with her. Odetta clapped the ball between her palms and hugged it to her chest.

'Did you like the story I wrote for you?' she asked.

'Yes, it was spellbinding.'

'I'm not pregnant, by the way,' she said, then threw the ball. It ricocheted off the wall above the door, and Brookes jogged forward to grab it.

'I'm glad to hear that,' he said, breath catching. The weight was lifted from him suddenly, but he felt no sense of relief. For so long he had been trying not to think about it. Now he only felt provoked. His body was full of violent heat, and sweat ran from his forehead.

'I told you I was because I wanted you to see . . . I wanted you to understand. I'm still very angry with you,' she said. 'I've been crying a lot.'

'Oh,' he said, and threw the ball again. You don't get to me like that, he thought. Not with that sentiment. But he felt his throat tighten with shame even so. Odetta missed her catch, fumbling in the air, and the ball dropped to the floor behind her and rolled away. Now she turned to face him.

'I trusted you,' she said. 'I thought you were on my side.'

'I'm on my own side,' Brookes told her, going after the ball. He heard her grunt, and caught her meaning. *That's what you think.*

A long lob from halfway down the room, but Odetta made no move to catch it. Brookes sprinted forward lightly and caught the ball as it leapt up off the floor. He paused, gulping breath, braced against his knees. Blood pulsed quick and hard in his head.

'I told you I was pregnant because I wanted to hurt you,' she said suddenly, fiercely, colour rising in her face. 'You think, don't you, that you can just do what you want . . . that you won't be affected by anything. You think nothing can get to you. It's for other people to suffer, not you.'

He glared back at her.

'I hoped at least you might have thought about me,' she went on. 'But you haven't, have you. You've just erased me from your mind. Rubbed me away . . .' She raised a hand and made a rubbing gesture in the air. 'Is that what you do?' she asked, turning to him. 'With people? With people and things when you're finished with them? You just rub them away when you don't care about them any more. Did you do that with your other women too? Did you do that with Carla?'

He shook his head slowly. An image came to him of bodies in flames, people stacked and burning in the streets of a bombed city. Any word he said to her would contain so much anger it would be hateful. There was no way he could explain himself.

'I suppose I should leave you to your game then,' she said. But lingered, finger twirling a loop of hair, waiting for him to speak. Brookes said nothing.

'You still don't know anything about us, do you,' she said.

'You're hardly the most forthcoming of families.'

'What do you think it's like for me?' she asked angrily, turning on him. 'Trapped in this place, rotting away? Just waiting for death . . .'

Brookes took a step towards her. 'Death?' he said, almost choking the word. 'What would you know about that?' He thought of the frozen corpses in the forests of the Ardennes. All the death he had seen. This girl, he thought, has no idea. Even the sight of the single corpse down there in the gatehouse had paralysed her. But she glared back at him, mocking and defiant.

'You really know nothing then,' she said quietly. 'I thought you might have guessed our . . . *dirty little secret.*'

'What? Tell me.'

'Why don't you make Mamma tell you? It's right there, after all. Go and find it if you don't believe me.'

She stared a moment longer, unblinking, then abruptly turned away. She had said too much.

'I'm going now,' she said.

Almost he spoke. The words were there, formed but not yet uttered. Odetta dropped her head, walking round-shouldered with a repressed urgency, and Brookes watched her leave the room. When he was alone again he straightened, stretched, then flung the ball hard against the far wall.

16

HE SAID NOTHING to the Baronessa that evening. Everything sickened him – the castle and everyone in it, all the secrets and the circular games. Lying in bed, unable to sleep, he felt himself glowing with taut rage. For so long he had felt himself unable to leave, to face once again the world outside the walls, that he had become almost one of the Barone's family, imprisoned by some mysterious compulsion that even now he was no closer to understanding.

Even if he said nothing to her, Brookes' mood seemed to have affected the Baronessa. She slept badly, rolling and shifting, mumbling sounds that never became words. Lying beside her on the great mattress, Brookes listened with gathering irritation. At last he flung off the quilts and got up, dressed quietly and went to sit in the chair by the window. Drawing back the heavy drapes a little he stared out at the night landscape: the snow was bright under a full moon, the forest etched black beneath. Nothing moved out there, nothing seemed to live.

The slight creak of a floorboard startled him, and he switched his attention back to the room. In the dark, Teresa was standing beside the bed. Only the pale phantom of her nightgown showed her move-ment – a strange drifting walk, unconscious and unwilled. Watching her, Brookes felt the prickle of superstitious dread, but he did not shift from the chair. The Baronessa knelt again before the dressing table, dropping to her knees and beginning to rock on her haunches. She looked like a penitent, like she was praying, swaying back and forward, her lips shaping silent words.

Brookes watched, fascinated. Teresa's head rolled, her body swayed, and now she reached up both hands and began to stroke the drawer of the dressing table with strange mechanical movements. Her body lacked the control of the waking mind – once again Brookes thought of a puppet. Her hands were stiff, pawing, and she was rocking more abruptly now.

'You want to open it,' Brookes whispered. 'You want to open the drawer.'

It was locked, he knew, and he had never seen where the key was kept. Fighting down the urge to try and force the drawer open himself, he waited and watched. Teresa's movements were be-coming more desperate, the low noise from her throat swelling to a keening groan. She sat up, her hands groping across the top of the dressing table, fingers outstretched. Brookes saw what she was reaching for: a silver powder compact near the mirror. He sat still, waiting, breathing slowly with his teeth rattling, as the Baronessa took the compact and clumsily opened it. The key dropped onto the carpet in a plume of spilled powder, and the tiny click of its fall was loud as a bell.

The noise seemed to confuse Teresa. The compact fell from her hands and she slumped back again, blank faced and silent. But Brookes was already beside her, snatching up the key and unlocking the drawer.

Inside were piled papers written in a close neat hand; letters, or a diary perhaps. Brookes lifted a wad of them from the drawer, but there was not enough light to read the words.

'What are you doing?' Teresa said, the words slurred and sleep-bound.

Beneath the papers were photographs, family pictures, smudgy grey in the faint light, shapes of smiling faces and formal poses. Brookes grabbed up a handful and threw them to the floor. Then, beneath the photographs, he saw the sheaf of documents.

'What are you doing?' the Baronessa said again, clearer this time, her face beginning to wake into confusion and fear. She was breathing hard, shudders running through her. Brookes snatched the documents from the drawer and went to the window. He threw open the drapes and a bar of white moonlight cut the room. The Baronessa shrank from it.

Regno d'Italia . . . Carta d'Identità . . . Thin brown cardboard with official stamps and the fascist emblem. Brookes flipped open each card and saw the portrait photographs of the Barone and his family. Beside each photo, inked in an official hand: name, age, date of birth.

Ettore Levi Almansi

Rachele Sonnino Almansi

Umberto Abramo Almansi

Isacco Almansi

Odetta Almansi

The names meant nothing to him at first. These were strangers, wearing the faces of people he believed he knew. For a few moments Brookes stared dumbly, frowning, opening one card and then another until finally, suddenly, he understood. He looked back at the woman kneeling on the floor – not the Baronessa Teresa Cavigliani but some other person he no longer recognised. She was clawing at her face, her shoulders jolting as she struggled from sleep.

'What are you . . . ?' she said. 'Who . . . ?'

But Brookes was already gone.

Assured in the darkness, he stalked quickly across the dining room and down the panelled corridor. Through the study and the library, he reached the door of the Barone's chambers. In his determination he wanted to throw it open and storm inside, but the door was locked. Instead he pounded on it, then stood breathing hard, clutching the bundle of documents.

'Who's there?'

'It's me,' said Brookes. 'Let me in.'

Another wait, long enough to stir a slow cold doubt. Then he heard the rasp of a match, and a narrow streak of candlelight showed from beneath the door. The lock grated, the door opened, and the Barone – the man who had called himself the Barone – stood there in his dressing gown.

'Come in,' he said.

A single glance took in the bedroom, obviously once an annexe of the library: books and glass-fronted cabinets all round the walls, a desk and chair, a folding steel bed. Brookes threw the bundle of identity cards onto the embroidered quilt. They scattered, falling open. When he looked up again, the man was holding a small pistol.

'Do nothing hasty,' the man said. He held the gun down by his side.

'Almansi,' Brookes said. 'Your name . . . I didn't understand at first. Maybe to an Italian it would be more obvious. A Jewish name, though, I believe.'

'It is indeed,' the man said. 'And frankly I'm surprised it took you so long to discover it.' He crossed to a cabinet against the far wall, casual and seemingly indifferent, the gun swinging at his side. Reaching behind the cabinet he took something in his free hand. When he turned back to face Brookes, he was holding a pair of identity tags, one green and one red, dangling on a leather cord. Squinting slightly, he lifted the discs closer and read what was stamped onto them.

'2207612 . . . Farrow, S.'

He flipped the discs into his palm and enclosed them in a fist, then looked back at Brookes with an expression of sly triumph.

'You?'

He threw the discs, and Brookes snatched them from the air.

In the grey of morning they gathered in the dining room, all of them around the long table in their accustomed places. Their new names sat awkwardly on them – the Barone a Barone no longer, but still Brookes could hardly think of him otherwise. Almansi, he thought, the man is called Ettore Almansi. Beside him, his wife Rachele was wrapped in a thick shawl, her face pale and bruised with sleeplessness. On the table between them, the discs and the identity cards. It was the brother, the doctor, who spoke first.

'I told you this man would bring trouble to us,' he said, addressing the table, excluding Brookes. 'I told you, Ettore! We should never have accepted him among us – now he knows this, he's even more of a danger to us!'

'We could hardly leave him to die,' Rachele said quietly.

Almansi held up a palm, silencing his brother's complaint.

'I'm sorry to have to tell you,' he said to Brookes, 'but I was aware from our very first meeting that your story was . . . suspect. You told us – do you remember? – that you were a British officer, and had escaped from a prison camp near Vercelli? I happened to know, however, that only enlisted men were held in the Vercelli camps. All the officers were confined much further south, across the Po. You really should have been more careful!'

'I'm sure you also had your reasons for deception,' Brookes said. He reached across the table and slipped a finger under the cord of the identity discs.

'Where did you find these?' he asked.

'Oh, my brother here picked them up from the mountainside while he was gathering wood. Months ago now. You see, sir, we've known for some time about your fabrications!'

'As I now know about yours, Signor Almansi.'

'Quite so,' said Almansi. 'So now you know our names, but we are still unsure of yours.'

Brookes remembered the first dinner he had attended in that same room, when he had been introduced to the family, his own halting account of who he was and where he had come from. Now he could speak with far greater conviction, but still his mouth was dry.

'I'm sorry to disappoint you, Signor Almansi,' he said, 'but my name really is Francis Brookes. And I really am an officer in the British Army. I was a member of the Special Operations Executive, working with the partisans.' He glanced across at Odetta as he spoke, sure that she must have told them all of this already. She barely blinked, but in her eyes he caught the knowledge that she had told them nothing. She had kept his secret to herself all this time.

'And who, then,' the doctor said, dubious, 'is this?' He pointed to the identity discs. Brookes picked them up, turning them slowly on their cord.

'Stanley Farrow,' he said, 'was a sergeant in the Royal Engineers. He died two years ago, in an internment camp in Switzerland for escaped prisoners of war, shortly after crossing the mountains. I was given his identity discs and paybook when I was sent to northern Italy. A false name, in case I was captured by the enemy – any checks would confirm that Sergeant Farrow was real, an escaped POW, and my actual role and mission would be unknown to them.'

'And yet you discarded this identity when you came here,' Almansi said. 'And gave us what you claim is your real name. Why would you do that?'

'When I threw these things away,' Brookes said, swinging the dics lightly before him, 'I thought I was about to die. If my body was ever found, I didn't want to be buried under another man's name. Then, when I found myself here, I didn't know what I might have said while I was feverish. Better to stick close to the truth in those circumstances. I didn't know who any of you were, of course, nor what your allegiances might be, so I obscured my links with the partisans and gave you the tale about escaping from the camp. That part was easy at least – it was the same as my old cover story.'

'But you neglected to change the location of the camp!' Ettore declared, with a rather smug gesture. 'So you are hardly the genius of espionage after all! I suppose we should be thankful for that, Captain.' For a moment he paused, head tipped back, and once more, very briefly, inhabited his old role. The Barone. Lord of Castelmantia.

'But you confess,' said the doctor, 'that you're the man the partisans are searching for? The man they say betrayed them?'

'I never betrayed them,' Brookes said quickly. 'Somebody else did that. We had some political disagreements, but I never betrayed them.

And now,' he said, tossing the discs down onto the table, 'it's your turn to confess, all of you.'

Almansi looked to each of his family in turn, as if silently asking their consent. Each of them gave the slightest of nods. But still he took his time before answering.

'Can you imagine, Captain,' he began, in a speculative tone, 'what it feels like to have your own country declare you an enemy? Your own country, which you have loved and fought for? Can you conceive what it is to be turned, overnight, from a prosperous and respected member of society into an alien, an undesirable? And not only you, but your whole family, your very blood – declared unsound, unwanted and suspect? Can you imagine what effect that might have on you?'

Brookes shrugged, keeping his eyes on Almansi.

'Of course you cannot,' the man said quietly. 'When the Race Laws were introduced back in '38, I was a lawyer in Turin and my brother Umberto was a doctor. We were forced to give up our professional practices, my children were forbidden to take public examinations and had to leave school. Still, we had many friends, and for several years our lives were not unduly difficult.'

'The difficulties grow,' Rachele said. 'It's strange. One scarcely notices them, until suddenly something happens and one realises that life has become unbearable. Something that cannot be assimilated into a mere change of circumstances . . .' She took a breath, shuddering slightly, her hands flat on the table before her. Just for a moment, the nakedness of her pain was shocking.

'My wife exaggerates,' Almansi broke in. 'We did not live badly. But one by one our friends stopped associating with us, my former clients pretended not to know me. We had no more dinner invitations. We were ordered to dismiss our servants. These things can be endured. We were at war by then, and everyone suffered in some way.

But then the Germans took control of Italy, and brought with them their own version of persecution . . .'

'We had the opportunity to leave,' Rachele announced abruptly. 'We could have gone to Switzerland. My husband insisted we stay.'

'It was the correct thing to do,' Almansi said. 'I could not desert my country.'

His wife gave him a look of fierce irony. 'Tell him about Vittorio,' she said.

'Vittorio, our eldest son,' her husband went on, turning to gaze at the photograph on the sideboard, 'was a very headstrong boy, rather political in the wrong way. He was arrested shortly before the Germans came and sent to San Vittore prison in Milan. And then . . .' a slight catch in his voice, something genuine through the weary posturing, 'and then, soon afterwards, we were informed that he had died. While trying to escape, we were told.'

'The Germans murdered him,' Rachele said. 'They knew he was a Jew. They came, and they just shot him.' She spoke calmly, the anger submerged deep in the stillness of long grief.

'He was very brave,' Brookes said.

'Brave, yes, he was,' Almansi replied, thin voiced. 'He was a good boy. Good son.'

His other son, Isacco, said nothing, and in his silence Brookes heard all the rage the boy was unable to express. Everything he could never become, gripped tight in the embrace of his family.

'And so,' Almansi continued, 'we had to flee. I still had some old friends I could rely on, and for several months they hid us. But we needed a secure place to shelter, and I recalled the one old contact of mine, a man whom I had once helped with a complex lawsuit, who owed me a favour . . .'

'The Barone of Salussola?' Brookes asked. Almansi nodded.

'Barone Paulo Cavigliani – the real one, that is – had departed for Sweden several years previously, but I knew that he owned the castle here. A mutual friend had been entrusted with the safekeeping. This friend communicated with the Barone, and we were duly installed. The people in the village know only that we are members of the Barone's family. And so, here we have remained ever since.'

'And the Black Brigades also believe this?'

'Comandante Battista,' Almansi said, with an expression of distaste, 'knows the truth, although his men know nothing of it. I am obliged to pay him generously to stop them finding out. He is a man of few scruples, and little faith.'

Brookes grunted, staring at the tabletop. That would explain the watchers on the far side of the valley, and the ritual with the lamp – Battista's insurance that the family did not try to slip away. Still he felt uneasy. It was a persuasive story, and one he wanted to believe. Impossible, though, not to suspect that Ettore was playing one more sleight of hand. But there was the evidence, the heap of identity cards on the table, the official documents of an abolished nation. He looked around the table, considering each member of the family – they appeared the same to him, even with their new roles.

Only when he looked at the boy did Brookes truly believe what he had just been told. Isacco, his non-Jewish name now discarded, sat upright and almost smiling, alive with truth, finally. His gaze was clear and assured, no longer surly and evasive but defiant.

'And you couldn't explain this to me when I first came here?' Brookes asked.

'Of course not!' Almansi said sternly. 'We didn't know who you really were or where you'd come from. We still don't! Because why should we believe you now? And if you left this place and were captured, how could we be safe? Should we have merely trusted that you would tell nobody?'

'Why should I have told anyone?'

'They would have interrogated you, Captain, as I'm sure you know well. Maybe tortured you, and if you said anything you would have placed all of my family in grave danger. I could not allow that.'

'And the rest of it, was that all acting? What about the business with the cards?'

'The cards are my own. The real Barone Paulo Cavigliani, I believe, is rather unimaginative, and would have no time for such things. Perhaps you would have found him a kindred spirit, Captain?'

'I feel rather close to him,' Brookes replied. 'After all, I assume I've been wearing his clothes these last few months?'

Almansi smiled, a little too pleased with himself. None of the rest of the family appeared entertained. Brookes himself did not know what to feel – amused, perhaps, or angry? Resentful, certainly, although it felt wrong. If the family's story was correct, they had good reasons for their deception. In fact he felt a sort of annoyed embarrassment, like he'd been caught doing something ridiculous. Ridiculous, he thought. That's how I feel. His unease must have been clear to see.

'You appear discontented, Captain!' Almansi said. 'Does it pain you so much to have been misled? You like to think you understand everything, don't you? You despise mystery. All this time you've been probing and questioning, and now you know why all this has been necessary – are you not glad? Are you not satisfied?'

'I suppose we sought to persuade ourselves,' Rachele said thoughtfully. 'We could see ourselves reflected in you. Our other selves. You allowed us to live the fantasy of being divorced from the world, of being safe . . . by being the Cavigliani family. Pure blood and privilege, Captain. An attractive combination, in these times. For a while it almost worked.'

At the sound of her voice Brookes felt a surge of disgust rise in his throat, a sense of dizzying absurdity. He wanted to laugh at them.

'And all this time,' he said slowly, coldly, 'you've conspired between you to maintain this illusion. With everything that's happened
. . .' He looked around the table, fixing each of them with his stare:
Rachele pale and resentful, Odetta watchful, Isacco and the two men
hard-faced and unyielding. 'With everything that's happened you've
kept up this deception, when at any time – at any time! – you could
have simply told me the truth?'

'No!' Almansi shouted, and slapped his hand down on the table,
his attempt at good humour abandoned. 'I could not allow you to
know the truth about us! Shall I tell you why? The fact of the matter
is this: if you had known, you would have *pitied* us. And I could not
bear the shame of your pity.'

'Oh yes, you couldn't bear that, could you,' Rachele said, mocking.
'What an insult to your pride!'

'The pride of us all,' her husband said. 'Our dignity.'

'Dignity!' Rachele spat the word. 'We could have escaped this
country when we had the chance, all of us. *All* of us, Ettore. Your
dignity kept us here! Your pride!'

Almansi leapt up suddenly, gripping the table with both hands. 'I
did what I thought best,' he cried, with pained emphasis. 'To protect
you.'

'To protect us!' Rachele almost laughed, astonished. 'We are all
under sentence of death, and you know it. This, Captain,' Rachele
said, turning to Brookes, 'is why my husband insisted we didn't reveal
who we really are. If you knew, if you could see what we had become,
then he'd be forced to admit that he was wrong. He'd be forced to see
the depths of his own ignominy!'

'You dare to speak like this in front of *him!*' her husband shouted,
flinging his hand in a gesture of dismissal.

'Yes, it's time he knew!'

'Tell him everything, Ettore, why not,' the doctor said, raising his voice now. 'Let him know it all!'

'Shut up!' Odetta screamed, standing up. 'All of you, just shut up!'

'Tell him everything, Ettore,' the doctor said again.

Almansi stood with his back to the table, shoulders tightly hunched. When he turned back, his face was hollowed with pain. He spoke only to Brookes.

'My family has experienced great suffering,' he said, his voice drained of feeling. 'We have made mistakes, and we must await our judgement at the due time. But you know the truth about us now, and you cannot ask for more. This conversation is at an end.' He paced towards the door, head down and dejected. Then he was gone.

'Don't go after him,' Rachele said, seeming to address them all.

Brookes threw his chair back and stood up. Before he turned to leave the room he caught Odetta's silent mouthed words.

'I'm sorry,' she was saying.

17

BROOKES LAY ON the huge bed, swigging red wine from a bottle. He thought about the Almansi family, people he knew and yet did not know, cleaving together in that leaking fortress, and realised that their desire to escape from the world's demands was similar to his own. They had walled themselves about with fictions, just as he had done, and made him into an unwitting audience for their theatre of self-denial. He could almost admire their will, their collective determination to construct the fantasy and live within it. Now that he had seen them exposed, scared organisms stripped and huddled together, he felt the weakness in himself.

He had believed himself to be strong, impregnable. All through his training, crouching in the grassy dunes under the abrasive salt breath of night, face smeared with black greasepaint, he had consumed everything they taught him and made it a part of himself. The code-book and the radio transmitter, the slick packed explosive and the detonator rods, the double-edged knife and the cheesewire garotte; all of it his body knew, his mind possessed, by instinct. To move with silent stealth, to know before sight or hearing, to act before conscious thought.

For years he had survived on the oxygen of self-belief, hurling himself forwards, point to point. How to survive, though, when no more points remained? When no plan, no mission, gave him purpose? This place, this castle, was nowhere, lost between the places on the map.

Several days had passed since the scene in the dining room, and the Almansi family were as assiduous in avoiding Brookes as their previous incarnations had once been. Rachele no longer lived with him in the master bedroom – his lover, the Baronessa Teresa, had vanished, and with Signora Almansi there could be no such intimacy. Brookes knew that she slept in her son's bedroom now, but he saw neither of them. Through the rooms of the castle he moved in perfect solitude, as if he threw some charged field around him that others could not enter. He imagined sometimes that they had all left him and he was truly alone there. The distant sound of a door closing, the exhalation of air from a room, the crack and sigh of board or banister might signal the presence of others around him, but they kept themselves hidden. Occasionally a dish of food was left for him in the corridor outside his room, but more often he would go to the scullery-kitchen and help himself to food, eating it out of the can, hardly aware of what it was.

The thought of further confrontation exhausted him.

Putting down the empty wine bottle, Brookes checked his watch. He was no longer sure whether it was day or night outside. Six, anyway. As he got up off the bed he heard a light tapping at the bedroom door.

The sound startled him, his reactions dulled by the wine, and the tap came a second time before he crossed to the door and opened it.

At his feet was a tray holding a parcel wrapped in gold tissue, a glass and a bottle of brandy with a bow tied around it. Further down the long gallery, beside the suit of armour, a figure stood waiting, dressed in an ill-fitting black coat and a white mask in the form of a leering face.

'What's this?' Brookes asked. The figure in the mask must be Isacco, he realised; the sight was so bizarre he could do nothing but stare. The boy pointed stiffly, indicating a small envelope propped on the tray beside the brandy. Then, before Brookes could speak again, the masked figure turned and walked quickly away.

Inside the envelope was a folded note, written in the familiar neat cursive.

> *Dear Captain Brookes,*
> *Please accept these gifts as a token of our goodwill. We would be honoured if you could join us for a small celebration in the dining room in one hour's time.*
> *Wear something unusual.*
> *Yours – the Famiglia Almansi*

They were already seated at the table when he reached the dining room, each of them disguised and masked, weird in the light of the branched candelabra. The figure at the head wore an oversized dinner jacket and a domino mask crested with tall black plumes; others wore robes made of damask sheets, and one of the men – Ettore or his brother, it was impossible to tell – had squeezed himself into a ladies' satin ballgown. Some of the masks were elegant, feminine, floating deathly pale in the candlelight, others were twisted and horrific, the faces of beasts or beastlike men. A rustle of laughter came from behind the masks as Brookes entered the room; he was wearing one of the fur coats from the armoire in the bedroom, a great heavy thing of pale beige. The sleeves were too short for him and he could barely lift his arms in the tight shoulders, but in the mirror he had presented to himself the slight resemblance of a bear walking on hind legs, and that seemed appropriately ridiculous.

There was another mask, a grotesque thing with a long hooked beak, waiting for Brookes beside his place at the table, and he put it on as he sat down. Dust went up his nose, and he sneezed. Where the masks had come from he could not guess; some forgotten recess of the castle he supposed, some locked cabinet or closet, relics of a long-ago Venetian carnival.

'*Buonasera*, Captain,' said the voice of Almansi. 'We're glad you decided to attend.' Brookes still could not make out which of the various figures was speaking, and the small eyeholes of his mask disorientated him even more.

'We hoped you wouldn't be too offended by our invitation. This is, you see, a religious occasion for us, although you'll be glad to know that all the pious aspects have already been concluded. Now we only have to enjoy ourselves!'

'Oh,' said Brookes, sounding unenthusiastic. There was food spread on the table: a big pot of macaroni, dishes of sweetened fruit and several plates of little pastries. He had already eaten the chunk of dry cake the family had sent him wrapped in gold tissue. He felt far from hungry. 'What's the celebration then?' he asked.

'Today is Purim,' Rachele replied. With a slight shock, Brookes realised that she was the figure sitting next to him wrapped in an enormous sheet, wearing a mask of porcelain white adorned with tiny red sequins, the face of a beautiful corpse. 'It's good you could join us,' she went on, her voice muffled. 'I'm afraid we were forced to celebrate Hannukah in secret, and tell you nothing about it. But today we must show charity and goodwill to strangers, and share our happiness with them.'

'Your happiness?' Brookes said. The man in the woman's gown, he now saw, was actually the doctor, Umberto. Odetta was at the head of the table, wearing the dinner jacket.

'Purim is a celebration of survival,' Almansi said. By a process of elimination, he was the figure swathed in red damask, with a deep hood covering his head. 'We remember the story of the virtuous Queen of Persia, which you might know if you've ever read the Christian Bible by accident . . .'

'Can't say I have.'

'Perhaps, Odetta, you could enlighten the Captain?'

The figure at the head of the table sat up in her chair, shrugging the loose jacket over her shoulders. She began to tell the story, almost by rote, like something learned in school. Told like that, broken up and deadened, it seemed an absurd farce, the plot of a comic opera. There was Assuero, the King of Persia, and his virtuous wife Ester. There was Haman, a genocidal general, and Mardocheo, 'a very wise Jew, who knew all the languages of the world.' And Haman schemed to kill the Jews, and somehow Ester stopped him, via a fiasco of disguises and misadventures, everyone pretending to be what they were not. Brookes was barely paying attention, but still the story stirred a memory in him. A school assembly, decades before – instructive tales from the Old Testament. He remembered – even with the names all different, and the story camouflaged with elaborations. The Book of Esther, he thought. Of course.

'And so the Jews were saved,' Odetta said finally, 'and Haman was executed by the King. And that's why we celebrate. The End.' She sat back again, as her mother and father politely applauded.

'But what this story really tells us about,' Almansi said from behind his mask, 'is the mysterious working of God in human affairs. The Jews of Persia were saved, it would seem, by human guile and intelligence, but in fact God had directed everything. His power was concealed, but made itself felt. His was, we might say, the hidden face.'

Strange way for a God to carry on, Brookes thought, but kept it to himself. Now wine was being poured, food ladled onto plates, masks pushed back or discarded as the meal began. Umberto, revealed in his female costume, could barely contain his laughter. The contrast to the mood the last time the family had sat together at the same table was extraordinary. Brookes, shedding his dusty mask, drank deeply and tried not to feel too uncomfortable.

The food at least was good, some of it obviously saved through the winter for just this occasion. Tinned peaches in syrup, almond and raisin cakes and little fried and sugared pastries that Rachele called 'Haman's Ears', all of it seeming sumptuous after so many meals bland or burnt. An almost pre-war luxury of taste. Brookes ate a little of each dish, letting the wine relax him, ignoring the odd little games and rituals that passed between the family members. When he felt he'd eaten enough he lit a cigarette and watched them, curious that they seemed so united now. What debates had brought them to this? What compromises had been reached?

'This must seem strange to you,' Rachele said, speaking quietly at his side. She had kept her mask on, eating little or nothing. The blank white face was turned very slightly, discreetly, towards Brookes.

'You seem to have resolved your differences,' Brookes said.

'We agreed,' she said, 'a truce, you might say. There are certain things I cannot forgive, but neither can we live at war with each other. And today is a joyous day. We needed to be together as a family.'

She raised the rim of the mask a little – Brookes glimpsed her chin, her lips as she drank.

'And what about you?' she asked. 'Are you still angry with us? We did deceive you terribly.'

Brookes waited a moment, letting the question hang between them, then shook his head. Even muffled by the mask, Rachele's voice had a slurred languor. She must have drunk a lot even before the meal, and was usually so abstemious.

'Tell me, do you miss her?' she asked. Then, in a darker voice, 'The Baronessa Teresa?'

'I do, yes,' Brookes said. He felt the intimacy between them. The others at the table were all talking among themselves. Nobody else could hear them now.

'I miss her too, sometimes,' Rachele said. 'A shame she had to go.'

The mask tilted upwards, and the candlelight caught the flash of her eyes in the sockets. Then she giggled, a strange sound from behind the expressionless face. Brookes, noticing the direction of her gaze, turned to look at the wall behind him. He was wearing his own mask pushed onto the top of his head, the beak sticking up – his wavering shadow had a huge obscene horn jutting from it. He snorted a sudden laugh, and the shadow-horn weaved. Rachele laughed with him, then reached up and grabbed the horn, pulling the mask down over his face again.

'I believe,' Almansi announced from across the table, 'that the gramophone behind you is now working, Captain. Perhaps you could wind it up and select some music for us?'

Grateful for the distraction, Brookes dragged himself free of the great coat and mask and went to the side table. A selection of heavy shellac discs in yellowed paper sleeves were piled beside the gramophone; all belonged to the real Barone, he supposed, like the pictures on the wall and the carnival masks and everything else in the room. The Barone's taste seemed eclectic enough anyway. He took one of the discs at random, wound the machine and dropped the needle into the moving groove. A pop and a hiss and then the music came dusty and distant from the canted trumpet.

'Mascagni,' Almansi declared. '*Cavalleria Rusticana*. A good choice!'

When Brookes turned back to the table, Rachele was already on her feet. Unsteady, shoving herself away from the table's edge, she dropped the white robe from her shoulders and stood dressed in her long silk evening gown.

'I want to dance!' she said, and held out a hand to Brookes. The music swelled, antique gold in the weaving light, and he took her hand and led her onto the open floor at the edge of the candle's glow.

'Take off the mask,' he said, but she shook her head and he saw the smile in her eyes. Holding each other at a formal distance they began to dance, shuffling slow circles as the music led them. Brookes drew her closer, feeling the slight tension before she relaxed her arms. The white mask swayed before him, the silk of her gown fluid in the shadows, and for a moment Brookes forgot his discomfort and allowed her to guide him, foot to foot, closer still.

'You're a *terrible* dancer,' she said.

Now their moving shadows were joined by others: Ettore had drawn Odetta from her seat and was dancing with her, the long tails of the dinner jacket swinging around the girl's knees. Circling, the two pairs passed and almost collided, then swung away on their separate orbits. At the table, Umberto was red-faced and grinning in his gown. Isacco sat with his beast mask pushed back, smirking with embarrassment.

'You two,' Ettore called. 'Join us!'

'Absolutely not! As Cicerone said, *only drunks and madmen dance!*'

Abruptly Ettore released his daughter and made a rapid dash to the gramophone, comical in his baggy robe. The music cut off with a shriek as the needle was lifted, then Ettore was placing another disc on the turntable.

'Dancing music!' he shouted, holding up the paper sleeve. *Musica Tradizionale di Sicilia*, the label read.

'Oh no, Ettore, not that!' Rachele said. The music began: guitars and mandolins, accordion and tambourines. Laughing, they plunged back into the dance, moving faster as the tempo picked up. Umberto got to his feet and grabbed Isacco's shoulder.

'You'll have to help me, young man,' he said. 'We'll do this together.'

Dragging the cringing boy after him, the doctor circled the table. Now they were all together, the dancing pairs breaking up, hands meeting hands. Stumbling with the rhythm, Brookes felt himself lifted, released from himself. Rachele held one of his hands, Odetta the other, the men linking them, and they were spinning in a circle. The music thrummed and they laughed together as the candles flickered and twisted in the candelabra and the room swung with their shadows. A cracked voice was singing in heavy dialect, and they tried to join in, yelling out their approximations of the words, tripping and swaying and crashing against each other. Everything was forgotten, everything forgiven.

Then, all too soon, it was over and the record hissed in an empty groove. The circle broke apart, each of them staggering away. Brookes was breathless and panting, not only from the exertion of the dance and the wine driving his blood. He felt the warmth, the hands in his own, a shared joy, and it stirred his heart. The doctor came to him smiling and threw his arms around him, hugging his shoulders.

Odetta still clasped his hand, and even Isacco was glowing with guilty pleasure. Rachele pushed back her mask and wiped her brow, exhaling loudly.

Silence returned, closing around them, and suddenly none of them could meet the eyes of the others. Over beside the table, Rachele stood with her husband. She took his hand.

From outside came the sound of a great breeze rushing through the night, rattling the shutters, and all of them glanced up as they heard it approach. Then the door swung violently open and the draught swept into the room, extinguishing all the candles in a single icy breath.

18

THE NEXT MORNING Brookes woke late with a dull headache. He had not drunk so much for a long time. Lying still, he tried to urge himself back into sleep, but his throat was parched. Getting up and struggling into his clothes, he went out into the painfully brilliant winter sunlight. At the well he drank from the pail, gulping the chill water straight down.

In the dining room he found the table still spread with plates and pots from the night before, and the sight of the congealed food made him queasy. The discarded masks lay on the table too, the costume gowns draped over the chairs. With the wine glasses and the empty bottles, the room looked like the aftermath of a student bacchanale. Brookes stood beside the table, in the space where they had all danced together. He coughed, remembering the evening with amusement, then spun around with his arms outstretched. Blood drummed in his head.

As he turned into the panelled corridor towards the study, he met Rachele coming in the other direction. Both of them hung back a step, then moved on, passing.

'*Buongiorno*,' Rachele said. Their eyes met briefly, with a flicker of warmth.

A fire was already burning in the grate, and Almansi was seated in one of the leather armchairs beside the fire.

'Captain,' he said with a weary smile. 'I've been waiting for you.' He gestured towards the other chair, and Brookes sat down. A few moments later Odetta came in, carrying a silver tray with two small cups of coffee and a bowl of sugar. She was blushing as she set the tray on the table between the chairs.

'*Good bye*,' she mumbled in English.

'You mean *hello*,' Brookes said. Odetta just shrugged and left the room.

Almansi sketched a dismissive gesture. 'A shame you made such little progress with the lessons,' he said ruefully. The silver sugar spoon rang in the bowl.

'I'm glad you've made peace with your wife,' Brookes said, uncomfortable. He had to remind himself that the man opposite him was a stranger now. He knew nothing of his intentions, nor what he might be capable of doing. The possibility of a long-crafted revenge was not unlikely. But Almansi just gave his same diffident smile as he stirred his coffee.

'She made her point,' he said. 'And now hopefully our experiment in hostility is at an end. It was very grievous to me, you know. The separation, I mean. I'm a firm believer that there is a natural order to these things that one disrupts at one's peril. Despite what my wife may have though, I was not happy with the . . . arrangement.'

How similar he seems, Brookes thought. Still the same baronial mannerisms, the delicate edge of formality; he had inhabited his disguise well. Or perhaps Almansi was still acting, but in some new role.

'And are you glad,' he asked, 'that you don't have to pretend to be somebody else now?'

'Glad? I'm not sure,' Almansi said. 'Being the Barone was . . . *fun.*' He used the English word, and it seemed to diminish the concept. He glanced around the room, assessing it. 'I'm sure, though,' he said, 'that I've appreciated this place more than the real Barone ever did. There are books in the library that haven't been touched for decades, maybe even centuries! He barely ever came here – just the occasional summer weekend, or a party for his city friends. I met him, actually, at just such a party. A rather obnoxious man, truth be told.

'My people have always had a strained relationship with the aristocracy,' Almansi went on. 'But they need us, as often as not, more than we need them.' Still the patriarchal tone. Almansi was surely wealthy; he could easily picture him as a community leader of some kind. As grand, in his way, as the real Barone must have been. He drank the coffee slowly, his head thick and clouded, watching Almansi over the rim of the cup.

'I believe I was right to come here,' Almansi said, 'despite what my wife tells me. I couldn't just run away, you see. I preferred a tactical retreat. I envisaged this place as a sanctuary, like the monasteries and hermit cells of the Middle Ages. Somewhere I could protect the rest of my family, and keep them safe.'

Brookes made an understanding noise. The man was trying to justify himself. He knew now why Almansi had waited here for him, sending Rachele from the room. After the scene at the dining table several nights before, he wanted to give his side of the story.

'You're aware,' Almansi went on, 'of what was at stake. The world was on fire. All I wanted was to save what I valued most, what I chose to bring from the destruction. A sense of order, and of calm. An appreciation for a culture and society that seems totally obliterated now. And my family, of course. It seems to me, you see, that truth consists of what we cannot bear to leave behind. We are what we cannot lose and still remain whole. Love, Captain – love of an ordered universe, love of God, whatever God might mean, and the love of the people I love most. Without that, I'm nothing.'

The phrase the Baronessa had used long ago returned to Brookes – *leave as you would leave a house on fire*. At the time, he had thought she was merely warning him, or perhaps even threatening him. Now, though, it occurred to him that Rachele might, perhaps unconsciously, have been telling him something quite different. He had not considered the old question, after all, banal but obvious. What would you save from a burning house? Take only what is most precious to you.

'Would you have done the same, in my position?' Almansi asked. Then, before Brookes could even consider, his expression changed. 'But of course you wouldn't!' he said, his voice suddenly loaded with contemptuous irony. 'For you, after all, there'd be nothing worth saving! Isn't that so, Captain? You believe nothing has any more value than that of expediency, no?'

Brookes set down his cup carefully. He felt tired, not in the mood for argument. And something in Almansi's words, if not his tone, had struck its target. An ache passed through him, deep and bitter, and he felt very much older suddenly.

'Last night,' Almansi said, 'when I saw you dancing, I believe I observed something different about you. While you were unaware. A side of you that remains hidden.'

'I was drunk,' Brookes said. 'Wasn't that the point?'

'You weren't all that drunk, I think. But you seemed happy.'

That was true at least. Brookes remembered it, and felt a guilty shame. It was a strange sensation, almost warm. He allowed himself so few opportunities for guilt of any kind.

'So what have I represented here?' he asked. 'You've been so eager that I stay. What place do I have in your perfect sanctuary?'

'Can't you guess?' Almansi replied. 'I am the representative of order and of hierarchy. Of fixed systems and the divine will. The Barone. You, on the other hand, represent chance. You are chaos, entropy, from the world outside these walls. You remained here to show me what I had escaped from. If I didn't have you to push against, I could have come to doubt my convictions. I could have given way to despair. I mean no ill will, of course! We're speaking, after all, as friends, aren't we?'

Brookes raised his eyebrows, heavily sceptical. It was impossible that Almansi could have forgiven everything so breezily. Impossible that he could treat all that had happened as an exercise in intellectual debate. He put a palm to his head, the remains of his hangover still pressing at his skull. Almansi was failing to conceal his satisfied amusement. Looking away, Brookes' eye fell on the lacquered box sitting on the side table. Almansi must have been studying his cards while he waited.

'You really believe in those things?' Brookes asked, pointing.

'Oh yes, certainly,' Almansi replied. He lifted the lid of the box and the sheet of covering silk, then brushed his fingertips over the pack of tarot cards. 'Although my interest has become much greater since I came here. Before, they were merely an amusement.' He lifted the pack of cards from the box and tapped them against the tabletop. A sharp brittle crack.

'Let's do it again then,' Brookes said. 'Show me the trick again, and perhaps in daylight I can see how you do it.'

'There's no trick,' Almansi said, his eyes narrowed. 'You choose the cards, not I.'

He passed the pack, and Brookes shuffled it. The cards felt inert, with nothing of the faintly sinister aura he had felt on the previous occasion, the restrained horror at the touch of old things. But then, as he shuffled, he sensed them changing, as if they were drawing warmth and life from his hands. He dropped the pack onto the table, face down, cut it and slid the top three cards into a line.

'Your choice, remember?' Almansi said.

As he went to turn the cards, Brookes hesitated. He felt a sudden nervousness, a dread of what might be revealed. Death, perhaps. Or the Lovers. Or the Knight of Swords again. He tried to think of some ironic remark to puncture the mood. Then he turned the cards over.

The Seven of Cups.

The Ten of Staves.

Judgement.

Brookes sat back, stupid with relief. He didn't much care for the third card, but the others looked innocuous. Seven bulbous gilt goblets on the first, and a lattice of staves – they resembled sceptres – on the second. Almansi was studying the cards gravely. So gravely that Brookes stifled a laugh.

'The past, here,' Almansi said, indicating the first card, 'shows temptation. The Seven of Cups presents a choice between virtue – the three cups to one side here – or the pleasures of vice, symbolised by the four brimming cups on the other. Perhaps this is a choice you've had to make?' He glanced up from beneath his thick brows, a meaningful pause. Brookes pursed his lips, unwilling to feel the implied scorn.

'And?' he said. 'What about the present?'

'Your present situation,' Almansi corrected. 'Look at the card. What does it say to you? The staves seem welded together, no? They resemble a prison gate. You desire something, but you feel trapped and frustrated. This could be the prison of the ego, perhaps, rather than a literal confinement. But whatever you want, it seems you cannot have it.'

This time the implication was overt, and Brookes shifted in the chair, nettled. Almansi was trying to provoke him again, but he was determined not to appear moved.

The last card showed a woman robed in black against a dark background. In one hand she held a sword, in the other a set of scales: Justice, quite obviously. But there above the head of the figure was a rider in black armour, galloping across a green field – the knight again from the previous reading.

'I always thought Justice was supposed to be blind,' Brookes said.

'Only in England, I believe,' the Barone replied, and grinned. 'The card relates, of course, to the future. Perhaps a test or trial lies ahead, or perhaps this is the destination you must try to reach. The outcome. A choice must be made, a balancing of good and evil, maybe.'

'I see our friend the knight has returned.'

'Judgement must sometimes be backed with force. But, you see, he is no longer reversed.'

'Am I supposed to find that comforting?'

'Find it however you like,' Almansi said, gathering the cards together and returning them to their box. 'It's for you to interpret these definitions, not me. But tell me something: do you believe we are judged for our actions?'

Brookes exhaled slowly, a cold nervous annoyance passing down his spine. The man was still trying to draw him out, to snare him into argument.

'I mean,' Almansi went on, tentative, a little uncertain, 'in some way beyond the human. I suppose what I mean to ask is rather, do you believe in damnation?'

'I believe in little beyond the human,' Brookes said slowly.

'But if one betrays oneself, betrays one's trust, hurts those one loves, chooses actions which one knows to be wrong and immoral . . . are we judged for that? Are we condemned? And if we are condemned . . . if we are damned . . . can we ever be redeemed?'

'I can't accept your terms,' Brookes said. 'Redemption and damnation. I don't accept them at all. I told you, I'm not a religious man.'

'Are we talking of religion? Are my other terms unacceptable too? What about conscience? Trust? Morality? What about love?'

'I know nothing of them either.' He felt grubby as he spoke. He expected Almansi to laugh, but the man opposite him looked wrapped in consideration.

Then he stood up abruptly, smoothing his suit. 'What you call religion, Captain, and affect to despise,' Almansi said, 'is what I call humanity. And I believe its judgement is as absolute whether you claim to believe in it or not.'

Clearly the debate was over. He might have changed his name, Brookes thought, but the man himself remains the same. Still the obscure grasping for supremacy and intellectual victory. Still the same lightly-veiled contempt. Brookes knew that he need have no fear of revenge just yet.

For Almansi, the game had not yet reached an end.

He listened a moment, the sound becoming clear above the last spatters of falling water. Twenty feet to his left, Rachele was leaning from the narrow window at the top of the stair turret. She had begun to applaud, a few sharp claps, when Brookes rolled onto his chest and started dragging himself up the angle of the sagging roof.

'What's the matter?' she called to him. 'Where are you going?' Brookes grasped at the tiles until he could hook his fingers over the ridge of the roof to pull himself up. He was high above the valley now, a hawk's-eye view, and .down in the cleft where the road came threading through the trees he saw them: four military lorries with tarpaulin-covered loads, motorcycles ahead and behind.

'What is it?' Rachele was calling to him. Then, as she heard the sound, 'Oh God, oh God get down before they see you! Get back inside, quickly!'

Releasing his grip on the ridge, Brookes slid down the slope of the roof, grazing his palms on the tiles and only just catching himself at the lower edge. In the courtyard below he saw Odetta running, waving up at him. Rachele waited, gesturing frantically, until Brookes had edged back along the roof and climbed through after her.

'Stay here!' she hissed at him, gripping his arm. 'Don't let them see you!' Then she turned and dropped down the curve of the stairway. Brookes waited a few moments, crouching in the low turret loft. The sound of the engines dropped as they laboured up the slope to the castle gates. From the rooms below, he heard running steps, a slammed door, Almansi's voice calling from the loggia. Then the first of the motorcycles was driving up the ramp from the gates and around into the courtyard. He stood up and went quickly down the spiral steps.

Nobody to see him now as he moved along the panelled corridor and into the study. Here he paused, hardly breathing, listening for the sounds from outside. He waited until he heard Almansi and the Comandante come in from the loggia, their steps on the dining room floor. Then he slid through the door into the library.

The voices came closer. 'We'll go into my room,' Almansi said, 'it's warmer there.' Brookes caught his breath, then crossed the library in four strides to the further door. It wasn't locked, and he went through into Almansi's room, easing the door shut behind him just as the two men entered the library. The room was small and dim, without obvious hiding places. As the handle of the door was turning, Brookes drew aside a curtain and found another, narrower doorway into a tiny dressing chamber. He had time only to dart behind the curtain before the men entered the bedroom.

They were silent at first, and Brookes glanced around the chamber: a roll-top desk with a green baize writing surface, a cabinet of bottles, and a window looking out into the courtyard. From where he was standing, pressed against the wall, he could see the lorries pulling up outside, each one reversing through the tyre-rutted mud, then the men in their black uniforms unloading long wooden crates from the back. The men carried the crates between them, across to the portico beneath the loggia.

'This was never discussed,' he heard Almansi saying from the next room. Then the Comandante's thin metal voice: 'There wasn't time. And besides, you're in no position to protest!'

'Attilio, please, I have my family to think of.' In the pause that followed, Brookes could almost hear the Comandante grinning.

'And your family are safe,' he said, 'because of me, right?'

'But I just don't know about this. It's dangerous. What if somebody comes?'

'Who? Who might come? The partisans? You were brave once, Ettore. Are you so fearful now? You don't have the heart for a little sacrifice?'

Almansi began speaking, fast and quiet, too quiet to make out. Edging along the wall, Brookes stood just inside the doorway.

'Where did you get them anyway?' Almansi said.

'Oh, we took them from the Germans. Most of it was ours originally anyway – those fucking cowards in the regular army who disbanded themselves after the armistice. The Germans were keeping it at a depot outside Biella, so we took it back off them. We disguised ourselves as partisans of course. Had to kill a few of them. My boys enjoyed themselves, actually – the fucking Germans have been treating us like shit for months now.'

'But the Germans . . .' Almansi said, pleading.

'Will never guess who took it!' the Comandante declared. 'They're finished anyway. That cocksucker Wolff's already negotiating with the Yanks in Switzerland, so we've learned, trying to pull his men back over the Alps. They're going to leave us to the Reds, Ettore. And you know what'll happen then.'

'I need a drink,' Almansi said. Creak of a chair as he got up.

'Good idea!' the Comandante replied. 'A drink to our new understanding!'

Brookes stepped back smartly as the curtain was whipped aside and Almansi walked into the dressing room. Pressed against the wall, he watched him open the cabinet and select a bottle. His pistol must be in here somewhere, Brookes thought. Probably in the roll-top desk. He wondered whether he could make a leap for it before Almansi turned and saw him. Probably not.

'You know what they're doing in Russia now?' the Comandante called from the other room. 'They've got four hundred thousand Italians in prisoner-of-war camps, and they're indoctrinating them with Bolshevist propaganda. Why d'you think they're doing that, Ettore?'

Almansi turned, shrugging, then froze as he saw Brookes standing against the wall. Brookes raised a finger to his lips.

'I . . . I don't know,' Almansi said.

'I'll tell you why. They're making an army, that's why! Think of it – nearly half a million trained soldiers, with their heads filled with Bolshevism, armed by Russia and sent back to Italy ahead of the Red Army! There are Bolshevist cells all over north Italy even now, just waiting for Moscow to give the word – only last month the munitions factories were on strike. They were flying the red flag over Turin! We think we've been at war all these years, but I tell you, the real war's only just beginning.'

'I see,' Almansi said, frowning. Brookes gestured over his shoulder. *Get in there.* Almansi swallowed hard, then walked back into the other room.

'So who's going to protect you, when that happens?' the Comandante said as the curtain dropped back. 'The Reds are across the German border already, so the Germans can't. The Yanks, you think? The English?'

'I don't know,' Almansi replied, sounding resigned now.

'Us, that's who!' the Comandante shouted, a steel bark. He banged his fist on a tabletop. 'Me and thousands like me, who won't just lie down and accept a Communist Italy! Men of action and courage, Ettore. You remember them?'

'I remember . . .'

'And the Allies . . . the Allies won't help us either. They'll try and keep order, in their feeble democratic way. But they can't stand up to the Reds! They'll try and disarm us, won't they? They'll try and cut off our balls! So now you see my plan.'

'You could have said something . . .' Almansi said feebly.

'*Said* something?' the Comandante cried. He was on his feet now, strutting back and forth – Brookes heard his boots banging the floor-boards. 'Have you really forgotten everything? Since when did these things needs to be discussed? Are we women? I thought, you know, Ettore, I really thought . . .'

'Please, Attilio . . .'

'I really thought you still had some juice in you. I thought maybe you were still the man you used to be. You remember those days? The things we did?'

'A long time ago.'

'No! Yesterday!' A crash, and Brookes tensed. The Comandante had kicked over a chair, by the sound of it. '*Faith lives forever,* or do you deny that now? You were a real man once – we stood together like brothers. Do you remember? When you had power? And when things went badly for you I put my head on the block to help you, does that mean nothing? I didn't care what you were. Didn't care about your *blood* . . . because I remembered the things we'd done, you and me. Back in '21 and '22 . . . Those days are coming again, Almansi. The mists are clearing, and it's time for the real men to step forward into the light! Italy must rise again . . . or are you afraid to do your duty now?'

'Duty,' Almansi said, grit in his voice. 'All I've ever done is my duty.'

'All we *can* ever do is our duty. We're soldiers. Even you, even your family. All of us are soldiers now, called to the flag. Cowardice will not be tolerated! Cowards and traitors must die! Absolute severity is the only way we can win! Totalitarian discipline . . . iron-willed strength. There is no pity any longer.'

'Please,' Almansi said again. The Comandante stopped striding and let out a crackling laugh.

'You are too weak, Ettore. Well, you have no choice anyway!' he de-clared. 'Who else can save you? Who else can you trust? I'm your only hope now! How d'you fancy your chances in front of a revolutionary tribunal, *Comrade?* If you're lucky they'd just kill you, rape your wife and daughter and ship your son off to one of those re-education camps in Siberia!'

'You're right. I have no choice.'

'Good! So let's drink to your lack of choice, shall we? We'll be seeing a lot more of each other, of course, once things start happening. I may have to send some of my men here to watch over everything. But I'll wait until we have more information on what the enemy are planning. It's important we keep this place quiet, don't draw anyone's attention to what we have here. But can I be certain your loyalty to the cause is assured?'

'As it ever was, Comandante,' Almansi said.

Brookes waited silently until the two men had finally left the room, then sank down against the wall. On his knees, he crossed to the window and peered out into the yard – the paramilitaries were gathering around their lorries, the Comandante marching back towards his sidecar. Huddled together on the steps of the loggia, Almansi and his family stood watching. The Comandante paused beside the well, then spun around and shot his arm out in a fascist salute.

'*Viva L'Italia!*' he shouted.

Almansi raised his arm and saluted back.

Down the steps to the courtyard, Brookes doubled back into the portico beneath the loggia. The sound of the convoy could still be heard moving away along the valley road. Light-footed, he ran to the far end where a narrow flight of steps descended through the flagstones. At the bottom was the steel door to the cellars, closed with a thick metal latch and a shiny new padlock. Brookes shoved at the door and hauled at the latch, but it was firmly shut.

A sound behind him, and he turned to see Odetta in the portico, staring down at him.

'What's in there?' she said urgently. 'What was in those crates?'

Brookes stepped back, then kicked at the door. The metal rang dimly but did not shift.

'There's another way in,' Odetta said. 'A tunnel. Follow me.' She was gone at once, and Brookes hauled himself out of the stairwell to see her jogging away across the churned mud of the courtyard towards the ruined keep. Calling for her to wait, he ran back up to the scullery and took an electric torch and an iron crowbar.

A mound of overgrown rubble led up to the door of the keep, the doorway itself an open arch piercing the massive medieval thickness of the wall. Inside, the building was little more than a shell, light filtering down from gashes in the roof high overhead, silhouetting the remaining rafters of the upper floor. The wreck of a wooden staircase hung in space, tilted sideways in the air, and the walls were pitted and blackened in places by old fires. Between the walls was a chaos of fallen roof tiles and the rubble of the collapsed upper floors. The whole place stank of damp rotting plaster and mould.

Odetta dragged her stockings up over her knees and started awkwardly through the rubble, shoving aside the dusty spars of fallen wood. As he followed her, Brookes saw the brick-lined pit in the corner, the steps that led down into it now heaped with debris and almost impassable.

'I've never been down there,' Odetta said. 'I don't really want to . . . but Papa says it leads to the cellars.'

Brookes moved past her and clambered down into the pit. At the bottom was a low brick archway, the decayed remains of a door standing half open and clogged with rubbish. He stepped over the threshold and switched on the torch. Rapid movement in the shadows as the torchlight penetrated the low tunnel beyond, illuminating the heavy swags of cobweb.

'I think I know what was in those crates,' Odetta whispered, climbing down to join him.

'You don't have to come with me,' Brookes told her. 'Wait here.' But she slipped past him into the tunnel, and in her eyes was a fierce determination.

Brookes started after her, the torch beam shining straight ahead. Odetta took his arm, ducking her head low to avoid the cobwebs. Together they stumbled forward into the throat of the tunnel.

'It stinks down here,' Odetta said. 'Like a grave or something . . .' Then she screamed suddenly and gripped Brookes' arm tighter. 'Sorry. Something brushed my leg. A rat, I think.'

'You can go back.'

He didn't see her shake her head. The faint daylight from the mouth of the tunnel was gone now, the walls curving imperceptibly. Then the floor began to rise, and Brookes tripped on a stone step. Odetta dragged him back upright, urging him forward as the ceiling dropped lower still. He paused, the torchlight wavering ahead.

'It's alright,' Odetta whispered. 'We can go on. We're nearly there, I think.'

A few more steps, and the torch showed steps ascending ahead of them. Trying not to inhale the rank air, Brookes climbed until he saw another archway ahead, and a small wooden door that he managed to shoulder open on the third attempt.

The cellar was still thick with disturbed dust, whirling in the beam of the torch. Beneath the massive stone vaults, the crates lay stacked in the middle of the room, a great chest-high buttress of them.

'Hold the torch,' Brookes said. He dragged one of the upper crates to the edge of the pile and started levering at the lid with the crowbar.

The wood splintered, and with a wrench of screws the lid came up. Inside was gleaming metal foil and the sudden scent of grease. Brookes ripped the foil aside and ran his hands over what lay beneath.

'The light. Bring the light closer.'

Odetta moved the torch, and the light spilled across the serried brass bullets packed inside the case. Brookes was already dragging another free of the pile.

'Oh God,' Odetta said. 'Oh God I knew it!'

The second crate was levered open, and this time there was a packing of oily straw. Under the straw, nestling together, were rifles. Polished stocks and steel bolts gleamed in the harsh electric light. Brookes opened more crates, flinging aside the shattered lids.

'Why have they left them here?' Odetta said. The beam of the torch wavered as her hand shook.

'The Comandante believes there'll be a civil war,' Brookes told her. 'He thinks the Allies will disarm his men and leave them defenceless against the Communists. This is how he intends to re-arm them. There's enough here for several hundred men, and he must have other caches elsewhere . . . Look at this,' he said. Odetta took a few steps forward and craned over. 'These are landmines,' Brookes told her, carefully lifting one of the heavy black discs from its packing. 'German landmines. And in here there are machine-guns . . . hand grenades, bayonets . . .'

Odetta was staring at him.

Brookes stood up, taking one of the guns from its crate. In the torchlight he examined it, checking breech and magazine. 'See this one?' he said with enthusiasm. '*Moschetto Automatico Beretta*, model 1938A. Very good gun. See the two triggers here? One's for single shot, the other for automatic fire . . .'

'Stop it!' Odetta cried. 'Stop talking like that! It's like you love all this!'

'I was just explaining,' Brookes began, then fell silent. He saw the look on her face as she watched him standing with a gun in his hands, the disgust and the fear.

'You're just like them, aren't you,' she said, holding her words steady. 'You're just a killer, like them.'

The torch swung down to the floor, and darkness rushed from the margins of the cellar.

20

IT WAS NEAR midnight when he heard the knock on the bedroom door. He had waited for hours, alone in candlelight, lying on the bed with the gun beside him. This time he would not go and find them. This time, he decided, they would come to him. Almansi knew what he had overheard. Brookes knew that Almansi could not attempt to conceal his knowledge now.

He was standing in the corridor when Brookes opened the door, dressed in his heavy tweed coat and carrying a torch and a walking stick. When he spoke he sounded hesitant and agitated, more than a little scared.

'You must help me, Captain,' he said. 'My daughter . . . Odetta's gone.'

'Gone where? How do you know? She could be hiding somewhere, surely. Have you looked . . .'

'No, no, she's gone,' Almansi said, then his words came fast. 'She didn't appear for dinner, and we thought she was in her room. But Isacco went to find her and she wasn't there. We searched the castle, all the places she might have been, but she was nowhere . . . Then we found that some of her things were missing, a coat and some other clothes, and a bag. She's gone, Captain. She's left the castle.'

'What about your brother?' Brookes said. 'Can't he help search for her?'

'Umberto is attending to my wife. She's taken it very badly. Everything that's happened . . . she had a sort of fit. Anyway, Odetta might be more inclined to listen to you than to any of us, I think.'

Brookes stepped back into the room and put on his coat. He picked up the gun.

'Please, leave that here,' Almansi said quickly. 'It won't do us any good, and my daughter might not like it.'

Brookes slipped the carbine under the bed.

'Let's go then,' he said. 'She's got at least three hours start on us already.'

Almansi turned off his torch as they left the shelter of the gatehouse. The night was clear, and the moon bright enough to show them the road and the rocky slopes ahead. Below, the valley was barred with mottled grey and the mountains were huge and pale under the snow.

'If we find her,' Almansi said over his shoulder, his breath steaming, 'I might need you to persuade her to return with us. That is, I might need you to use force. Would you do that?'

'We'll see,' Brookes replied. 'First we find her, then we'll see.'

The other man was walking fast down the slope, almost jogging, striking out with his stick. Brookes looked across the valley at the little clutch of cottages, dark and dead now it seemed.

'You must have hoped she would appear in time for your performance on the balcony?'

'What?' Almansi replied with fierce incomprehension. He threw up his hands. 'How could we think of something like that?' He turned to stare up at the cottages, shaking his head. 'They didn't come,' he said, 'but they know . . . they must know.'

'Is there anywhere she might have thought to go?' Brookes said. 'Anywhere close to here she might be heading for?'

'I don't know. She had friends in Novara, and in Turin, but both places are too far . . . I don't know where she's gone.' Bleak desperation in his voice. Inside the walls of the castle, his daughter's disappearance would have been a crisis; out here in the freezing night, it was catastrophic.

They reached the level area where the road curved back on itself before dropping into the valley towards the village. A short distance down the slope, Brookes saw the stand of trees he had sheltered behind on the night of his own attempted escape, when he had witnessed the family's ritual with the lamp on the balcony. Beside him Almansi stood leaning on his stick, breathing hard as he gazed into the vastness of the valley.

'She must have gone down there,' he said, sounding unconvinced. 'To the village, perhaps. Don't you think?'

'I've no idea,' said Brookes. He waited, hands deep in his coat pockets, for Almansi to make a decision. He was very tempted to return to his room in the castle.

'But what do you think? Should we split up? You must have some idea!'

'No,' said Brookes. And even if I had, he thought, I wouldn't tell you.

Something caught his eye then, away up the valley to the right. A quick flash of light, cut by trees or high rocks. He said nothing, but kept watching the place where the light had been.

'I don't know, I don't know . . . she could be anywhere!' Almansi was saying, shaking his head, the enormity of the space outside the castle seeming to overwhelm him.

'She's up there,' Brookes said, pointing. The flash came again, quick and vivid, a white spark in a great dark void. Odetta too must have an electric torch, and either she was in a deep cleft in the mountain or was only turning the torch on occasionally to pick out the path ahead. But Almansi was already moving, plunging down off the road and beginning to scramble across the face of the slope, calling for Brookes to follow.

There was no way of telling how far away the flash of light might have been, how far up the valley Odetta might have climbed. But she was climbing, certainly – not following the road towards the village but scaling upwards into the empty wilderness of rocks and thick forest that lay above the castle. After a moment's hesitation – he saw the light blink again and noted its position – Brookes went after Almansi, leaping across the gullies scored in the hillside. Very soon he had passed the other man and was pushing on ahead, reaching out to grab at stunted trees and brambles. Behind him he heard Almansi toiling, breath loud and hoarse, the steel ferrule of his stick clashing on the rock. Then even these sounds had fallen behind him, and Brookes climbed alone. He felt the strength in his limbs, his heart powering the blood in his veins.

He had no idea how long he climbed: perhaps twenty minutes, perhaps an hour. Then he reached a level area, a slight hollow between low tree-lined spurs, and halted to look around him. The night was absolute, and as he listened he could make out the sounds of Almansi below him once more, the rattle of dislodged stones, the crack of brittle branches. Brookes sat down on a smooth boulder, his determination ebbing away. He lit a cigarette. A few minutes later he heard the cry from the valley below.

'Odetta!' The sound rang back, echoed off the mountains: *ta . . . ta . . . ta . . .* Almansi cried out again, then once more began climbing.

'Brookes!' he called, stifling the panic in his shout with difficulty. 'Brookes, where are you? Can you hear me?'

Brookes waited, smoking in silence until the man had almost reached him, then called back. Almansi scrambled up the last slope into the hollow.

'Have you seen . . .' he gasped, gulping lungfuls of cold air, 'any sign of her?'

'We won't find her like this,' Brookes said calmly. 'She could be anywhere up there on the mountain. We'll have to wait here till dawn.'

'Impossible! We have to find her now!' Almansi, still fighting for breath, struck at the ground with his stick.

'Don't be ridiculous. You'll just end up falling over a cliff in the dark.'

Almansi made a dismissive spitting sound. 'What do *you* know?' he said. 'She's my daughter!'

'And what do you think she's running away from? Me?'

Brookes caught Almansi's contemptuous gesture – the thumb and forefinger pressed together. 'You understand nothing!' the man said, a sudden and surprising ferocity in his voice.

'On the contrary, I think I understand everything very clearly now.'

Brookes stood up and crossed the hollow in two long strides. Raising his arm, he shoved the man's chest with his open palm. Almansi staggered back, then tripped to fall sprawling on his back.

'Sit down, why don't you?' Brookes said casually. He made no move towards the fallen figure, but in his blood he felt the quick thrill of violence, of physical mastery. He willed himself to calm.

'Now,' he said. 'Perhaps we can talk frankly? What better place for it, up here on a mountain in the middle of the night?'

Almansi was watching him warily, a hunted caution in his eyes. Brookes kicked the fallen stick away into the shadows. Slowly the other man sat up, wiping dirt from his palms.

'Tell me about the past,' Brookes said. 'Tell me what you did.'

'You must have guessed most of it,' Almansi said in a near whisper. He rubbed his face, then dragged himself back until he could sit against the trunk of a tree. For a long time he was silent.

'It began after the war,' he said at last. 'I had the sense – I told you I was an idealist then – that Italy had been cheated. In England I heard young men mocking my country, and it filled me with shame. I knew what we'd lost in that war. When I got back home I felt powerless. We all did, I think. I began working as a lawyer, but I was just waiting for the moment to come. The call to duty. It's hard to explain now . . .'

'I understand,' said Brookes. 'What then?'

'In 1920,' Almansi said, 'I joined the Fascist party. We were part of a squad, a blackshirt action group, Battista and me. Actually he was my junior then, but we were both ex-soldiers. He was my strong arm, so to speak. We did things that were . . . discreditable in hindsight, I suppose. We were young men, on fire with patriotism. We called it patriotism. Perhaps it was just violence. Anyway, I was noticed by the hierarchy and given an official position. By 1928 I was Provincial Secretary of the National Fascist Party in Turin. Two years later I moved to Novara and met Battista again – he was chief of the local militia. We worked together.'

'Worked together?' Brookes said.

'I sat behind a desk,' Almansi said, 'wearing my uniform and official sash, and I directed the beating and torture of others. I decreed imprisonment and intimidation. I arranged wealth and honours for my associates and saw that anyone who had crossed me or the party in the past paid for their error. Battista did the work on my behalf, and he enjoyed it all immensely. We made a good partnership, he and I. I've always been able to exude an aura of sober authority, or so they tell me. I don't appear to be a thug, in short.'

'And you became rich, you and your family.'

'Oh yes, of course. I was already wealthy, but it was more than money. It was the prestige. The best schools for Vittorio and Odetta, invitations from the highest levels of society. I did it in the name of Italy, of course. I believed in the new order. I believed that harsh measures were needed to restore my country to greatness.'

'Of course you did,' Brookes said quietly.

'I even,' Almansi went on, a slight quiver as he spoke, 'continued to believe after '38, when the Race Laws were introduced. I thought it was all a mistake, or a ploy by the regime to expose traitors. Not *all* Jews – not us, certainly. Just some Jews, the bad ones, the Zionists and the agents of . . . oh, who knows? International capitalism? I denounced them, the *bad Jews*, you see; I gave evidence of their crimes against the state.' He tensed suddenly, suppressing a shudder, and raised his hand as if to cover his face. 'Rachele, she is sensitive, she felt some . . . horror. She begged me to leave – we had the chance – but I would not flee Italy like that. It was a test of my loyalty. I wrote letters to Mussolini and the other hierarchs, claiming exemption for my family. For a while, it was granted – I was a war veteran, a long-term Fascist. I'd even been awarded a medal for the March on

Rome . . . But soon that door closed on us as well, and by then it was too late.'

'And she's never forgiven you?'

'How could she not hate me? Think what she has lost. But what could she do? My wife, Captain, is a very traditional woman. As fixed in her sense of duty as me. She would do anything to keep the remainder of our family together, whatever the cost. And so she came here with me.'

'Battista brought you here then?'

'Yes, he helped us escape when the Germans came, soon after . . . soon after my son died. He'd made himself custodian of the castle when the Barone left, but didn't have the men to garrison it, so he installed us here. We were to keep quiet, never go outside or communicate with anyone, and his spies would keep watch over us from the other side of the valley. Back then he was thinking of contingencies, I believe – if the war went badly for Germany, he could produce us as evidence. The Jews he saved from the Nazis. A possible amelioration for his crimes. And of course, there was the money . . .' He laughed. 'You could call me a benefactor, I've funded him and those animals of his for months. And then there were the things only I knew about; things he had done for Italy. Maybe, also, in a way he did it for brotherhood. Who knows?'

The two men sat silently for a while. Almansi's head was sunken onto his chest, and the moon lit one side of his face, drawing a pale grey sickle over his cheekbone.

'I suppose you had a similar idea in mind for me,' Brookes said. 'You would save me, and if the Allies won you could claim that as exemption for your own past.'

'Maybe, yes,' Almansi said. 'But you see, Captain, it goes further than that.' He sat up a little, and in the moonlight he face was twisted into a grimace. 'At first my hands were tied. My daughter found you: how could we not take you in? After that, my family's safety was my main concern. I had to keep you close, you understand. But then I came to see a greater potential in you. I had been, I realised, a tyrant. I had oppressed and maltreated others, used my power in the interests of evil. I felt that I was condemned to a slow damnation, and wanted an end to it. In short, Captain, I wanted you to be my judge.'

Brookes was speechless, disarmed. He heard Almansi's dry chuckle.

'But in order to judge me, you must first understand what I'd been . . . You had to become the tyrant yourself. And it seemed to come naturally to you – to oppress me and my family, to abuse our trust. I suppose you thought your only option would be to exert yourself over us all. So many times, as you lay with my daughter and my wife, I wanted to kill you . . . I could have killed you. I had a gun, I could have put a bullet through your skull. Once I stood beside you while you slept, with the gun to your head . . . But I resisted the urge, Captain. I showed mercy and humility, even when I was goaded. I remained passive. I did all this as a penance. So when this moment came and you knew everything, *you* could judge, who are the same as me.'

'And you family knew about your ideas?' Brookes asked with disgust. He saw the slight shake of Almansi's head. 'You used your family for that?'

'They were aware of the means, if not the end. But I knew when first I saw you that you were the man I needed. As if you'd been sent to test me, and to judge me. I could see it in your eyes, you know, and hear it in your voice. Such a facility for lying! I knew you were a killer, Captain, a man without moral qualms. I could almost believe there was something supernatural about you, like you were a force of destruction against whom I must fight for my soul!'

Brookes got up and paced closer to where Almansi was sitting.

He felt a slow steady gathering of force in his body, an idling potential for harm.

'You wanted me to punish you, that's all,' he said.

He took another quick deliberate step and saw Almansi pull himself upright. There was something in the man's raised hand: moonlight glinting on steel. The pistol.

'Don't come any closer, Captain,' Almansi said softly.

'What are you going to do with that?' Brookes said. 'Shoot me? Ever shot anyone before? I doubt it.' He stepped closer again, and saw the gun barrel wavering in Almansi's hand. 'You know,' he said, 'I've seen a lot of men shot with pistols. At least half of them shot themselves by accident . . .'

He lunged, closing the distance fast, his hand snaking out to grab Almansi's wrist. A tightening of muscle, almost a reflex, and Almansi yelled and released his grip on the gun. Before the man could fall Brookes had flipped the pistol into the palm of his hand and brought the reversed butt hammering down on Almansi's head. He felt the solid concussion of the blow up his arm. Breathing hard, he stood with the pistol raised, wanting to strike again.

Almansi was writhing on the ground, clutching his head and his injured wrist, his legs kicking at the dirt. Brookes lowered his arm; there was blood on the pistol butt and streaked on his hand. He flung the pistol away clattering into the darkness.

'Is that what you want?' he hissed at the man beneath him. 'You want more like that?' He was poised, ready to kick and stomp. Waves of energy coursed through him, hot and powerful, and he felt his face contorted into a terrible snarl. 'All the death in the world,' he said, 'and you want to play games with it. You want special exemption! But if you want to suffer, I can arrange that . . .'

Almansi's attack took him by surprise, the man springing against his legs. Brookes hit the ground rolling, kicking and trying to struggle upright. Almansi clung on, his hands clawing up until he could grasp Brookes by the throat. Brookes punched hard, but the grip did not slacken, fingers digging into his windpipe. Neither of them made a sound – except the steady heave of their breath and the rattle of the stones beneath them, they fought in silence. Almansi's strength was extraordinary, powered by despair and anger, his face a mask of moonlight.

Then suddenly there was a shock of light, a hard electric glare flooding over them. Brookes got his legs beneath him and scrambled backwards – a last quick punch drove Almansi to the ground. Odetta stood at the lip of the hollow with the levelled torch. 'What were you *doing?*' she was saying. 'You're insane! What were you *doing?*' She advanced carefully towards them, keeping the light on her father.

Almansi crawled across the hollow until he could prop himself against the tree again. His face was dark with blood and he groaned as he moved.

'I heard you,' his daughter said. She held the torch with both hands, like a gun, pointing at her father. 'I heard what you told him. Why didn't you tell him everything? Why didn't you tell him the worst of it?'

'What would be the good of that?' Almansi said through bared teeth, shielding his face from the light.

'Just tell him!' Odetta screamed, and her voice echoed back off the mountains. 'I want to hear you say it!'

Almansi was shaking his head now, pulling himself further back against the tree as Odetta advanced on him. He let out a strange high whine.

'It was your son, wasn't it,' Brookes said. 'The eldest one, Vittorio. It was you that informed on him.'

'He was a *traitor!*' Almansi snarled, turning from the light. Between his daughter and the stranger he crouched at bay, savage and desperate. He was a different man now, the last vestiges of the Barone sloughed like a dead skin. 'He wanted to betray his country . . . he wanted to betray *me!*'

'So you had him sent to prison,' Odetta said with slow cold fury. 'To be beaten and tortured . . . for the sake of your *country*,' she spat the word in his face.

'To be cured!' Almansi shouted. 'And returned to me . . . obedient. A good son! A loyal son! How could I know what would happen?'

'You have never, ever been sorry!' the girl shouted. 'Never once have you said sorry for what you did!'

She moved suddenly, the light from the torch swinging up and then wheeling, blinding as she threw it. Brookes heard the torch strike Almansi, then the bulb burst and the light cut off.

'*Maledetto, bastardo!* I loved him, my brother, and he died because of you!' Almansi was scrambling upright as the girl leapt for him; he tried to swat aside her assault, but his strength was gone. For a few harsh breaths they struggled, vague forms in the swirling darkness. Then Brookes threw himself forward, colliding with them and forcing them apart. Almansi dropped to the ground – Odetta still fought, almost unconscious of who she was grappling with. For a moment Brookes gripped her wrists, forcing her arms down, then she too sank as her legs gave beneath her. He stood above them both.

Staring down into the valley, he felt emptied now, completely alone and still. He had a sense of having reached an end, but not having achieved anything. He considered that he could walk away from all this and it would mean nothing. But he was responsible, and he had to make the decision. The man and his daughter crouching in the hollow behind him were his concern now.

'Can you walk?' he called to Almansi.

The man began dragging himself upright using the tree trunk. 'My ankle,' he said. 'I've twisted it, I think . . .'

'We need to get back to the castle,' Brookes said. 'Odetta, you'll have to help me carry him.'

He expected her to refuse, but the girl got up in silence and took her father under one arm. Between them they hoisted him and began stumbling forward. Almansi hung, dragging his injured leg, groaning and pleading. Through the moonlight on the empty slopes they struggled back towards the castle. Twice they had to pause as Almansi vomited, doubled gasping and choking, braced against the mountainside.

'I never wanted it,' Almansi was saying, weeping out the words. 'If I'd known . . . if I'd ever guessed. I loved him too, you have to understand that . . . I'm sorry . . .'

'Hush, papa,' Odetta told him. 'Be quiet now. I'm sorry too.'

Brookes did not want to listen. The violent spirit, the spirit of punishment, had left him now. He could almost feel pity for the broken man clinging to his side – or not that man, but rather the Barone that he had once been, the proud armour that he had used to conceal his disgrace. As they reached the lower slopes, Odetta went on ahead to pick a path through the scored boulders and the scrub. Anger and shame wrapped her, tightening her shoulders and quickening her steps. Several times she slipped and scrambled back upright without a word.

Hours, or so it seemed, before they reached the gates once more. Brookes was exhausted, his legs burning from scrambling down the treacherous slopes lugging Almansi's mute weight. As they scaled the ramp to the gatehouse they saw the orange glow beneath the arches, the three figures waiting for them there in the light of the paraffin lamp.

The doctor stood at the centre, a hand on the shoulders of Rachele and Isacco. He was stiff, authoritative, a man of science ready the take command of the situation, but it was Rachele who spoke first.

'Where have you been?' she said as they approached. 'What have you done?' In her voice, in her eyes, Brookes recognised the slow blur of morphine. Umberto tightened his grip on her shoulder, steadying her.

'You'd best come inside, all of you,' he said.

But before another word was said Almansi slipped his arms free and lurched forward, falling to his knees on the cobbles. In the lamplight his face was stripped and rigid – with bloodied hands he reached out to his wife, to his son. He gripped their clothes, dragging them to him, sobbing apologies. His wife, his son and his brother gathered close around him, their faces moving from confusion to pity. Only Odetta stood apart, averting her eyes from the wreckage of her family.

Back in his room, Brookes retrieved the machine carbine from under the bed and checked it. Not the best tool for what he intended – on the table was a bayonet in a scabbard, brought with him from the arsenal in the cellar. He drew the blade free, tested the edge with his thumb then slipped it into his belt. With the carbine slung on his back, he went outside again.

He had been halfway back to the castle, lugging Almansi across his shoulders and trying to follow Odetta's rambling course amongst the rocks, when he realised the importance of something he had almost forgotten. The watchers on the far side of the valley; they were guardians as well, with the means to report back to Battista if anything seemed wrong. Not a telephone – there were no wires to the cottages – but certainly a radio transmitter. The family's non-appearance that evening would already have been noted and passed on.

Even so, he had to will himself onwards. It would be easy, he told himself, to leave this place and disappear. Whatever troubled affection he might have felt towards Almansi and his family had surely been nullified now. The game was over, and there had been no winners. But even as he turned these thoughts in his mind, examining their flaws, he knew he had no choice, not really. He had nowhere to go – the course of his actions had pushed him to this point. He would throw over the balance, shatter the fragile stasis that had held the castle and its occupants, himself included, for so many months.

Down the side of the valley in a series of bone-jarring leaps rock to rock, he reached the stream in the cleft, loud and fast with white melt-water now. He crossed where it narrowed and began to climb again. He almost wished that the cottage up there would be deserted – perhaps Battista had pulled back his watchers when he left with the convoy. Adrenaline ran fast in his body, but Brookes knew how tired he really was. His reactions would be slow, but he had the advantage of surprise. Through ice-brittle air and bare trees petrified by the moonlight he climbed slowly, guarding his remaining strength. As he approached the cottage, scaling the last slope to the little footpath that led to its door, he heard the faint sounds of radio music and saw the needle of light between the closed shutters.

There would be two of them at least, probably three, but they had no guard or sentry keeping watch outside the cottage. Brookes slid up to the wall and pressed his back against it, then drew the bayonet from his belt. From within the shutters, rich in the thin air, he smelled hot food and the warmth of men. With the blade in his fist he moved along the wall, then around the corner and up to the doorway.

He heard the hushed voices, the electric drone of the radio, felt the radiance of orange lamplight and heat. The door was thin wood, latched shut on the inside. Calm now, prepared, Brookes silently counted to ten.

Then he took a step back and kicked open the door.

21

THEY WERE WAITING for him when he returned; the whole family in the light of the candles in the big bedroom.

'He has blood on his face,' Almansi said, but his voice carried no expression. He sat on an upright chair beside the window, a bandage around his head and a red bruise under one eye.

'What have you done, Captain?' Rachele asked. Her eyes were bright with the drug, but she towered among the others. The dynamic had shifted again, dizzyingly. She was in charge now. Perhaps, Brookes thought, she always had been.

He took the bloodied knife from his belt and dropped it onto the carpet. Odetta stifled a scream.

'There's nobody watching you now,' he said. 'You can leave whenever you want.'

'No, no no,' the doctor said, stepping forward. 'You don't seem to understand. That isn't part of the arrangement here at all. We can't just leave!'

'You've broken the rules,' Rachele said slowly. 'You've put my family in danger.'

'There are no rules any more,' said Brookes.

But they were all on their feet now, even the vacant Almansi, even his silent son. They were standing and moving towards him gradually, and he felt their fear and their determination. With everything thrown down, he was their only focus in the confusion. He was their only enemy now – the threat that could unite them. He slung the machine carbine from his shoulder and slipped off the safety catch.

'What's this?' Rachele said. 'Are you going to kill us all now? Do it then . . .' She was stepping steadily closer as she spoke, her hands raised as if to take the gun. Brookes tightened his grip on the stock. His finger found the second trigger, the one for automatic fire. The family were circling him. Brookes glanced at Odetta, and saw the terrified compulsion in her eyes. He glanced at Rachele and saw nothing.

He thumbed back the safety catch and threw the gun to the floor.

'What's going on?' he said flatly. Even as he spoke, he heard Odetta's warning cry. He struck out backwards, his fist already seeking its mark, and felt the blow connect as he turned.

'Sorry,' he said, as the doctor staggered back clutching his face.

But they were all around him now, poised, driven by desperation.

'Give up, Captain,' Rachele said. 'You can't fight us all.'

Brookes leapt for the door, shoving the doctor aside. Out into the long gallery with his head down, he collided with the far wall. Fatigue was aching though him, a helpless, dizzying despair. His foot

caught one of the rainwater buckets and it spilled, clanging. Shouts
from the bedroom, thudding steps behind him – he began to run,
but only managed two strides before a body hurtled against his back
to trip him and bring him down. Falling, Brookes threw out a hand
and grabbed for the suit of black armour against the wall, but the boy
was clinging to his legs and the momentum of his fall could not be
checked. The armour tilted and crashed over, rattling into disarray.
The halberd toppled with it, catching Brookes on the temple.

He hit the floor hard. For a moment he was floundering in confused chaos, trapped in the articulated joints of the metal – he hurled
it clear, and Isacco released his legs just long enough to punch him in
the stomach. Brookes heard the doctor shouting *Hold him! Hold him!*
and then the weight of several bodies came down onto him, beating him to the floor. His head was bleeding and his arm was being
wrenched behind his back.

'Be careful,' Umberto was saying.

Brookes felt the wadded towel pressed over his face, gagged at the
sudden fumes of the chemicals and the whirl in his head. He
thrashed backwards, and felt the hand forced against his neck and the
lurching slide into unconsciousness, then he stopped struggling and
knew nothing.

He awoke lying on his back in daylight, in his old room in the tower.
The ceiling seemed much higher than he remembered, and that
puzzled him for a while. There was no pain or confusion – he felt
lucid, his head very clear and empty as if washed by pure water. He
decided that the ceiling looked higher because the mattress had been
placed on the floor, and when he tried to move his leg he found that
his right ankle had been shackled to the water pipe he had once used
to earth the wireless set.

Brookes tried to speak, but his voice escaped him. As the anaesthetic ebbed from him the pain returned, a web binding his body. He began to sweat, and to drag his leg compulsively against the chain. But he was spent and he knew it, his muscles raw and his bones bruised. Struggling to sit up, he stared at the chain on his ankle. It looked like a pair of police shackles, but he could not make the effort to wonder where the family might have found them. Sinking onto the mattress, he clenched his jaw and rode out the pain until he slipped back into unawareness.

'They didn't know when you'd wake up,' Odetta said as he opened his eyes again. She was sitting cross-legged against the far wall with a blanket around her shoulders. 'There's a tray there with food and water. You can just reach it, I think.'

'Explain to me what happened,' Brookes said. 'I don't remember too clearly.'

Odetta didn't answer for some time. Brookes rolled onto his shoulder and glared at her. 'You killed the men in the cottage over there, didn't you?' she asked.

'Yes,' he replied.

'Mamma thinks you did it on purpose, so Battista will come back and . . . punish us, I suppose. She thinks you were going to run away and leave us to the Black Brigade.'

'She thought wrongly then. Battista won't be coming here. And I have no plans to go anywhere.'

Brookes shifted his leg, and the chain rattled against the metal pipe.

'Don't move, you'll hurt yourself,' she said, starting forward a little. 'I'm sorry about what happened. I had no choice, really. None of them trust me any more anyway.'

'Free me then. Get the key and unlock this chain.'

'I can't,' Odetta said. 'I couldn't do it. I want to but they'd never forgive me.'

With a canine snarl Brookes lunged forward, throwing himself off the mattress until the chain rang taught and held him. Odetta shrank back against the wall.

'They're my family,' she cried, 'and there's nobody else left.'

'Tell them they have to leave! Tell your father.'

'He won't go. He still believes he did the right thing coming here. If he left . . .'

'If they won't leave then go yourself – get away from here!'

But she was shaking her head, turning from him. Groaning, Brookes dropped onto his back again. He could hear that she was crying and he waved her angrily from the room. After a moment, the door closed quietly behind her.

Later, when the day had sloped into evening, Brookes found that by sliding the chain along the pipe he could get his leg beneath him and sit up. The pipe itself was old iron as thick as his arm, mortared into the wall at one end and curving around and down through the floor at the other. Hauling himself up to a crouch, he gripped the pipe with both hands and heaved at it, trying to rip it from the wall or the floor, or even to bend it, but it was immovable. The furniture had been taken from the room as well – not a chair or a table leg he could break and use as a lever. And with every movement the shackle dug into the flesh of his ankle, raising dark welts. Brookes pounded the pipe with his fists, then punched the wall until the plaster cracked and his knuckles were bloody. Finally, slumped against the wall in an anguish of hopelessness, he abandoned the effort. He lay down again on the mattress and waited for morning.

He was not aware of having slept, but when he opened his eyes his head was full of dreams. Someone was holding him down, pressing him into water or mud – he remembered being shot in the forest, and the taste of the wet dirt in his mouth, the smell of rotted leaves. The shadows flickering above him were the ferns that sheltered him and Carla; he felt her face beneath his palm, and the warmth of her escaping life. Closing his eyes tightly again, he caught each image and held it in his memory, as if he could relive it. He saw Commissar Bruno raise his gun, the vivid green of the forest behind him. Then he was running along the tracks on the bridge at Gattinara, hearing the whine of the approaching train through the steel rails. The separate memories bled together, became one, became something like a life. His father's funeral in the English cemetery in Florence, Carla wrapped in a blanket in the village billet the day before the attack; Odetta laughing as she ran naked back to the bed from the fireplace.

But all these images were not his life. They were a mask, no more than a thin brittle shell, and beneath them were the things he no longer wished to admit. Beneath was the truth which he had been trying to suppress these last months, ever since he had arrived at the castle, perhaps even before that. If he chose only to remember these things and not the others, the great swathes of his life and his experiences which darkened and compromised him, perhaps he could cease to be that other person entirely – that other person had a different name and a different history, and Brookes had come to hate him.

Then he was awake properly, plunged back into the present, and the weight on his body was the pressure of his own arm, and the shadow above him that of the shutter shifting in the wind, and he was alone.

'Do you enjoy killing people?' Odetta asked. It was the next day. Possibly two days had slipped by – Brookes felt the stubble on his jaw and tried to judge how much time had passed.

'I used to, yes,' he told her, already feeling the anticipation. It would not be long now.

'And what changed?' she said.

'I don't know,' he replied. 'There'd always been a reason I suppose, some objective. But before I came here I killed somebody accidentally, and it felt out of my control. I didn't own death any more. It owned me. If that makes sense.'

The girl said nothing. She was sitting against the wall again, as if she still wanted to keep her distance from him. Between them was the tray of food and the flask of water she had brought with her and he had ignored. The room was full of clear daylight, and from outside came the sounds of birds singing.

'Nobody can choose the sort of person they are, can they,' Odetta said.

'I've tried to,' Brookes replied. 'All my life I've tried to do that.'

'It's a sort of fantasy, isn't it,' she said. 'If we could just change our names and our backgrounds, rearrange everything and become somebody different... If we could become somebody better. Like living here, since you came – pretending to live another life. We almost convinced ourselves, I think. But in the end it's never something you decide for yourself. Vittorio tried to fight against it. He tried to do something . . . There are so many things I wanted to tell you before, about him. I wished I could be like him myself, but I never could, I didn't have his strength. And then they killed him.'

'Because he broke the rules,' Brookes said.

'Yes, that. You understand how Isacco came to think like that. How can you explain these things to a child? It's a sort of comfort, to believe in order, however impossible. But when everything you do is a crime, when even existence is a crime, any kind of fantasy is better than the truth.'

Brookes recalled what Almansi had said about trying to salvage something of life from destruction. Whatever you cannot bear to leave behind, that is what you are. He knew now that the memories he had been reliving over the last few days had been just that: the things he could not bear to lose. But those memories meant little, divorced from what they tried to conceal. He felt the lack in himself, and the inability to belong anywhere, or to anyone. All that he had been given, all that he could have loved, he had torn apart, not with wanton joy but with a savage desire for denial.

'There was a time . . .' Brookes began, then stopped speaking. He frowned, uncertain how to continue. 'I was with the partisans,' he said. 'We had orders to blow up a bridge, a railway bridge, outside Gattinara. There was a German munitions train in a tunnel up the line, hidden from the Allied planes, and that night it would be sent south to resupply the troops in Milan. As soon as we heard the train was moving we went to the bridge and laid charges, gelignite along the rails and beneath the girders. I was in charge of that part of the operation. As soon as the train was on the bridge, we set off the explosives.'

Another long pause. Brookes felt his mouth dry, but didn't want to move from the mattress to reach for the water jug. Odetta sat perfectly still, watching him. He could not meet her eyes.

'The Germans,' Brookes went on, 'had found out about our plan. Somebody told them. They held the munitions train back in the tunnel and sent another in its place, diverted from a different line. The train we blew up was filled with Italian factory workers and their families – men they'd conscripted to work in one of the power stations further north. They were sending them back to their homes. We didn't realise until it was too late. We heard them, though. All of them screaming, packed together in the freight wagons as the bridge collapsed under them. That was how we knew what we'd done.'

'It wasn't your fault,' Odetta whispered.

'Oh no, the Germans did it on purpose. They knew it would damage the partisans' cause. But I don't even know how many died that night. I set the charges with my own hands, and I don't know how many I killed.'

He wanted to say more, but even now he held back. His eyes tight shut, he felt Odetta take his hand. She was squatting on the floor beside the mattress.

'But it was the Germans who killed them. It was their fault. They killed my brother too. They started this. They're to blame for all of this. Not my father. Not you.'

But Brookes was shaking his head, trying to tell her how wrong she was. And he wanted to tell her everything. He wanted to confess himself, and in that moment lay bare all that he was and had tried to conceal. But his nerve failed him and he said nothing.

'You're crying,' she said quietly. 'I did not think I would ever see that.'

An hour after dawn, and the sound rose through the stillness of a spring-like day. *Here it comes*, Brookes thought as he lay on the bed. *Now it begins.*

He sat up and made a last desperate attempt to wrench the iron pipe from its housing. It was useless, and his ankle ached as he struggled to stand. He managed to drag himself into the embrasure of the window, then pulled open the inner shutters.

Craning his neck until his face met the window glass he saw the vehicles, the car and the lorry flanked by motorcycles, as they turned onto the last rise before doubling back towards the castle gates. The car was a field-grey Mercedes: four men inside, and there would be more soldiers in the lorry. Then the vehicles were out of sight below the castle gatehouse and he let himself drop from the embrasure. He sat still, nursing his raw ankle, waiting.

The noise of the engines seemed to pass beneath him, then on upwards into the courtyard. He heard shouting, but could not distinguish the words. A long silence followed. Water dripped somewhere, the shutters rattled above his head. Would this, he wondered, be the end? Tensed for the sound of gunfire, he stared hard at the door, willing it to open, hardly caring who came to find him.

He waited so long that when the sound of running footsteps reached him he almost believed it was some auditory hallucination, created by his own expectations. But then the door flew open and Odetta was rushing across the room to throw herself down on the mattress beside him. She was holding a ring of keys.

'The Germans are here,' she said, in a rushed, gasping whisper. Her face was swollen, eyes black-ringed and wet, and she was trembling violently as she fumbled with the keys. 'They're in the dining room.' Her voice was rising in pitch, closing on hysteria. Brookes took the keys from her shaking fingers and unchained himself.

'What happened?' he said, seizing the girl by the shoulders. Tears flowed down her face as she told him.

'I was watching from the window. They've arrested them as fugitive Jews – they have to go with them to the barracks in Novara. Papa told the officer that he was a friend of Comandante Battista, to contact him to explain everything . . . but the officer said Battista's already been arrested for treason. He said he'd already *paid the highest penalty . . .*'

Brookes massaged his ankle, then got up. He stood in the

middle of the room flexing his shoulders, testing his weight on the injured leg.

'It wasn't going to happen like this,' he said, as if to himself. 'You weren't supposed to be here when they came.'

'What?' she said, baffled for a moment, then shook her head violently. 'Franco, listen to me: I can't leave my family, but you have to escape! They don't know you're here, but they said they'd search the whole castle. You have to go now, out the side door at the bottom of the stairs. You can get away before they see you, but you have to go now!' Odetta was on her feet, grabbing Brookes by the arm and trying to drag him towards the door.

'Please,' she said, sobbing. 'Please go . . .'

Together they left the room and went down the stairs, Brookes slow and almost casual as Odetta begged him to hurry. At the base of the stairs she pulled open the heavy door to the courtyard, but he made no move to follow her. He placed a hand on top of her head, leaning to kiss her brow.

'Thank you,' he said.

Then he turned and began walking along the corridor, towards the nursery and the great hall and the rooms of the castle beyond. Odetta went after him, running at first but then slowing, falling back.

'Where are you going?' she called weakly after him. 'Don't go that way! The Germans are there, what are you doing? You can't fight them! Franco . . .' Her words died, her steps faltered, and she watched him as he walked away from her. Something about the way he moved unnerved her suddenly. He was calm, limping slightly but still purposeful. Across the distance of the great hall she watched him, the back of his head and the set of his shoulders.

'What are you going to do?' she said, but the words were a whisper. Then she was running after him again.

Up the stairs and along the passageway, Brookes moved steadily, determined. Trailing behind him, Odetta felt the first slow horror stealing through her, the reeling dizziness of vertigo. She could hear the sounds from the dining room now, the voice of the German officer talking in his bad Italian, her father answering back quiet and cowed. If she fell to the floor now she would not have to witness it, she thought. If she ran away she could be free of all this. But she could not leave. She walked in Brookes' path, following him mutely along the passage and out into the open light of the dining room.

The German officer was sitting at the table, helping himself to the remains of their breakfast while the family sat and watched him. As Brookes walked in he put down his cup and jerked upright, calling an order to the soldier by the door. The soldier stepped forward at once, raising his gun.

Brookes spoke to the soldier, and the gun was slowly lowered.

Poised in the doorway, her ears burning, Odetta watched Brookes march up to the table and stand stiffly before it. She heard him address the officer. She could not understand the words, but recognised the language. Brookes was speaking in German, and in that moment Odetta knew that everything she had believed was wrong. She knew that Captain Francis Brookes did not exist; that the man she had called by that name was somebody else, somebody alien. When he turned briefly towards her, noticing her still waiting in the doorway, even his face looked different.

He looked at her with the eyes of the enemy.

22

THE GERMAN OFFICER, Oberleutnant Carl Reincke of SS-Polizei-Regiment 15, remained seated at the dining table. He was young and pink faced, with thinning yellow hair and very pale eyes, and he said nothing as he listened to the man standing before him. His long coat was thrown open to reveal the decorations on his uniform, the iron cross and anti-partisan medal pinned to his breast pocket, the SS runes sewn beneath it. His hand rested lightly over the pistol on the table.

From where she was sitting Odetta could not hear a word of what the man she had called Brookes was saying, even if she could understand the language. It could be a silent tableau, she thought – the man standing stiffly with his back to her, like a soldier at attention, and the officer mutely facing him, gazing up with his pale dead eyes.

The rest of the room was stilled too: her father sitting at the end of the table, arms and legs tightly crossed and his bruised face a ghastly grey; her mother hunched in her gown, covering her eyes; Umberto and Isacco standing against the wall. There were three other soldiers in the room as well. One of them, in a cap and camouflaged trousers, waited behind the officer, holding a thick leather satchel or document briefcase. The other two wore helmets and long motorcyclists' coats, and carried submachineguns. Odetta had not dared glance at them as she crossed the room to sit beside her mother, but now she forced herself to look away from the scene at the table and focus instead on the sleeve of the soldier standing nearest her. The rough grey wool of his coat was embroidered with a green spread eagle inside a wreath of oak leaves. She stared at the symbol, trying to clear her mind of everything else. The soldier barely seemed to notice her.

An eagle, she thought, and tried to remember why this seemed significant. She recalled the day that Brookes had come to her room for the first time and they had seen the bird circling over the valley. But already there was the deception of memory. The prince of lies, she thought. The deceiver. But she felt no anger, and her fear was so enormous that she was barely aware of it any more. Instead she felt merely dazed, slightly sick and untrusting of everything around her. None of this is real, she told herself. Everything is a lie.

Abruptly the officer stood up and walked around the table, picking up his gun and cap. He motioned to the soldier with the briefcase to come with him, then followed the man towards the far door.

'We need to use your study,' the man said to Almansi, in Italian. Odetta felt the shock of his voice, the familiarity of it. Her father nodded once, and the group left the room.

Odetta jumped in her seat as she felt the touch of her mother's hand. Rachele's hand, binding with her own, fingers interlacing. Nobody made a sound. One of the two remaining soldiers crossed the room in his long heavy coat and perched on the edge of the table with the gun across his lap. He took a cigarette from the pack on the table and lit it, then smoked with the cigarette stuck between his lips. He stared at each of them in turn through the smoke, eyes narrowed and his face impassive beneath the helmet's rim. Odetta's father was stooped over in his chair, folded up on himself, mashing his brow between his fingers. Her mother's lips moved, forming silent words. She was praying.

For a long time nothing happened. The smoke rose from one soldier's cigarette; the other cleared his throat and ground the nailed sole of his boot slowly against the stone floor. Odetta felt unable to breathe. Only when the silence had become unbearable, and she felt the long-held scream rising in her throat, did she hear the men returning from the study. The door opened, and the officer snapped out an order to his men.

The soldier perched on the table looked bemused, but only for a moment. Then he got up, tossed his cigarette onto the floor and all of the men went out onto the loggia. The family were left alone in the dining room.

'Could somebody explain?' Umberto hissed. 'Rachele, you understand German.'

'I understand nothing,' Rachele said. 'Not any more.'

And so they waited, beaten by their own silence. From the loggia they heard the Germans talking, then the shouts of command and the noise of the engines starting.

They're leaving, Odetta thought. They're all leaving. But she kept her eyes on the floor, locked into the swirling weave of a frayed rug as she listened to the sounds of the vehicles departing – first one motorcycle, then another; the car, then the lorry, then the last two motorcycles. Gone.

She looked up, and the man was standing in the middle of the room, his hands braced against the table.

'Who are you?' her father said. 'If you're not Francis Brookes?'

'Brookes died a long time ago,' the man said. 'Actually, I killed him.'

'And you? You're some kind of German agent?'

'My mother was German,' the man said. 'Father was English. So I'm both, or maybe neither.' He looked tired as he spoke, worn down, sagging against the table. He took a cigarette from the packet the officer had left.

'And what about us?' Rachele asked. 'You told them we were under your protection.' Her husband let out a long sigh through his teeth.

'I bluffed them a little, yes,' the man replied.

'When you killed those men in the cottage across the valley,' said Almansi, with sudden vigour, 'you used their wireless transmitter, I suppose? You informed your superiors of Battista's plan, and about his raid on the arms depot. You knew they'd arrest him, and then they'd come here.'

'A brief anonymous message, yes,' the man said. 'And by the time it took effect I intended you all to be long gone. Just as I intend you to leave this place now.'

Slowly, instinctively, the family drew together, crossing the room to sit at one end of the long table with chairs gathered close. Odetta sat beside her mother, clasping her hand, Almansi and Umberto to their left flanking Isacco. Facing them at the far end, the man seated himself in his black throne-like chair.

'First tell us why,' Rachele said. 'We can't leave until you explain.'

The man checked his watch. He closed his eyes in slow, deliberate calculation.

'There's time enough,' he said. He scrubbed his hand through his hair, then across his stubbled jaw. 'When my father died I had no relatives back in England, so I went to Germany instead. This was the early '30s. While I was there I heard one of those . . .' he paused, circling his hand in the air as he searched for the correct word in Italian, 'those *rallies*,' he said. 'I heard Hitler speaking.'

Odetta heard her mother's cry. The man continued.

'I can't explain now what I heard,' he said, 'or the effect it had on me. Something about the hatred of it captivated me. The rightness of the hatred. I didn't really care what he was saying, or why, but it had a sort of magnetic unreason . . . All of those people there, thousands of ordinary people, felt the same. The rules had all been changed. The world had been made different.'

'You became a Nazi?' Umberto asked, incredulous. The man nodded, eyes closing again – it could have been a proud expression, or one of shame.

'I joined the party in '34, under my mother's maiden name. For a while it didn't make much difference. Several years later I was contacted by the *Sicherheitsdienst* - the intelligence branch of the SS. As a native English-speaker, I was very valuable to them. I was trained by them. After the war started I was sent to North Africa to infiltrate the British army intelligence networks. Two years later, after the allies had landed in Sicily, I was picked up by a submarine and taken to Rome, then on to Florence and Verona.'

'They must have trusted you a great deal,' Almansi said. 'From what I've heard of SS intelligence, they don't suffer fools.'

'I wasn't a fool. I was one of their best field operatives. I was only found out once, by an intelligence officer named Brookes. That was in Tunisia, but I escaped, and by the time I reached Italy I had a new cover name and identity. I was sent north to link up with the partisans. My new role was that of an escaped British prisoner. My orders were to locate and execute several prominent figures in the partisan high command – mostly communists. I was to implicate the British in the killings, and cause a total breach between the partisans and the allies.'

'So you did betray them,' Almansi broke in, 'just as they believed.'

'No. No, I didn't. As it happened, I never got close enough to these men to carry out the order. True, I sent several reports back to headquarters in Verona, but fewer as time went on. By then, you see . . .' He broke off again, gazing into space. For a few moments he said nothing, lost in consideration.

'I didn't behave as I did out of love for Germany,' he said. 'Or hatred of England. I had no real ideology. It was my life, that was all. I loved the game of it. I enjoyed the freedom and the subterfuge. I enjoyed the risk. I came to look down on those who wore themselves on the outside, so to speak. I was one of the select few, moving through the world without having to obey its laws. Without having to obey any laws.'

'You make it sound so idyllic,' Rachele said bitterly. 'Being a spy and a murderer.' The man at the end of the table smiled, almost wistful.

'It was my dream,' he said. 'A very powerful dream.'

'And what? You woke up?'

'Something like that, yes. Things happened which were out of my control.'

Odetta felt the quick heat of realisation: she knew now who had informed the Germans of the plan to blow up the bridge at Gattinara.

She knew now why it had affected him so deeply. He had not planned it; events had slipped from his hands.

'I could not continue as before. So, I made contact with an American secret service cell operating around Lake Orta,' the man said. 'I intended to work for them as a double agent, in return for an amnesty. Actually I didn't care about the amnesty – I felt my trust had been violated. I wanted revenge. The Germans, however, discovered that one of their field agents was giving information to the enemy.'

'There were several agents, then?' Almansi asked. 'But they guessed it was you?'

'They didn't,' the man said. 'SS intelligence don't make guesses. They just decided to execute everyone. Somebody passed information to the commander of my partisan brigade that I was a spy and a traitor. They must have assumed that the sentence would be carried out promptly, as they usually are, without too many questions asked. But it didn't happen. And so I came here, to this place.'

The man gave a last indifferent shrug and sat back in his chair. Beside her, Odetta noticed that her father had his hands tightly clenched.

'You think you can have everything your way?' he said with sudden vehemence. 'You think you take what you want from the world and use it however you wish, lie and betray everything and remain impervious? You have conspired,' he said, snarling the word, 'in the destruction of a world and a culture, and talk about it like you have no responsibility! My people,' he jabbed his fingertip down onto the table, 'my family, have been threatened with extermination, and you talk of games and acting roles? You talk of freedom and choice? How can you be so *vicious*?'

The man shrugged again, unmoved. He lit another cigarette.

'All my life,' Almansi went on, 'I've tried to protect my people, to protect my family. I may have been misguided, I made mistakes, but I acted in good faith, from motives that were at least once noble. You, though – all you've done is cause destruction and death. You have deceived and betrayed everyone, even the Germans, who made you what you are! And you've gloried in it all! Now you expect us to – what? Believe you? Thank you? We don't even know your real name!'

'I'm nobody,' the man said. 'I have no family, no people, no country and no faith. I am without hope. When I die, I'll leave no trace in the world. Back on the mountain, before I came here, I was ready for that. Now I think differently. This is my choice, it's what I've decided.'

'He told the officer,' Rachele said in a level voice, 'that the partisan leaders were coming here. That this castle was a *rendezvous* for their high command.'

The man was laughing silently. 'I didn't know if they'd believe me,' he said. 'But I mentioned certain high-ranking names, gave the correct code words . . . I stressed the utmost importance of the Oberleutnant leaving here with his men and not approaching until he received orders from headquarters in Verona. He had no way to communicate with his superiors, so had to trust my word. I spun them quite a story.'

'Something you are clearly very adept at,' Almansi said.

'Quite so. Besides which, I hold the official rank of SS-Hauptsturmfuhrer, so technically I'm his superior. But within the next few hours he'll report back, and very soon the truth will become apparent. It won't take them long to discover my identity. Then they'll come to find me.'

Rachele stood up, pushing back her chair. 'How long?' she said. Brookes looked at his watch again.

'Within five or six hours, I'd estimate,' he said. 'You should leave now. Gather only the barest essentials.'

He took a folded map from his pocket and tossed it along the table, then began to speak quickly, not looking at the family. 'This is a map the Oberleutnant gave me – all the roadblocks and checkpoints are marked. You'll take a lane branching off from the main lakeside road between Verbania and Ghiffa,' he said. 'You will reach it by sundown if you take the road through Civiasco. The lane leads to the sanatorium of San Martino di Monfalchetto, overlooking the lake. The man who runs the place is named Bertozzi – he has no scruples, and you'll have to pay him very highly, but he'll shelter you. The war will soon be over, and nobody wants to help the Germans if they can avoid it. I take it you have money, Signor Almansi?'

Odetta's father nodded once, then picked up the map and studied it.

'What about you?' Rachele asked. 'Are you coming with us?'

'No, I'm staying here. The Germans will search until they find me, so I'm not safe to be with. But this castle belongs to me now, and I'm ordering you all to leave.'

He stretched himself on the chair, hands behind his head.

'The Lord of Castelmantia,' Almansi said, looking up from the map with a slow smile.

Now the castle was loud with the impending departures. Rooms and corridors echoed the noise of slamming doors and running feet, suitcases thrown from wardrobes, Almansi repeatedly shouting '*Leave it! Leave it behind!*'

In the courtyard, Umberto had already brought the big Lancia from the garage; it stood waiting, the engine idling, Isacco sitting in the rear seat with his single small suitcase clutched to his lap.

In her turret room, Odetta stood before the window looking out at the valley for the last time. She felt a heady sense of unreality – the Germans had been there, and the man had sent them away, and now they were really leaving and the roads were open before them. The possibility of escape was maddeningly close, so close it felt cruelly like an illusion. Gazing into the cleft of the valley, she felt suddenly giddy with dread and grabbed at the windowsill to steady herself. The valley yawned wide and threatening. She turned quickly from the window, snatched her coat and suitcases from the bed and ran down the narrow stairs to the lower landing.

The man was still in the dining room, sitting in the big chair at the table drinking cold coffee and smoking. A pack of large playing cards were spread before him and he stared at them with a blank expression. Odetta dropped her cases near the door and sat on them, watching him.

'They'll kill you, won't they,' she said.

'They'll try,' the man replied without glancing up.

'Come with us. We can escape together.'

An almost imperceptible shake of his head. Who was he now, Odetta wondered. What role had he slipped into? He was a stranger to her, wearing a stolen body. She remembered the times they'd lain together, in his bed and hers; the textures of his skin, the newness of him.

From the surrounding rooms she could hear the rest of her family, busy with their packing. She wanted to cross to the table and touch the man – just a touch of her hand, to satisfy herself that he was real. Almost she did it, but as she stirred herself to stand she felt the fear again, the wrench in her gut. Her face was hot, and she wanted very much not to cry. A sound from the door, and she turned to see her father coming in from the loggia, wearing his thick tweed driving coat and hat. Rachele followed a step behind him.

'I took your cards, Almansi,' the man said, gathering up the pack. 'Your *tarocchi*, while I was in the study earlier. You'd better have them back.' He dropped the cards into their silk-lined box and closed the lid.

'Thank you,' said Almansi, taking the box.

'I kept one, if you don't mind.' He held up one of the cards. A mounted figure in black armour.

'The Knight of Swords,' Almansi replied. 'Although no longer reversed, I see.'

The man slipped the card into his jacket and sat back in the chair. Then the two of them faced each other.

'You seem to have offered us life,' Almansi said, 'but I cannot find it in my heart to thank you, or to forgive you.'

'I've done what you wished, haven't I?' the man replied. 'I've judged you. I've made my choice.'

For a while Almansi did not speak. From outside came the noise of the car revving, Umberto's hurrying shout.

'Can I ask why?' Almansi said. The man considered, scratching his jaw.

'Call it love, perhaps,' he replied.

Odetta felt her scalp tighten as if a cold breeze blew down her neck. She knew what the man meant, and what he did not mean.

'You told me once,' the man went on, speaking to her father, 'that love is the only thing worth saving. Do you remember? I have nowhere to go now, and nothing left to betray. Your family is the only thing of value I can save. That's my victory, Signor Almansi. That's how I win.'

Almansi nodded. 'I concede,' he said. 'Keep the card, it's yours.'

Then he turned and walked from the room.

Rachele waited until her husband had passed, then went to

the table. The man stood up, and for a moment they held a very formal distance.

'He won't thank you,' Rachele said. 'But I will.' She moved closer, placing her hands on the man's shoulders, then kissed him on the lips.

'Goodbye Captain,' she said, then followed her husband into the courtyard.

Now Odetta alone remained. She stood up, gathering her cases, then paused. Any word she could say would be unbearable. Instead she just looked at him as he dropped back into his chair. He took the card from his pocket and studied it, then turned to see her waiting by the door. His face told her nothing. If he speaks to me, she thought, if he only speaks to me I'll stay with him. She felt the weight of the suitcases in her hands, wanting to drop them and cross to the table, tell the man that she would not leave. What she felt then was something greater than the love she had imagined before.

Then he winked, a quick smile. *Go*, he said silently. And before she made a sound Odetta ran from the room, out across the loggia and down the steps to the courtyard, where her family waited for her in the car.

He stood between the arches of the loggia watching them go, their last nervous glances around the protective enclosure of the castle, their last uncertain waves as the Lancia turned in the courtyard and away down the ramp to the gates. Only when the sound of the car had died away along the valley and the tense silence of the empty castle had returned did he walk back inside. As he moved through the chambers he saw lines of fire, positions of attack and defence, sabotage and ambush. The fabric of the castle was alive to him, transformed into a field of battle.

In the master bedroom, where the great armoire stood open with silks and furs spilling from the doors, the dressing table cleared and the floor scattered with bottles and vials, he found the machine carbine leaning against the wall in one corner. He took the gun and descended to the courtyard. Down the steps beneath the portico, he stood before the sealed metal door to the cellar. Taking careful aim, he closed his finger around the single-shot trigger. The blast shattered the silence, the lock bursting from the latch. He kicked the door open and went into the cellar.

Two hours later he had dragged what he needed up from the vault. His belly was tight and empty, but he felt no hunger or fatigue. Working fast, he stripped the cases and piled the weapons along the damp flagstones of the portico: rifles and submachineguns, mines and grenades. One case held four anti-tank grenade launchers, another held blasting gelignite. He took thin steel wire from the storeroom and bound the grenades together into clusters; he loaded belts of gleaming ammunition into the breeches of the machineguns, checked every bolt and every magazine. Then he began heaving the weapons together and carrying them to the positions he had selected: stairways, window apertures, doorways and corridors, turrets and balconies.

He buried landmines all along the road leading to the castle gates, then under the gates themselves he slung the clusters of grenades, dangling like swollen iron fruit in the shadows of the stone arches. He scraped shallow holes in the gritty dirt of the courtyard and laid more mines, then ran quickly along the loggia, through rooms and up stairs, moving from one position to the next. The castle was sown with weaponry.

The sun was dropping in the sky, a last pinkish light over the snows of the mountains, as he stood waiting in the gatehouse. He carried two grenades in his belt, a machine carbine slung across his back and a grenade launcher over his shoulder. Nothing was left now but waiting. Soon he would hear the first of the cars driving up the valley, the first of the hunters coming to trap him. There would be many more after them.

He lit a cigarette and squinted into the sunlight.

23

THE FIRST TIME she passed, Odetta missed the turning in the road. Driving further, she reached a petrol station and asked directions. *The castle?* she asked the attendant. *How do I get to the castle?* The man scratched his grey jaw and denied in his knotty dialect that any such place existed, but then almost as an afterthought waved her back down the road and jutted a stiff palm off to the left. She turned the car, drove back, and found the narrow, branching road.

The valley looked completely different now, of course. Summer, and the trees were all in full leaf, the ground radiating heat and light and life. Eight years had passed since Odetta had last been there, and her memories were of a cold and barren place. She was driving a blue 1949 Fiat Topolino – it had been a wedding present from her husband – and the little round car purred happily as it took the curves of the rising road. Odetta hummed a tune to herself as she drove, something she had heard on the radio at home that morning. But as the trees opened ahead of her and the flanks of the mountains massed into their familiar forms, she felt the tightness in her shoulders and the rapid motion of her blood.

She had left her husband and two young children back at their house by the sea on the outskirts of Genoa, intending to drive to Turin and visit her mother. Alone for the first time in months, the idea of making a detour did not form until she was nearing Alessandria – then, before she could think clearly about it, before her nerves could halt her, she turned the car northwards towards the mountains on the far side of Piemonte. All that long drive she had avoided thinking about what lay ahead, and what she might feel when she returned there.

The events of those years were no longer discussed or mentioned. It was easy to do that, to let it all slide into a gulf of forgetting; the trauma of war, and the confused period immediately afterwards, had left few unaffected. Not many people in Italy cared to be reminded of what they had been, or what they had allowed themselves to become. Even victory, even peace, seemed fatally compromised now. And it was only in those first months after the ceasefire that the extent of the damage had become apparent: the slaughter and the deportations, the many thousands of dead. Odetta's husband had lost half his family, sent away to one of the camps in Germany, reduced to tiny details in the vast accounting of death.

Odetta had been relatively lucky by comparison. Her father had died in his bed in 1948. Rachele now lived alone in the big flat in Turin, stately in elegant black, saying nothing to deny the rumours that she might be related to the aristocracy. You could, it seemed, be whatever you wanted in the New Italy. But if Odetta ever mentioned her lost brother, or those months they had sheltered together in the castle, her mother's face would close, her neat smile vanish. Nothing would be said. Isacco was at university in Milan now, and Umberto had moved to Rome. Scattered, the family chose their own amnesias, and regarded the past only in solitude.

Another turn and the village appeared, two rows of little cottages huddled along the roadside, small and mean and grey despite the green forested slopes and the weight of summer sunlight. Odetta eased her foot off the accelerator, slowing the little blue Fiat as she passed the last of the houses. Rising ground and thick trees still hid the castle. She drove a short distance further, then pulled over to the verge and shut off the engine.

Climbing from the car she smelled the thick, sappy breath of the forest. It was an effort merely to raise her eyes from the road, but still there was nothing of the castle to be seen. She began to walk, swinging her red purse on its long strap, trying to keep the tune of the song in her head. A few paces more, another bend, and Odetta saw the road barred with a rough wooden fence and gate. A sign nailed to the gate read PRIVATE PROPERTY. NO ENTRY.

She paused a moment, standing in the road under the full burden of the sun. She saw butterflies circling in the shadows between the trees, heard birdsong. Then, squaring her shoulders and pulling up her skirt, she stepped up onto the rungs of the gate and swung herself over.

Humming still, she walked steadily forward up the curving road. It was very overgrown here, tall grass and brambles pressing in from either side, the faint tyre ruts baked almost to nothing. Nobody had come this way in a long time. Keeping her pace steady and her eyes on the ground ahead, Odetta passed the switchback bend in the road. Only then did she stop and look up at the castle.

She believed she had known what to expect. Not the same place, of course, unaltered after eight years, but something that she recognised. Instead she saw desolation.

The road up to the gates was cratered with great pits, full of tangled bushes now but looking as if something once had grabbed and scooped at the hard ground. Further on, the gatehouse was a jagged black stump, the arch gone and the masonry above fallen in grassy ruin. The walls of the castle itself were still standing, rent with holes. Ivy covered the old stone, massing around the ragged gaps, parting only in places to show the marks of fire.

Odetta walked carefully up the road, around the craters and over the fallen lumps of masonry. She reached the gate and looked between the standing piles of stone, worn teeth in an old jaw, into the courtyard. Arms spread for balance, she climbed over the heaped rubble and through the gates. The courtyard opened before her, a dry jungle of rank grass and ruin. In the centre, beneath the shattered shell of the keep, the remains of several wrecked vehicles stood choked with weeds, metal twisted and stained with rust.

Odetta moved slowly across the courtyard. A few arches of the loggia still stood, hanging alone in space above the broken walls. Everywhere the stone was pitted and gouged – bullet holes, she guessed, or the effect of grenades. The upper floors of the buildings had all collapsed, piling timbers mottled black by the flames into the rooms beneath. Under Odetta's feet, broken glass and fine rubble crackled and creaked. She reached the portico beneath the arches and stood in its shade, staring around her. A chunk of pitted stone lay where it had rolled against the inner wall; she recognised the head of the angel which had stood above the well. The rest of it had been blasted to pale shards.

Closing her eyes, she listened hard into the silence, as if she might hear some echo of the extraordinary fury that had ripped the castle to ruins. Her imagination conjured gunfire and shellblast, the screams of the wounded, the roar of falling stone. She flicked her eyes open again, her throat tight and her head ringing.

Now, as her vision adjusted to the shade, Odetta could make out the remains of stone steps rising from the wreckage inside the main building. Picking her way carefully, aware of the unstable masses of stone balanced above her, she passed through the doorway to the stairs, then began to climb. This was the base of the stairway which once led up to her own room in the turret, although looking up into the slanting light she could see that the turret itself had been destroyed. Climbing to the top, she found a short remaining flight of wooden steps still clinging to the masonry; up again, as far as she dared on the groaning treads, she reached a hole broken in the wall and looked out over the valley.

This was the view she had seen for so many months from her room in the turret – the same configuration of mountains and trees, the same swoop of sky and white peaks in the distance. Odetta leaned against the wall, trying to ease the weight of her body off the broken stairs. Fumbling in her purse, she found cigarettes and a lighter. For the first time she allowed herself to remember what had happened in this place.

She thought of the man they had left here – the man she had called Franco, or Captain Brookes. He was as strange to her now as he had been when she saw him last, sitting alone in the dining room staring at the tarot card of the mounted knight. So often she had thought of him since then – all those long moments of solitude, lying in bed beside her sleeping husband, or walking in the grounds of their house, listening to her children playing. All through these eight years she had thought of him, felt him close to her, closer even than her own skin; a new skin she wore in this new and reborn country. She remembered that last moment in the dining room, and her desire to remain with him in the castle. Often she felt that she had stayed, or that in some way she had taken the place of the man, becoming him while her family departed. She felt him unfolding inside her.

A sound startled her, and Odetta grabbed at the broken wall to keep her balance. A figure was moving across the courtyard, parting the tall weeds and bushes. Once the initial shock had subsided, and the more rational fear had risen in its place, she ran quickly down the steps and back across the rubble to the arches beneath the loggia.

It was a man, old and dressed in worn clothes, with a sack across his back. A man from the village, Odetta realised with faint disappointed relief, come to the castle to scavenge just as the villagers had always done. As she watched, he leaned into one of the burnt-out vehicles and dragged free a scar of metal, dropping it into his sack. When he straightened up, he saw her watching. She thought he was about to run, but after scanning the surrounding ruins and assuring himself that Odetta was alone, he approached her.

'Are you lost, Signorina?' he asked, his voice cracked and his language tangled with the local dialect. Odetta told him that she was not lost.

'Exploring then? A tourist, from the cities?'

'Something like that,' Odetta said, holding herself very erect, aware that her clothes were badly dirtied from scrambling through the rubble. The man looked inoffensive, but one could never be sure.

'What happened in this place?' she asked. 'Does anyone know?'

'Yes,' the man replied, drawing out the word. 'We all know, who saw it. Back in the war. Germans blew it up.'

'Why would they do that?' Odetta said, trying to keep her tone

neutral. She feared the man would spin her some elaborate fable –
then recognised her city prejudice. Even so, she thought he looked
the type.

He dropped his sack to the ground and gazed at the broken walls.
Then he began to speak, moving his hands in circling, clawing gestures, as if he was trying to draw something from the air.

'There was a man here,' he said, scratching out the words. 'A partisan, or an American maybe. He was hiding here and the Germans
came to get him. We watched them going through the village – first
a car, then lorries with German soldiers, lots of them. The valley was
full of fire, smoke. Terrible noise. . .'

He paused, his face tightening into a brief grin, then cleared his
throat. 'At night they brought up more soldiers – a whole battalion,
my brother said: SS Police with Black Brigade men and militia. Up
here they came, soon as dawn broke, and then it all started again
. . . sounded like there was a whole division of partisans, not one
man. In the end the Germans brought tanks and artillery, put
them just down there where the road curves – then they shelled the
place to rubble. When that was done they came up here again with
grenades and dynamite and bombed whatever was left. Fire took
everything else.'

Odetta was silent, staring back over her shoulder now at the blasted
rooms and collapsed timbers. She could almost discern the point where
her imagination ended, where anything in her own experience departed.
All that lay beyond were these ruins, these pitted walls.

She thanked the man, gave him a handful of cigarettes, then
walked slowly back through the courtyard to the gatehouse. Slowly
she climbed down onto the road and gazed across the valley at the
bare rock of the mountains and the scars of bright snow above. He's
gone, she thought, and for the first time she truly felt bereft. He's

dead. She closed her eyes again and tried to summon a memory of him – willed herself to imagine the touch of his hand on her shoulder. Then a crack of stone jerked her back to awareness and she turned quickly.

The man from the village was clambering down from the gatehouse, nodding to her as he passed.

'Where did he die?' she heard herself saying. 'The man who was here. Where did they kill him?'

The man seemed to smile, although the bright light made his expression hard to judge. 'Oh,' he said, 'nobody knows that. After they'd finished, the Germans and fascists went all through the place taking away their dead and searching for his body, but they found nothing. Didn't seem like he could've escaped, or hidden anywhere and survived – they had the place completely surrounded, you see. In the end they gave up searching. I've looked all through here myself over the years, and never found anything.'

'Nothing at all?'

'Not a scrap, Signorina. Almost like there never was anybody here. Or maybe he just went up in the smoke and away over the mountains, eh?'

The man grinned, then continued down the road into the valley. Odetta looked back into the courtyard, then at the shattered wall above her. Her eyes were suddenly wet, and she brushed the tears away before they broke. She would leave now, she told herself, and never return to this place. All that had happened here was gone. All that remained of him was inside her now, as if he had surrendered himself to her keeping.

Odetta smiled to herself, and felt the warmth of what she possessed. She would walk down to her little blue car at the bottom of the hill, drive to Turin and see her mother. Then, maybe tomorrow, she would make the long journey home, back to her family and her friends and her two little boys, taking with her all the things she had never told, and would never tell, her handsome smiling husband in their big house by the sea.

Acknowledgements

I would like to acknowledge the assistance of the Arts Council during the writing of this novel. Thanks also to my agent, Laetitia Rutherford at Mulcahy Conway Associates, and to my editor, Becky Senior at Old Street Publishing. I am very grateful to all those who gave me advice, encouragement and support; in particular I would like to thank Nikita Lalwani, Polly Tuckett, Nathaniel Matthews, Sam Harvey, Jason Bennett, Emma Hooper, Ros Cook, Rick Hewes, Brendan Donaghy, Dean Ryan, Philippa Heap, Alessandro Anastasi, Ivor Brennan, Valentina Muscusco, Laura Caggegi-Guidone, Chris and Kath Matthews, Neville Attkins, Victoria Arber, Richard Bohane and Ruth Orson.